**Jason lifted his hand to Kyla's face. "I don't like you being here."**

His touch overwhelmed her senses. And quite possibly her reason. "We both need to find answers," she said. "You have your strengths, I have mine. Unless you'd rather ask me to use my connections at the DA's office to help with your case."

"I'm an ex-con, Kyla. Not a current one. I'd never ask you to compromise your ethics or career."

"Said the man about to break into a private office without a warrant." But she got his point. Throwing his past in his face certainly wasn't going to get either of them what they wanted. "We'd better get moving."

"Why?"

She glanced at the crowd in the sleazy nightclub. "Because our suspects are done arguing and look ready to move." She reached up and stroked her hand down the side of his face. "I like this, by the way. The beard. Super sexy."

"Careful, Kyla." He caught her wrist in his hand and turned his lips to brush against the sensitive skin. "Mixing business with pleasure is never a good idea."

Dear Reader,

Some couples are just meant to be. When Kyla Bertrand, who first appeared as Simone Armstrong's paralegal in *Reunited with the P.I.*, I knew two things: one, that Kyla needed her own story, and two, her hero had to be someone who would not only want her but *need* her. As a newly promoted prosecutor, Kyla has a lot to prove, but she's willing to put her entire career at risk when her friend's death is labeled an accidental overdose. Suddenly, she's seeing things from the other side. More importantly, she needs help if she's going to uncover the truth.

Enter Jason Sutton, ex-felon turned PI who has still to prove himself. Jason's made a lot of mistakes in his life, but he's paid for them. He knows better than most that the world is a harsh place. Not everyone sees him as redeemable, but Kyla isn't one of those people. She never has been. She's always seen him for who he truly is: a good man she can rely on. Falling in love isn't only inconvenient, it's complicated, which makes for a super fun story to write.

I hope it's as much fun for you to read.

*Anna J.*

# THE PI'S DEADLY CHARADE

---

## Anna J. Stewart

# HARLEQUIN®
# ROMANTIC SUSPENSE™

Recycling programs
for this product may
not exist in your area.

ISBN-13: 978-1-335-73825-7

The PI's Deadly Charade

Copyright © 2023 by Anna J. Stewart

All rights reserved. No part of this book may be used or reproduced in any manner whatsoever without written permission except in the case of brief quotations embodied in critical articles and reviews.

This is a work of fiction. Names, characters, places and incidents are either the product of the author's imagination or are used fictitiously. Any resemblance to actual persons, living or dead, businesses, companies, events or locales is entirely coincidental.

For questions and comments about the quality of this book, please contact us at CustomerService@Harlequin.com.

Harlequin Enterprises ULC
22 Adelaide St. West, 41st Floor
Toronto, Ontario M5H 4E3, Canada
www.Harlequin.com

**Printed in U.S.A.**

Bestselling author **Anna J. Stewart** can barely remember a time she didn't want to write romances. She's been a bookaholic for her whole life, and stories of action and adventure have always topped her list, especially if said books also include a spunky, independent heroine and a well-earned happily-ever-after. With Wonder Woman and Princess Leia as her earliest influences, she now writes for Harlequin's Heartwarming and Romantic Suspense lines and, when she's not cooking or baking, attempts to wrangle her two cats, Rosie and Sherlock, into some semblance of proper behavior (yeah, that's not happening).

**Books by Anna J. Stewart**

**Harlequin Romantic Suspense**

***Honor Bound***

*Reunited with the P.I.*
*More Than a Lawman*
*Gone in the Night*
*Guarding His Midnight Witness*
*The PI's Deadly Charade*

***The Coltons of Roaring Springs***

*Colton on the Run*

Visit the Author Profile page at Harlequin.com for more titles.

For Sarah Palmero,

For your straightforward advice and encouragement.

# *Chapter 1*

"Kyla Bertrand?"

Distracted by winning her first trial argument, Kyla stopped just outside the Sacramento County courthouse. She turned, pushing her shoulder satchel behind her and watched a trim, middle-aged woman with a straight silver bob emerge from the other side of the glass doors. Kyla recognized her face, but couldn't place her. "Yes?" Kyla's gaze shifted to the shield the woman wore on the waistband of her practical black suit. Ah, now she remembered and shifted from guarded to welcoming.

"Detective Lorna Peterson." The woman offered her own pleasant smile. "I was hoping to catch you in court, but you'd already left."

"Yeah, sorry. I need to talk to my supervisor before she takes off for the day." After almost ten years as Simone Armstrong-Sutton's paralegal, Kyla got more than a little thrill from reporting to Simone in the capacity of a prosecuting attorney. "What can I do for you?"

"Why don't we sit for a moment?" The sudden solemnity in Detective Peterson's voice had Kyla on alert.

"What's wrong? Is it my parents? Did something happen?" She instantly dug into her bag for her cell phone. Had her dad been cleaning the gutters again on that stupid ladder?

"No, it's nothing like that. I apologize." Detective Peterson let out a sigh, then turned longing eyes on the coffee cart nearby. "On second thought, I could really do with a jolt. It's been a long night and even longer morning. I promise I won't take up much of your time."

"Okay." Intrigued, Kyla joined the detective on the short walk across the gnarled mulberry tree laden courtyard. The high-back cement benches basking in the mid-fall prelunch sun provided an odd kind of maze throughout the area. October in Sacramento was one of Kyla's favorite times of year and as she waited for her own nonfat mocha, she took a moment to enjoy the cool air that was such a relief after another brutal valley summer.

The look of bliss that crossed Detective Peterson's face when she took her sip of coffee had Kyla grinning to herself as she retrieved her own order. The detective stuffed a paper-wrapped croissant into her suit pocket and gestured to one of the benches nearby. "Thanks. I've been trying to cut down on the caffeine, but my system's fighting back."

Kyla resisted the urge to check her watch. She'd already texted Simone to say she was on her way and she hated being late. "Do you need to talk to me about a case?"

"Yeah, right, sorry." But the detective didn't look quite as flustered as she sounded. She dug into her other pocket and pulled out an evidence bag. "We found this on the body of a murder victim early this morning. She didn't have any other ID on her, so I'm at a bit of a loss. Lab's backed up, so running her prints is taking longer than I'd like."

Kyla accepted the plastic bag and looked at the card with worn and creased edges. She was uncertain what the detective thought she could offer as far as information until she saw her own name looking back at her. "It's definitely my card, but it's pretty old. I stopped handing these out two, maybe three, years ago?" She turned the bag over. Whatever had been scribbled on the back of the card was obscured with grime and age. "It's my paralegal card. I'm an attorney now."

"I thought you looked familiar. You've been with the DA for a while."

"Nearly ten years." Kyla smoothed a finger over the plastic covering her information, wishing she had an answer for the detective. "I started in the mail room when I was still in high school, then worked as a paralegal and assistant. Finally earned my prosecutor's stripes." She managed a quick, almost regretful smile. It seemed callous to be happy about her success when someone— someone she might have known—had recently lost their life. "I must have handed out hundreds of these cards." She'd been so proud of the title of executive administrative assistant, but even more touched that Simone herself had given Kyla the business cards as a promotion gift. Knots of unease tightened in Kyla's stomach. "This woman you found, do you have a picture of her?" At the detective's hesitation, Kyla pressed harder. "I'm assuming since you didn't lead with that, the victim's in pretty bad shape."

"Doesn't get much worse if I'm honest," Detective Peterson said. "It's not an image I'd want stuck in anyone's head, especially since I don't think she's identifiable. I knew the card was a long shot."

"But you still tried." And that, Kyla knew, was what had established Detective Lorna Peterson as one of the most dedicated detectives in the Sacramento Metro Police Department. She hadn't become as jaded as a lot of other detectives had over her twenty-plus years on the force. "And you knew I'd ask."

Detective Peterson's lips twitched. "I had a hunch." She pulled out her phone, tapped her screen, then handed the device to Kyla.

Kyla accepted the phone, but took a long, deep breath before she focused on the brutal image. Her years working as Simone's assistant had honed her detachment skills. Simone's propensity for taking on the toughest cases exposed Kyla to some of the most violent imagery and particulars that would make even the most experienced crime writers cringe. Boss, mentor and friend, Simone had wanted to make sure Kyla knew exactly what she was getting into by pursuing a career as a criminal prosecutor. All that preparation, however, didn't stop Kyla from flinching as she examined the photo of the brutally beaten woman. Kyla's blood went cold. This woman hadn't just been beaten.

Someone had wanted her obliterated.

Anger coiled around Kyla's disgust and snapped her back to reality.

"I won't have a more detailed description until the coroner's completed her exam," Detective Peterson said.

"All I feel safe in saying at this point is she's Caucasian, brunette, brown eyes, five foot six, about a hundred fifty pounds. I can't even guess her age."

"She can't be much older than me." And yet this young woman's life was over by twenty-eight. Why? Who was she? And why did she have Kyla's business card from years before? "Is there anything else you can tell me?"

Detective Peterson hesitated. "Hers was one of two bodies found in an alley about a block away from Night Crawler—"

"The nightclub off K Street?"

Detective Peterson's eyebrow arched. "You know it?"

"Hard not to." Kyla shrugged and sipped her almost forgotten drink. "It's not my scene, but I've come across it where some of our cases are involved. The owners aren't exactly considered pillars of the community." Both Vice and Narcotics had several investigations into various employees and customers over the years. Last she'd heard, the FBI wanted a piece of the action. All that said, Kyla couldn't think of one acquaintance who frequented the club. "You said there were two bodies?"

Detective Peterson nodded. "We've identified the male as a Kevin Dowell, age twenty-two. He's got a sheet—multiple arrests going back to before he could walk practically. Small-time stuff, nothing major. Drugs mostly. Been in and out of rehab a good part of his life. Name ring a bell?"

"No, I'm sorry." Still, something about the card, about the age of it, niggled at Kyla's mind. "There must be a reason the woman had my card." Call it a sign, call it a coincidence, but Kyla wasn't the type of person who could walk away from unanswered questions. Especially when it came to victims of violent crime. "Maybe seeing her in person would jar something loose. I could come down to the morgue." She handed the bag and phone back to the detective, who looked as surprised as Kyla felt having made the offer.

"You sure you want to do that? That's not an easy place to go."

"I've been there before." More times than she cared to count. It definitely wasn't her favorite place, but if she could help figure out who this poor woman was… "No one deserves to die unnoticed."

"On that we can agree." Detective Peterson pushed the evidence into the pocket of her suit jacket. "I'll arrange it with the coroner. Would three this afternoon work for you?"

Kyla was finally able to glance at her watch without feeling rude as they got to their feet. "That should be fine." She ran a nervous hand down the waist-length flowered scarf she'd tied in her hair that morning. Color was her solution to the darkness, to the despair and the reality she potentially faced every day. Wearing the bright, tropical flowers and prints always gave her a little light to focus on when days got dark.

"I'll make sure the coroner does what she can so this isn't too difficult for you." Detective Peterson glanced toward the street as traffic began to pick up for lunch. "You know where it is and where to go?"

"Yes. I'll see you at three."

"Great." The detective gave her a quick flash of a smile. "Gives me time to head back and fill in my lieutenant. Appreciate your help, Ms. Bertrand."

"Kyla, please." Kyla cleared her suddenly tight throat. Her father always said that with the good often came the bad. It was, he told her, the universe's way of balancing things out. Also the universe's way of reminding her never to get too comfortable or complacent. As excited as she was about her future, she needed to remember there was a present to deal with.

And it was that thought she carried with her on her walk to the DA's office.

After dropping her bag in her newish, windowless office, she headed back through the cubicles and hallways, clutching the fabric of her orange maxi-dress in one hand. She found her replacement, Penny Eddington—all five-foot-two power packed inches of her—spinning in her chair, cell phone glued to her ear beneath the tumble of black curls.

"Mom, I can't ask about vacation time when I've only been here a few weeks." Penny caught sight of Kyla. Her eyes went wide and she overcompensated. When her foot caught on the carpet, she pitched out of the chair and face planted on the floor. Her cell phone went flying and Kyla, unable to stop the laugh from bubbling free, set her cup down to help her up. "I'm sorry," Penny whispered, hands covering her flaming cheeks. "I'm so, so sorry. That was unprofessional and rude and—do you hear voices?"

Kyla retrieved Penny's phone and pushed it into her hand. "Tell your mother you'll have a week off at Christmas and we'll see about wrangling you a few days around Thanksgiving." That was less than a month away. It should be enough to mollify even the most demanding of parents.

"Thank you," Penny whispered and rubbed her nose. "Um, sorry about the chair thing."

Kyla shrugged. "Why do you think I wanted one that

spins? Is she in?" She gestured to Simone's closed door. Without waiting for an answer, she pushed it open. "Hey, Simone. I'm sorry I'm late. I had a visit—what's wrong?" She closed the door behind her and hurried to her friend who was standing at her window, looking down at the hustling traffic outside, a wadded up tissue in her hand. "Is it Vince?" Given Simone's husband was an in demand private investigator, it was possible he'd been injured. "Was he hurt on a case? Is he…?"

Simone waved her hand and shook her head. "It's nothing. Sorry. Vince is fine. I'm just having a bad moment."

"You don't have bad moments." After almost a decade, Kyla knew how to manage her boss. Her surrogate big sister. Her friend. "What's going on?" Kyla guided Simone over to the chair behind her glass desk. The office, much like the woman, was pristine, organized and classy. Amidst the awards, degrees and citations sat framed photos and mementos of her best friends and their families, a testament to a life fully led.

Sacramento's own Avenging Angel, a nickname Simone had earned with countless won cases that had put dozens of criminals behind bars, didn't only not have bad moments, she didn't have bad days. And she definitely didn't cry for no reason.

"I told you, it's nothing." Simone dabbed at her eyes.

"It must be something." Kyla scooped up crumpled papers and dropped them into the trash can, where she saw something that had her bending down. She reached out and pulled out the plastic test stick. Tears pricked the back of Kyla's eyes. "Oh, Simone." Simone and her husband, Vince, had been trying for over a year to have a baby. There had been tests and schedules and doctors' appointments and shots. Now there was a stick that showed none of it had worked. "I'm sorry."

"It's still early, I know. I mean, what's a year of trying, right?" Simone flipped her long blond hair behind her shoulders and straightened her fuchsia and white spattered silk blouse. "I just thought for sure this time... I'm six weeks late. I mean, good heavens, we've been trying like crazy." She swept her fingers under her eyes and gave a quick, albeit dim smile. "TMI, I know."

"As if it's a surprise you and Vince have sex." Kyla dropped the disappointing test back into the trash and covered it with the papers. "That's why we call you guys the window rattlers."

Simone laughed, a real laugh this time, only to have her eyes fill again. "Allie called."

"I thought she and Max were in Hawaii on vacation."

"They are. Allie's pregnant. She just found out and couldn't wait to share her news."

Ah. Kyla took a deep breath. There it was. Simone, Allie and Eden—three women tied at the hip, no, scratch that. The three friends had been tied at the heart since they'd met in kindergarten. Now, Eden and her husband Cole's baby girl, Chloe Ann, was closing in on her first birthday and Allie was about to join the ranks of motherhood, leaving Simone, who Kyla knew had always longed for a family of her own, trailing behind.

"Maybe you and Vince are just trying too hard," Kyla quipped.

Simone stopped and arched a brow.

Kyla rolled her eyes. "I mean maybe you're just too focused on getting pregnant. You two should take a hint from Allie and get away, forget about doctors and tests and baby making, and just reconnect. Go somewhere and turn off. Something might present itself. Don't you have like a million years of vacation saved up?" More than three weeks, if memory served and Kyla's memory *always* served.

"I have to admit, the thought crossed my mind." Simone blew her nose. "We haven't had any real time away alone together in a while. That wouldn't be giving up, right? Not trying for a while." Hope sprang into Simone's eyes and eased the weight around Kyla's heart. "I mean, if it's meant to happen, it'll happen."

"Exactly."

"Maybe next weekend will work if he's done with his case," Simone mused. "Hey, how did your appearance go in Judge Madison's court?"

And just like that they were back to business.

"Great. He denied the defense's request for a change of venue, so I offered another plea deal. Not as favorable as the last one of course," she added, making certain Simone knew she'd learned from her mentor's example. "If they don't take it—" and she really hoped they didn't "—jury selection will begin a week from Monday." Her first trial as first chair. The training wheels were off and she was on her way. Excitement and dread battled for control of her pulse.

"Excellent. A few more attention-grabbing cases like this carjacking and you'll be well on your way to earning that level four qualification you want. We should celebrate. How about a late lunch?"

"Don't you and Vince have lunch plans?" Kyla asked.

"Not today. If I'm going to convince him to take some time off, I need to let him work."

"I can probably do dinner." Kyla nibbled on her bottom lip. "Something's come up I need to take care of this afternoon." With everything else Simone had going on, Kyla didn't want to worry or distract her with Kyla's potentially futile trip to the morgue. Knowing Simone, she'd insist on going with Kyla.

"What's going on? You have a hot date? Oh!" Simone beamed. "Did you meet someone?"

Kyla had to wonder if Simone and Mirabelle Bertrand, Kyla's mother, were commiserating over Kyla's love life again. Knowing Mirabelle, it wouldn't surprise Kyla at all. "Considering you turned me into a workaholic, exactly when would I have had time to meet someone? So how about dinner?"

"Dinner's out." Simone's face twisted. "I'm meeting with Ward. I think he's going to tell me he plans to run for state attorney general."

"You think he'll try to get you to change your mind about running for DA again?"

"I have no doubt." Once upon a time, Simone would have jumped at that chance. Now, her ambition had taken a backseat to her determination to focus on family and friends. They knew all too well how quick life could turn. "Rain check?"

"Of course. I still need to have you and Vince over for dinner. You haven't seen my new place yet." Kyla headed to the door. She needed to finish up with her notes for the day before heading to the morgue.

"Let's aim for in a few weeks once things settle down," Simone said, glancing at her calendar. "I'll find a way to make it work for all of us."

Jason Sutton stepped out of the Sacramento County morgue on Broadway just as the afternoon sun slipped behind a bank of clouds. The slight ease in warmth had him stopping, lifting his face to the sky and taking a deep breath.

Rarely did a day pass that he didn't take a moment to appreciate the crisp breeze and the fall leaves as they dropped from thin-branched trees and scattered onto the sidewalk. As a former guest of the state prison system, there was a time not so long ago he wasn't sure he'd ever breathe free air again.

The entire buzz of the coming holiday season lightened his mood. Halloween was around the corner. His favorite time of year. He'd already decorated not only his own second story apartment with creepy and comical jack-o'-lanterns but also his brother's bar, The Brass Eagle. Cobwebs were strung across the doorways and windows, and new, mini pumpkin candles were flickering on the tables. He'd strung up a couple of ghosts on the ceiling so they hovered above the bar, flowing white gauze catching in the breeze whenever someone opened the front door.

If there was a pumpkin left in the valley, it wasn't because he hadn't tried to buy it. He'd even managed to persuade Vince to host a Halloween themed night, provided Jason oversaw the bar that evening. As excited as he was to implement some fun menu ideas and activities, all of Jason's celebratory anticipation had taken a backseat when he'd started a missing person's case last week.

He could have called the morgue, inquiring by phone to see if a body matching sixteen-year-old Bess Carmody's description had been found, but he'd wanted to check in person. A life was worth far more than a phone call and besides, coming down for a face-to-face inquiry helped him to establish his own connections in the medical examiner's office. He could only ride his big brother's successful private investigator coattails for so long. If Jason was going to make it on his own in this business, he was going to have to step out of that large shadow Vince Sutton cast. Not an easy thing to do as an ex-felon.

The good news was Bess wasn't here. The bad?

The more Jason learned about Bess Carmody, the more convinced he became she eventually would be. The girl wasn't just a troublemaker. She was in trouble. The kind of trouble Jason himself was all too familiar with.

Jason needed to find her before it was too late.

How ironic that his first case had him searching for a kid with a string of juvenile offenses Jason had been guilty of himself well before sixteen. Breaking and entering, vandalism, possession of pot. Truancy. Resisting arrest. The last had earned her a three week stint in juvenile hall.

Once upon a time he could have matched Bess crime for crime, delinquency for delinquency, with one big difference.

Jason was eventually held accountable for his offenses while, even now, Bess's parents continued to chalk up her bad behavior to growing pains and normal teenage rebellion. The Carmodys' high-priced connections and seemingly bottomless finances had earned Bess probation with the juvenile courts, far from the years in prison that had finally kicked some sense into Jason.

Normally his first stop would have been Bess's probation officer, but Bernice Yablonski, a twenty-plus year veteran of the department, was currently on extended family leave and not due back before next week. Until then, Jason was pretty much grasping at straws and hoping for a break that would get him the information he needed to bring Bess home.

The two years since he'd been released had been tough, but the support he'd found with his brother and sister-in-law, and by extension their friends, had helped him get his footing. But nothing would ever completely remove the stigma of his past.

Once a con, always a con. Something he was determined to prove wrong. All he needed was a chance and Bess's case gave that to him.

His cell phone vibrated in his pocket. Probably Vince checking in on him again. His brother seemed more anxious than Jason about this case. A case Vince hadn't seemed particularly eager for Sutton Investigations to take. Understandable considering Vince's history with missing kids. It had been Jason, after reading Bess's file, who couldn't say no.

That his brother agreed to let Jason accept this case for himself was something Jason did not take for granted. He knew Vince's private investigation business had taken a hit when he'd made Jason a full-time employee. Having a convicted felon on the payroll didn't exactly instill confidence. Being instrumental in helping track down a group of escaped prisoners as well as aiding in the rescue of an undercover FBI agent a few months ago had repaired a lot of the damage and earned them some loyalty from both the local PD and the Feds. Still, Jason wasn't about to let his brother down after Vince had placed so much faith in him.

A familiar flash of bright color bolted around the corner toward the front door of the morgue.

*Kyla.*

Jason's insides did that odd little dance whenever he spotted the pretty prosecuting attorney. As always, he slammed the door shut on any romantic possibility. Talk about pie in the sky dreams. She was so far out of his league they weren't even in the same universe. Besides, no way would he burden Kyla—or any other woman—with the emotional and historical baggage that dragged behind him.

It couldn't matter that the beautiful woman had captured his attention from the moment he'd met her, shortly after his release. Or that he found himself coming up with endless excuses to talk to her about…well, anything. They'd become friends. Flirty friends maybe, but that's where he'd told himself it had to stop. Even as he worked to redeem himself and his reputation, there was no getting rid of the darkness that, at times, swirled to the surface. He tried hard to keep himself in check, but he'd be lying if he said there weren't times his temper flared.

He'd grown up around explosions of anger. He didn't want Kyla to see any of that kind of volatile unpredictability.

Kyla radiated everything that was good in the world. She was also his stark and constant reminder he'd spent a good portion of his life inhabiting the shadows of the world she fought to expose.

Nope.

He had no business even thinking about getting involved with Kyla.

And yet…

And yet she had an amazing, pulse-kicking, stomach tightening laugh that made him smile. But he wasn't smiling now, not as he watched her move. Kyla's normally fluid, graceful movements seemed stilted. Jerky even. Something wasn't right.

"Kyla?" He left his car and headed back to the building, catching up to her as she pulled open the heavy glass door. His hand covered hers on the handle. "What are you doing here?"

"Oh, Jason, hi." That smile of hers broke through every dark cloud threatening to hover around his heart. "I, um." She stepped back to let someone walk out. "I'm meeting Detective Peterson. I might be able to identify a body they found near Night Crawler early this morning." Kyla tucked a springy black curl behind her ear and smoothed a hand over the narrow neon band that kept her hair back from her round face.

He'd heard about the bodies on the news. What did they have to do with Kyla? "Is this related to your carjacking case?"

"No. This is something…" She grimaced. "Different. I'm sorry. I'm already late. Can we talk about this when I'm done?"

"I can walk and talk." He followed her into the reception area.

Kyla shook her head. "You don't have to come with me. Really, this isn't anything you want to…" She trailed off as Detective Lorna Peterson looked up from her cell phone. "Detective. Sorry I'm late. Traffic was, well, traffic was typical." Kyla shifted her oversize turquoise bag on her shoulder. "Jason, I'm fine, really."

"So am I." Whatever was going on was definitely out of the norm for Kyla. He didn't know all the requirements of her job, but he'd never heard of her needing to take a solo trip to the morgue. "What's going on?"

Detective Peterson gave him a long, dubious look. One he was all too familiar with. He held out his hand and kept his expression neutral. "Jason Sutton."

"I know who you are." Detective Peterson shook his hand after a brief hesitation. "You're working for your brother these days, aren't you? Keeping out of trouble?"

Would there ever come a time when the unspoken accusation and the in-your-face doubt didn't hit him like a ton of bricks? It was the condescension he hated most. Like he was still a foolish adolescent trying to deal with the life he'd been dealt. "Yes, ma'am." He'd found politeness went a long way to earning even a tidbit of respect, especially where law enforcement was concerned. Even if his words were tinged with the tiniest hint of sarcasm. "I thought I'd stick around for Kyla. Moral support."

"I doubt you can help her identify a body."

"No," Jason said without missing a beat, or without missing the irritated gleam that sparked in Kyla's dark brown eyes. Not at him, he realized and took the boost of confidence. She was annoyed with the detective. "I can wait here if you'd rather, Kyla. Or go with you." He looked directly at Kyla. "Your choice."

Knowing what he did about Kyla, he suspected she was having an argument with herself. She didn't need anyone's help, and she certainly didn't need him holding her hand. But she also didn't appreciate it when people looked down their noses at others because of their pasts. It was one of her best qualities. Even as a prosecutor, she looked at the evidence before she cast judgment.

"I'd actually be grateful if you'd come with me, Jason, thanks," Kyla said. "Detective? Lead the way."

"All right." Detective Peterson angled him another

look before leading them through the staff only door. They navigated the aisles of cubicles, through another pair of doors into a hallway. Jason kept his eyes on Kyla as they bypassed TV monitors displaying in-progress exams and autopsies. The smell always got to him. He'd never been able to adequately define or describe it, but there was nothing else like it. A combination of chemicals and decay covered by the oh so familiar aroma of disinfectant.

"Wait here a minute." Detective Peterson instructed and left them alone in a locker room with long benches. She opened the door labeled *autopsies*, stuck her head in and called out to the attending coroner. "Okay, she's ready for us. Kyla, you can change your mind. This is going above and beyond—"

"You can't help this woman until you know who she is." Kyla straightened as if stiffening her spine. "I want to identify her if I can."

Jason's admiration for Kyla took a giant leap into the stratosphere. It was evident by the pinched expression on her face that she didn't want to do this; she felt she had to. She was going to do what was right, because that's who she was. It's who she'd always been. He doubted she'd ever made any decision, even when she was a kid, that would have derailed the future she'd focused on for herself.

"It shouldn't take too long." Detective Peterson opened the door and motioned for them to go inside.

Jason kept a hand close to Kyla's elbow, uncertain of her previous experience when it came to visiting the morgue. He'd been here far too many times, beginning when he was eleven and a local patrol officer had tried to scare him straight. How Jason wished it had worked.

The blinding bright light of the overhead lamps almost made him think of his sunglasses. They weren't led back to the cold storage where many identifications took place, but instead to a metal table where a scrubs-clad thirty-something woman waited for them.

"I'm Dr. McEwan." The brunette with frizzy, untamed curls greeted them. "I've cleaned her up as best I can. Detective Peterson said you might be able to identify her." Dr. McEwan stepped to the side and left Kyla and Jason to look down at the body, which was draped with a simple white sheet from shoulder to toe. The victim's damp hair hung in wet ropes over the edge of the steel table. Her skin was the shade of death; not quite gray. Not quite white. The bruising on her face, neck and shoulders was extensive and had Jason wincing. He really hoped Kyla didn't know this woman.

Kyla stepped forward. Jason forced himself to remain where he was—close enough to be there if she needed support, yet letting her do what she needed to do. She inclined her head, reached out a hand and brushed her fingers lightly over the woman's cheek. When her shoulders straightened and she gasped, his hope vanished.

"Julia." Kyla's whisper scraped against his heart. She lifted her chin, eyes slightly panicked and dazed when she met first Jason's and then Detective Peterson's gaze. "I think this is Julia Summerton. We were roommates at Sac State. That must have been why she had my card."

"When was the last time you saw her?" Detective Peterson asked.

"Two, three years ago?" Kyla looked back at the woman on the table. "We had lunch. Reconnected. Then we lost touch again. Um." She pressed her fingers into her temple before she recovered. "Julia has a tattoo, a dancing penguin, on her right hip."

"Doctor McEwan?" Detective Peterson asked.

Dr. McEwan stepped forward and lifted the sheet to expose the tattoo. "I'm sorry."

"She dropped out of school." Kyla spoke as if no one else had. "There were family issues. Money was tight. She lost her grant. Government cutbacks. She moved out halfway through our junior year, but she was doing okay when we last spoke. I might have some pictures from back then. I never throw pictures away."

"That would be a big help, Kyla. Thank you." Detective Peterson moved to usher her and Jason out of the room, but Kyla reached out to stop Dr. McEwan from covering Julia back up.

"What's that on her right arm?" Kyla pointed to the red band around the skin on Julia's bicep.

"A welt." Dr. McEwan moved around the table and lifted Julia's arm into brighter light.

"A recent one," Jason observed. Something niggled in the back of his mind. Something familiar he couldn't quite snap in place. "It's like someone's ripped something off her arm."

"How…" Kyla cleared her throat. "Was she beaten to death?"

"I can't be certain until I complete my exam," Dr. McEwan said. "But my preliminary findings tell me, given the number of broken bones in her face, there should be more bruising."

"Meaning she was probably beaten after she was dead," Jason said, grateful for small mercies.

"Then how did she die?" Kyla asked.

"I'm leaning toward an overdose," Dr. McEwan said. "There's some—"

"No." Kyla shook her head, her voice defiant. "No, that's not possible."

"Kyla—" Jason touched her arm and nearly jumped when she turned on him.

"Julia would never have done drugs. Never. I knew her, Jason. There is no way."

"You said you haven't seen her in almost three years," he reminded her before Detective Peterson could. "People change, Kyla. That's a lot of life to live." He should know. He'd lived multiple lifetimes in his almost three decades.

She wrenched her arm free from his hold. "It hasn't been long enough that Julia would start doing drugs. I want to know what the lab tests say when they come in." She swung on the doctor. "Can I know that?"

"I—" Dr. McEwan looked to the detective.

"I can let you know what they are when they come in," Detective Peterson said. "In the meantime, let's let Dr. McEwan get back to work."

"She wasn't an addict. She didn't do drugs." Kyla let herself be guided back into the hall where the monitors continued to run current exams. "I don't know what's going on, but there's no way Julia died of an overdose."

"The tests are going to say what they're going to say." Jason tried again. "I know how hard this is, Kyla. I've been there—"

"You have not been *there*," she snapped. "Not where Julia's concerned. If drugs killed her, she didn't take them voluntarily. Someone must have given them to her. Shot her up. Overdosed her on purpose."

Jason's eyes widened and his disbelief had anger

flashing like flint in Kyla's gaze. "That's a pretty big conclusion to come to without any evidence. Or is there evidence we don't know about?" he asked the detective.

"I've told you everything I know," Detective Peterson said. "Kyla, thank you for coming down. For giving her her name back. That'll be a huge help. And so will any pictures you can find of her."

"Her parents will have to be told." Kyla was shaking now, and she drew her arms around her, hugged her elbows in. "Her father's been ill for as long as I've known her. I'm not sure if they still live in the area—"

"I'll take care of it," Detective Peterson said. "Let me take care of her. I'll find out what happened to your friend, Kyla. I promise."

Kyla nodded, but there was an odd coolness in her expression. "Thank you."

"Come on." Jason gently steered her down the hall and back outside. "Kyla, I can only imagine what you must be feeling."

"Anger," Kyla spat as she stalked to the parking lot. Jason hurried after her, not entirely convinced she should be driving just yet. "A friend of mine is dead and she shouldn't be."

"I can see how upset you are. Kyla, hang on. Wait." He grabbed her hand when she reached into her purse for her keys. "You need to stop a minute and catch your breath. I know she was your friend and I know you only want to…" She only wanted to what? He couldn't read her mind, but he knew grief when he saw it. It cascaded off her in waves so thick it nearly drove him back a step.

"There is no chance that Julia was using drugs," Kyla seethed. "Impossible. Her older brother died of an oxy overdose when she was sixteen. She was majoring in psychology so she could help kids like him. She wouldn't even take aspirin, Jason. Beyond that, she wouldn't do it to her parents."

"All right." He wasn't going to argue with her. How could he when he didn't know much more than what he'd heard in the last few minutes? "Let's say that's true. What can you do about it?"

"What do you think I'm going to do about it?" She ripped her keys out of her purse and clicked open the door. "I'm going to find out who murdered my friend."

# Chapter 2

"You grind your teeth any harder and I'm going to call the dentist."

Jason glanced up as his brother dropped a stack of junk mail into a recycling bin near Jason's desk. The beady-eyed skeleton Jason had hung on the wall behind him cackled and rattled his bones.

Vince glared and shook his head even as Jason grinned. His brother had been spinning like a top all morning, tidying and straightening and triggering Jason's allergies by dusting. Vince had even gone so far as to desalinate the coffee machine. Jason clicked the second window on his screen closed. "What?"

"Something's bugging you." Vince Sutton walked around Jason's desk and peered over his shoulder at the information on Jason's computer. "You always get overly quiet when you're puzzling something out. You find something on Bess Carmody?"

"Maybe." Jason flexed his fingers. He didn't like what he was coming up with, but he wanted to find a way to handle it himself. "Took me a few days but I finally got Bess's cell phone records." He refrained from telling Vince his frustration had nearly driven him to hack the cell phone provider's server.

"I thought her parents were going to help you with that."

"They were too busy packing to catch their flight to Cancún. Time-share reservations," he added at Vince's blank stare. "Yeah, I know. With folks like that, no wonder Bess took off." It wasn't the first time she'd disappeared. But this was the first time she hadn't come back. After ten days, rather than going to the police to report her missing, they'd approached Vince. Despite Jason's lack of trust in the police, he wasn't so disillusioned that he didn't think a report might actually have helped.

"What do the phone records tell you?" Vince asked.

"That her cell hasn't even been on for more than two weeks." From what he knew about teenagers, existing without a cell phone wasn't a physical possibility. "I did talk to one customer service rep who was willing to ping the phone's last location."

"And?"

Jason bit the inside of his cheek. He hadn't mentioned his meeting Kyla at the morgue, or her parting comment that, Jason had to admit, had kept him up the past couple of nights. "A nightclub on K Street."

"Only club I know of is Night Crawler." Vince stopped, glanced over his shoulder at Jason and cursed. "That place is bad news."

"So I've heard." If his brother agreed with the sentiment, Jason was going to have a fine line to walk. Vince and missing kids were not an ideal combination, which explained Vince's reluctance to take the case in the first place. But Jason had wanted to prove himself, get his feet wet so he could stand on his own in this industry. He also wanted to bring Bess home, safe and sound. "You heard about the two bodies they found near the club?"

"Hard not to," Vince said. "Still, Night Crawler." He shook his head. "The O'Callaghan brothers have a pretty nasty reputation and have since they hit town, what, five years ago? You name it, they're into it."

"Unlike the Sutton brothers." Jason attempted to keep the tone light.

"Yeah, well, we keep things legal around here." Vince slapped a hand on Jason's shoulder. "Mostly legal, anyway. You start sniffing around that place, you be careful. Word is those brothers are connected and not in any way we're set up to deal with. Watch your back, yeah?"

"Understood." Jason appreciated that Vince didn't err on the side of over-protection. He'd trusted Jason, all but considered Jason's stint in prison as nothing more than a blip on the radar of his kid brother's life. But it was more than a blip. One day Vince was going to have to accept that. Still, Jason didn't believe in coincidences. In the past twenty-four hours, Night Crawler had popped up twice. First with Kyla's friend, Julia, and now with Jason's missing teen.

Ignoring the coincidence would be tantamount to reckless negligence.

And if *he* felt that way… Jason shifted in his chair. He could only imagine what Kyla was thinking about now.

Jason watched, slightly amused, as his brother returned to his desk and began to straighten it. Again.

"You due for an inspection or something?" He'd never seen Vince quite so fastidious before.

"No. Just keeping busy. I closed my case last night. Nervous energy."

Marines didn't get nervous. Not even ex-marines. Not that there was such a thing. His brother wore his service on his sleeve, from the brass eagle moniker on the front door of his bar, to the military-style buzz that left his head just shy of shiny. Vince still ran five miles a day and maintained his business with a ruthless precision any commanding officer would have approved of. In other words, Vince Sutton did not do nerves.

"Simone mentioned taking some time off down in Monterey. Her folks own a beach house down there." Vince hesitated. "With you talking about the O'Callaghans. You think you'll be okay on your own for a week or so?"

"I'll be fine." Despite the trust, even after two years, his brother still hovered occasionally. Still…worried. Jason understood and even appreciated it, to a point. But there was nothing his big brother could do about the ghosts that haunted Jason. "Why do you look like there's a guillotine about to fall on your neck?"

"Because my wife lobbed the 'you plan it and I'll pretend to be surprised' idea at me and romance isn't exactly up my alley."

"Then work on your presentation." How was it that Jason—an ex-con with a penchant for computer tech, hacking and an affinity for fortified water—had more of a romantic streak than his former military brother? "Surprise her with some wine and flowers for when you get there. Oh, I know. Get her a box of those brownies she likes as her invite. And if that fails, beg." Jason grinned. "You're good at that, aren't you?"

Vince grunted, but inclined his head in approval. "That could work. The brownies I mean. Good idea."

"Maybe you could say that as if I didn't just master putting on socks." Still, Jason found himself marveling at the life his brother had made for himself.

Who would have thought, given their upbringing that either Sutton brother would have found anything close to happiness and marital bliss? Not Jason, that was for sure. Okay, so it had taken Vince and Simone two tries to get it right, but marriage number two seemed to be an entirely different story than their first attempt.

"Don't worry about me," Jason assured him when Vince looked like he was going to argue about leaving town. "I'm probably tied to this computer for the foreseeable future." He was planning to research the heck out of Night Crawler and the O'Callaghan brothers before he even thought about stepping foot inside the club. "I can get those brownies today for Simone when I pick up my lunch."

Vince's mouth twisted. "I don't know why you insist on spending money on food when there's a fully stocked kitchen downstairs in the bar."

"Because you mostly serve carnivores." Jason turning vegetarian after his release from prison had been one of many things that confounded his brother. "Vary your menu in the bar a bit more and we'll talk." He grabbed his keys. "Well? You want me to grab them? I can drop it off at her office on my way back here."

"Yeah." Vince scribbled a few choices on a piece of scratch paper and added the name of Simone's favorite bakery—the one that had done their wedding cake.

"Let's go with a gift box of those brownies. Wait. Let me write her a note." He grabbed another sheet and, after a brief hesitation, scribbled something down and folded it more than was necessary. He snatched it away when Jason reached for it. "Not for your eyes."

"Please." Jason scoffed. "I stopped reading your love notes to girls when I was…" Vince's expression dared him to continue with that lie. Jason chuckled, pocketed the note and headed for the door. "I'll be back in a bit."

"No, no, no. That's not right." Kyla scribbled out yet another sentence and added a *NO* in capital letters. This was not working.

Splitting her attention between her upcoming case and Julia's pending autopsy results had made her as unproductive as a hyperactive kindergartner on the first day of school. She jumped as one of the paralegals darted by and slapped a comical black cat wearing an orange witch's hat on Kyla's door. Kyla's mouth twisted.

Halloween gave her the creeps.

She glanced at her computer screen, waiting for an email from either the coroner or Detective Peterson that seemed destined never to arrive. The website for Night Crawler was minimized in the bottom right corner of the screen. Its splashy, obnoxious graphics flashed and blinked, distracting her, taunting her, convincing her that's where she'd find answers about her friend's death.

Her opening statement for the jury she'd be seating next week had yet to coalesce in her mind, let alone on paper. Every time she thought she'd found the right hook, she found herself doing another online search. And, as temptation had proven too much, she'd even stayed late last night to access any files in the DA's office that even mentioned Night Crawler. This morning, she'd siphoned through two years of junk email in case she'd missed a message from Julia that would shed some light on why her friend would have made it a point to have Kyla's business card with her.

Other than a disturbing amount of suspicious—and unproven—criminal activity at the club, she'd come up with an absolute zero for results. Every time law enforcement came close to building a case, whatever witnesses they had either recanted or vanished and the entire process would start over.

Until she read that report, until she spoke with Detective Peterson again, there was nothing more she could do about Julia's death. She nibbled on the end of her pen. Or was there?

"Okay. Stop. Get that thought out of your head. Focus, Kyla. Fo. Cus." She took a deep breath and then released it.

She needed to get her opening statement not only finished, but polished so she could start practicing. But no matter how hard she tried, she couldn't get the image of Julia's body out of her head.

There was no way Julia had died of a drug addiction. No. Way.

She ripped off the sheet of paper from the pad, crumpled it up and chucked it across the room.

"Let me know if that actually helps."

Kyla glanced up to find Jason Sutton standing in the open doorway of her office. She shifted, reached for her mouse to close the screen, but it had already gone dark. Kyla waved him in and instantly the space seemed to shrink.

Space was a kind word for the tight quarters—with

barely enough room for a desk, two chairs and a tall metal filing cabinet, all of which were piled with files, notepads and books. But it was hers. She'd earned it. And she was slowly making it her own. "Hey." She dropped her pen, surprised at how easily a smile formed on her lips. "What brings you by?"

"Delivery run for Vince. Brownies for Simone. Cute cat," he added and hefted a cardboard tray in his hand before setting it on her desk. "Thought maybe you could use a pick me up, too."

"Well, that was nice of you." Her mood brightened as his cheeks went red. She'd bet half a month's pay he had no idea how cute he was when he blushed, even behind the beard. *Oh, stop*, she ordered herself. Cute thoughts about Jason Sutton were only going to get them both into trouble.

Lots and lots of trouble.

As she plucked the coffee cup free, she hid her own smile. It was so easy to be around Jason. Even though he made her nerves jolt, she'd mastered her ability to conceal her reaction to him. Past not-withstanding— and his was a doozy—Jason was what her mother called a nice guy. When Mirabelle Bertrand told him that to his face, his ensuing blush had proven her right. Polite, presentable. Conscientious and a bit of a goof. He could also be more intense than most of the men she'd been interested in in her on-again, mostly off-again social life.

In recent months, that baby face of his had been transformed by the full beard he now sported and slightly too long brown hair. She'd often found herself trying to come up with an excuse to touch it, to tame it, and always, so far at least, refrained from giving in to temptation. But now, she found her resistance to be on shaky ground.

With a sturdy build and a spark in his eye that noted an appreciative if not guarded skepticism of life, Jason Sutton reminded her of a certain shield-wielding superhero; a man determined to make amends and right the world's wrongs.

A man who, strangely enough, saw both sides far more easily than she ever could. There definitely wasn't anything wrong with that.

Or with him.

She pulled the handles of the small paper bag apart and would have let out a squeal if she hadn't been at work. "White chocolate blondies." She reached in, broke off a piece, and stared at it lovingly. "How did you know these are my favorite?"

"I'm a detective, remember?" He glanced around for somewhere to sit.

"Just move those wherever." Kyla gestured to the stack of files on one of the two chairs. "I owe you for this. You've saved me from the toxicity of the break room." She really needed to get her own coffee machine in here. She removed the lid and took a deep breath of caffeine enhanced chocolate. "Double shot mocha?" When he started to respond, she held up a finger, sipped, sighed and relaxed. "It's perfect." Glancing at her phone, she noticed the time. "My brain always dips around now. So you saw Simone?"

"Just for a minute. She was heading out to a meeting." He shook his head. "To be honest, delivering for Vince was an excuse. I was worried about you. How are you doing?"

"Me? Fine." She started to shrug, then saw his eyebrow arch. "Okay. I'm doing okay."

"Really?" He didn't look convinced. "Seeing your friend like that—"

Kyla held up her hand, then gestured to the door. Jason reached back and pushed it closed. "Thanks. I haven't told anyone about Julia, especially Simone. You didn't say anything to Vince about her, did you?"

"No." Jason's response had her breathing easier. "I figured if you wanted them to know, you'd tell them."

"Yeah, I will tell them. Just not yet." She sipped more coffee. "I don't want anything derailing their getaway plans."

"You know about that?"

"I know everything about those two," she joked without laughing.

"This I've heard," Jason teased with a slight smile. "I also wanted to tell you I was sorry."

She inclined her head. "For what?"

"I didn't mean to sound like I wasn't taking you seriously yesterday. Or that I didn't hear you about Julia. I did. If you say she didn't do drugs, I believe you. I do. So. Yeah." He cringed. "This sounded better in my head when I rehearsed it."

The idea that Jason had rehearsed talking to her was probably the sweetest, most unexpected thing she'd ever heard.

"I appreciate you saying that." She hoped her smile was enough to close the subject. "You're forgiven."

"Have you heard from Detective Peterson?"

"A couple of times. Perfunctory updates. Once to thank me for the pictures I dropped off at the station." It was hard keeping the edge out of her voice. Detective

Peterson was a good cop, but if that toxicology report came back positive, she wouldn't have the time or inclination to pursue Julia's death based solely on Kyla's opinion. She'd close it and move on and Julia would be forgotten. "I'm sure when she has information to share, she will. Until then, I have a trial to prepare for."

"So you're letting Detective Peterson handle it?"

She ignored the doubt clinging to his words. "I don't have another choice." She imagined the smile she offered was bitter.

"You're not one to give up so easy," Jason said in a way that surprised Kyla. "What about Cole or Jack? Maybe they could—"

"I tried." She grimaced. "I called both this morning, hoped maybe they could find something out for me considering they've worked with Detective Peterson before, but they told me the case was in good hands and that I should drop it."

"That seems…odd." Jason's brows knitted.

Didn't it, though? Detectives Cole Delaney and Jack McTavish had always been willing to do a little digging, at least for Simone or Cole's wife Eden—an online crime blogger with a penchant for investigating cold cases. When Jack's murder-witness-turned-wife had him putting his own career on the line to protect her, there had been no question or hesitation. And don't even get her started with the chances they took with Allie Hollister, who went missing back when Jack got shot.

But when Kyla asked for help with Julia's death? Suddenly she was met with a stony, disappointing wall of silence and avoidance.

"Odd doesn't begin to describe this whole situation. But I can take a hint." Kyla pinched her lips together.

She wasn't about to say something that would get back to Vince and thus Simone. Nor was she going to let this go. "That reminds me, what were you even doing at the morgue the other day?"

Whatever optimistic light had been shining in Jason's eyes dimmed. "I'm working on a missing person's case. Sixteen-year-old named Bess Carmody. Girl's got a past that could put mine to shame."

"Runaway?"

"Looks that way."

"You don't sound convinced." Kyla could practically see the wheels turning in Jason's head.

"Runaway makes it sound simple and from what I've learned, there's nothing simple about this girl. I've got a lot of unanswered questions. Tell me something."

"Sure." She sat back, holding her cup between her hands.

"Bess was in therapy when she went missing. What are the odds...?"

"Zilch."

"But I didn't finish—"

"Asking me how you could get your hands on her medical records? Yeah, you and Vince are cut from the same cloth." She circled a finger in the air, aimed between his eyes, at that tiny wrinkle that appeared whenever the Sutton brothers were trying to get away with something. "You knew the answer before you even asked and I will confirm that, legally, you're out of luck. The only way you could see those files would be if her therapist waived confidentiality—"

"Her parents couldn't? Not that they would," Jason added.

Kyla shook her head. "HIPAA regulations. Bess is

the patient, end of story. It would be up to her to waive privilege and given she's a minor, even that would be tricky. The only thing that could supersede the regulations is her death and that could become a legal battle if her doctor decided to make it one."

"I'm not planning on going down that road." Instead of looking disappointed, he shrugged as if she'd just presented him with a challenge. "I guess I'd best let you get back to work. Oh." He stopped and turned. "Do you know if there's going to be a funeral?"

It took her a moment to understand his question, then felt ashamed she didn't catch on right away. "I don't. Not yet. Detective Peterson said she spoke with Julia's mother yesterday. I guess her father passed away last year and she's all alone. I'm planning to call Mrs. Summerton myself." From what Detective Peterson had said, Kyla had the feeling Julia's mother wasn't in the best of health and the news about her daughter had hit hard. Kyla had mentioned getting permission from Julia's mother to access her friend's house but was informed, without going into detail, that it wouldn't be necessary.

"If there's anything I can do to help, let me know," Jason offered.

"Thank you." The offer touched something inside of her. "I will. Thanks again for the coffee and blondie."

Jason's smile didn't quite reach his eyes. "Anytime."

Kyla was lying.

Jason kept the uneasy thought at bay until he was back in his car. Sheltered from the fall warmth in the three story parking lot, he sat back and stared out at the buildings across the street.

She wasn't lying about everything, but when he

asked about her letting the police handle Julia's death? Yeah. He frowned. She was definitely lying.

He'd caught a glimpse of her screen before it had blanked out, saw she'd had the website open for Night Crawler. And at least one of the case files on her desk he remembered had featured Night Crawler as a place of interest.

If she was keeping things quiet, that meant she planned to do whatever she was thinking about on her own. Alone. Without any help. Without any backup.

She probably figured she didn't have a choice given her two go-tos, Detectives Jack McTavish and Cole Delaney, had turned her down. Jason turned the key and started his car and headed back to The Brass Eagle.

Kyla wasn't foolish. Not by any stretch of the imagination. But he knew how reckless people got when emotions were involved, and of course Kyla was emotional about Julia's death. Especially when she wasn't getting the answers she wanted.

He had a little time, at least he hoped he did, to get a bead on Night Crawler and what really went on there. She had a case to think about and prepare for while she decided on what her next move was going to be. So yeah. He had a window of time.

But when she did make her move, Jason planned to be right there.

Whether she wanted him to be or not.

# Chapter 3

Nearly twenty-four hours after receiving the coroner's report as an email from Detective Peterson—an *email*, not a phone call as was promised—Kyla was still mad. It had shifted into a measured, steady, blood-boiling seethe that had taken most of the day to bring down to a simmer.

Toxicology reports were still pending, but preliminary results led to a ruling of death by misadventure, meaning they were ruling Julia's death an accidental drug overdose.

Case. Closed.

Kyla gnashed her back teeth. Exactly what she'd been expecting; been dreading. She'd wanted to be wrong, but she'd witnessed enough in her ten years in the DA's office to expect anything other than what she got.

But she was going to get her answers.

Beginning tonight.

Kyla straightened up and ran her pinkie under her lower lip to erase the smudged color. The thick dark liner that had taken her half an hour to apply was staying in place around her eyes; the stark silver eye shadow was a perfect match to her discoball of a go-go dress she'd found on the clearance rack of Evangeline's in Old Sacramento.

She'd no sooner reached for the handle of her car to slip out of the vehicle when her cell phone rang. Shoot. If she didn't answer Simone's ringtone, Simone would know something was wrong. Kyla rarely, if ever, went out on a Saturday night.

Sitting back, she pulled out her phone and answered, doing her best to erase the frustration coating her throat. "If you're calling me," she said in way of greeting, "clearly the beach isn't working for you."

"Ha ha." Simone's snort had Kyla smiling. "It's actually great down here. Should have done this months ago."

"Yeah, well, wait until you're well and truly relaxed before you declare the trip a success. What's up?" *Keep it easy. Keep it quick. You have places to be.* "You cleared your desk off before you left yesterday."

"It's not about work. Exactly. I was looking through my emails. Saw the weekly police report come through. Julia Summerton." Simone's tone gentled. "Kyla, you knew her. Why didn't you tell me?"

Kyla's stomach dropped. She should have realized Simone would remember her one-time college roommate. Simone remembered everything. "You have a lot going on." Kyla tried to sound nonchalant. "I didn't want you to worry."

"Kyla." Simone sighed. "We're family. You should have told us. We could have been there for you and instead—"

"Instead you're putting your focus where it should be—on Vince and my future honorary niece or nephew." Kyla leaned over to peer up at the blinding lamppost over her car. "Simone, I promise. We can talk about it when you get back, all right?"

"If you're sure." Simone clearly didn't approve of that option. "What about the funeral? If it's next week, we can come back—"

"There isn't going to be one," Kyla said. "I'm taking Julia's ashes to her mother in a few weeks. Her mom already arranged for Julia to be cremated as soon as the body is released." If things went as planned, she'd be delivering Julia back home along with some answers for her only remaining family member.

"They haven't released the body?" Simone's disbelief had a new alarm ringing in Kyla's brain.

"I was told it was pending," Kyla said. "Why? Does that seem strange?"

"Not necessarily." Simone spoke in her prosecutor's voice. "They could be waiting to see if they need more tests. What about the man they found with her?"

Kevin Dowell. Kyla frowned. "I didn't ask." And she should have. "I'll do that next week. Simone, really, you shouldn't be calling me about this." She glanced at her watch. "It's almost eleven on a Saturday night. Surely Vince has other plans for you?"

"Vince is busy unpacking his things."

"Vince finished unpacking in about three minutes last night." Vince's voice echoed in the background. "Give me the phone, babe."

"But I don't—"

Kyla curled her toes in the too-high, glitter-coated ankle-breaker sandals.

"Kyla." Vince's voice carried that concerned big-brother tone he'd adopted years before, when he and Simone had first been married.

"I didn't tell her on purpose," Kyla explained before he could accuse her. "I want you guys to have this time to yourselves."

"I appreciate that. We appreciate it. Yeah, a beer would be great. Thanks. Hang on." Kyla squirmed in her seat, listening to the sound of a sliding door opening and closing. "How are you? Really?"

Kyla closed her eyes. He sounded just like Jason. "I'm working through it."

"Uh-huh. Well, if working through it causes you some problems, you call Jason, all right?"

"Call Jason for what?" She cringed at the squeak in her voice. "Vince, I'm not—"

"Your friend is gone and from what Simone told me, there aren't any clear answers. I'd bet good money you aren't spending your usual Saturday night alone, curled up on the couch with Loki and reading him B-I-N-G-O."

"That's a song and we both know I don't sing." She pinched her lips closed. She hated lying to the people she cared about.

"Kyla?"

"Yes?"

"I get it. I do. Just be careful. I mean it. Don't make me bring Simone back early to identify *your* body in the morgue."

Kyla's entire body went cold. He knew. How did

Vince know she'd been to the morgue? Had Jason said something to his brother after all? "I know what I'm doing, Vince." She flicked a finger against one of her giant hoop earrings.

"I guess we'll find out, won't we. I'm a call away. Always."

He hung up before she could respond. Afraid she'd chicken out, she grabbed the small clutch that was big enough to carry her fake ID and her cell, along with a lipstick and some cash, and pushed out of her car.

Her thick heels clacked along the sidewalk as she rounded the corner toward Night Crawler. Her parents had been surprised when she'd decided on working for the DA's office rather than becoming a public defender or working with a firm for social change, but Kyla had worked with Simone and so many others enough over the years to know that prosecutors were fighting for change, too. From inside the system. And that, Kyla was convinced, would help her make a difference.

The club was easy to miss with its obscure metal door and rusted oversize hinges. The pulsating beat thrumming, heavy enough to make the cement vibrate, kicked her into gear and reminded her why she was here. And who she was supposed to be: a college dropout looking for the friend who had recommended Night Crawler to her as a place to…start over.

Night Crawler definitely kept a tight rein on the appearance factor and promoted the club as a hot spot where kids of the wealthy and powerful hung out. Drawing customers from as far south as the Bay Area, Night Crawler had become one of the go-to spots for people looking for a "private" good time.

The line to get in was long and peppered with college students and some kids clearly too young to be legally admitted; to a passerby, it looked like Night Crawler was any other trendy club with its share of fans and anxious partiers.

But she had no doubt there was far more to this place than met anyone's eye. Speaking of eyes. She stood close to the entrance, hand on her hip, and pouted.

"Pretty lady like you should be smiling." The tall, buzz-cut, bulky bouncer standing guard at the end of a red velvet rope offered her a grin that had his round face looking like a carved Halloween pumpkin.

"Hard to smile thinking I'll be stuck at the end of this line all night." She sighed.

He crooked a finger. Heart hammering, she walked over, smelled the odd combination of liniment oil and tequila. "You got ID?"

"I do." She pulled out the fake one she'd created online. He barely glanced at it, his dark eyes flickering. "You think I'll find my Prince Charming in there?" She noted the name embroidered on his black T-shirt. "Clyde."

"Maybe you'll find him out here."

"Maybe I will," she teased back.

The intermingling tattoos on his cyborg-sized biceps caught against the dim light of the overhanging bulb. He waved her through, silenced the protesting crowd with a glare that had Kyla shivering, then reached out and pulled open the door for her. The music instantly blared fullblast; the heavy techno-bass thrummed low in her belly. "You be safe, you hear?"

Oh, she heard. But only barely.

The instant she stepped inside, her smile faded. Marble tile coated the floor of the narrow dark hallway leading to the winding staircase. Glittered walls gleamed and reflected the strobing and spinning lights which caught the sequins of her silver dress and lit her up like a firecracker. She walked to the beat, scanning the crowd and throngs of people mingling in groups and along the waist-high iron railing.

She couldn't see enough space between people, they were packed into the space so tightly. Ugh. She straightened her shoulders. So not her scene.

Downstairs, at the far end of the dance floor, private rooms hosted parties and upscale socializing opportunities. This was a dealmakers' den. For all kinds of deals, she'd bet.

She glanced at her watch. The owners, brothers originally from back east, were rumored to make an appearance every night. Her research, meager as it was, told her Colin and Liam O'Callaghan couldn't have been more different if they'd been born on separate planets. Liam, the older brother by ten months, rarely interacted with anyone outside the private rooms whereas Colin, more handsome and oozing charm, spent a good portion of his evenings mingling with the clientele on and off the dance floor.

Kyla descended the stairs, trying to appear as if she was looking for someone. She had questions to ask, on the sly of course, about Julia. About Kevin Dowell who, until recently, she'd discovered was a part-time employee for the place.

All she needed was some information to pass along

to Detective Peterson—enough that Julia's case didn't stay in a file as cold as her body.

Kyla remembered hearing Vince say he learned a lot more just by hanging around and listening than by asking intrusive questions. Maybe that was worth a shot.

She maneuvered her way over to the glass-topped bar and settled onto a stool.

The bar was crowded, but not as packed as the dance floor or the surrounding tables. The normally stale air associated with the club scene didn't have a chance against the pure oxygen she suspected was pumped in through the ventilation system. Delayed reaction to the alcohol and frenzied socializing meant more drinks sold, which meant longer nights for the patrons.

*Money, money, money*, Kyla thought. The bottom line every time.

She made herself comfortable and set her clutch on the bar. The nerves that had accompanied her jangled to life. Her pulse kicked into high speed in her throat. Since passing the bar exam last year, she spent most nights catching up on work. Whatever nights she did go out were quiet events with good food and wine, and often ended with an alcohol-induced realization that her bed had been seriously cold on one side for far too long. Those lamentations had been replaced by Julia's death; it was not just the guilt at having let a friendship lapse, but that despite all Kyla's hard work and mapped out plans, her own life could take an unexpected turn at any moment. Talk about a sobering wake-up call.

Someone jostled her from behind. When she glanced over her shoulder, she barely had time to catch a glimpse of the well-dressed man moving onto the stool next to her before a bartender approached.

"Evening." The tall Latina behind the bar gave Kyla a wide, welcoming—and evaluating—smile. Her name tag read Lola. "You're a new face. What's your name, sweetheart?"

"Darlene." Kyla crossed her legs, resisting the urge to shift forward. Lola was stunning, with shiny black hair she wore braided all the way down her back and a skintight red leather dress that exposed just the right amount of sienna-toned flesh to draw attention. "I'll take a Cosmo, hold the vodka and triple sec."

"You've got it," Lola yelled with a nod.

"Busy night!" Kyla yelled back.

Lola rolled her eyes and shrugged, and a few moments later set a martini glass filled only with cranberry juice in front of Kyla. "New band!" Lola yelled back. "On in about an hour. What brings you here?"

Kyla sipped her drink. "I'm looking to invest in a 401(k)."

"You want a job?" Lola's eyes went wide. "Word is the coffee house up on 14th and J is looking to hire. Maybe check it out?"

"What's wrong with here?" Kyla asked. "I saw on-line they're looking for something called a Temptress. Maybe I qualify?"

Kyla noticed Lola's jaw clench before she poured three shots of Scotch. She angled an appraising look at some of the dancers on the floor. "That job's not for a smart girl like you."

"Maybe I'm tired of being smart," Kyla challenged. "Maybe I'm just looking for some fun."

Temptresses, as she'd learned via Night Crawler's social media accounts, were hired to make the club as profitable as possible by ensuring the customers had a memorable time—while spending as much cash as possible.

They also had tattooed bands around their biceps.

In the exact same spot where Julia's body had displayed an angry welt.

It was a threadbare connection, but one Kyla had clung to.

"There's nothing fun about what those girls do," Lola said.

"I heard Temptresses make good money," Kyla said.

The man behind her seemed to be having trouble keeping his balance on the stool. Kyla gnashed her teeth. *If he bumps into me one more time…*

"They can," Lola said with a sidelong glance that told Kyla she was skirting the edge of suspicion. "That's not a job that always stays on the dance floor."

"Oh?" Kyla feigned surprise. If Night Crawlers was a front for prostitution, that would explain Vice's interest in the place. Dread pooled sick and sour in her stomach. Julia hadn't gotten caught up in that life had she? "I'm just looking to make a little money to pay off my college loans. Nothing…extracurricular."

"None of my business what you do." Lola's tone suggested, however, that she definitely did not approve of Kyla's choice of potential employment.

Kyla looked back over her shoulder and watched the suffocating crowd gyrating to the deep, undulating beat of the music. She lost count of the number of bicep tattoos she saw on various young women. "It does seem like there's already enough of them on the floor."

"Boss likes to keep at least a dozen in rotation." Lola's trepidation seemed to vanish. "It's a job people like to hang on to, if they can deal with the consequences the next morning. Not sure that's you, considering your beverage of choice." Lola inclined her chin toward the cranberry juice. "Just consider what you might be getting into."

"Appreciate the warning." Kyla's mind raced.

"You want anything else, you flag me down, okay?"

Kyla nodded, immediately missing the comfort and protection of having someone to talk to as Lola moved off. The man behind her elbowed her as he turned on his stool. No way was that an accident.

"Look." Irritation surged through her as she spun on her stool and glared at him. "If you can't stay in your own space…" She'd suddenly recognized the all-too familiar blue eyes glaring back at her. "Jason!"

"Announce it to the world why don't you." Jason Sutton picked up his glass and downed the amber liquid that was left. "What are you doing here, Kyla?"

"Darlene. And I could ask you the same question." He was the last person she expected to run into at Night Crawler. "Did Vince send you?"

"If Vince knew I was here, he'd probably read me the riot act," He turned his head and she couldn't hear the rest of his thought. "I'm working. That girl I've been looking for?" His gaze flickered to Lola, then back to Kyla. "Last place her phone pinged was here. Not only that—" he picked up his drink and took a healthy swallow "—something told me you were going to show up."

She arched her brow at him and lifted a shoulder. "So? I'm working, too."

"Not officially, you aren't." He reached out and took hold of her hand, entwined their fingers as he drew her closer. The air froze in her chest. Every bit of skin where he touched her suddenly felt warm. "Relax, *Darlene*. We're just two people at a bar testing the waters."

"I, um." Why couldn't she think? Because this wasn't the Jason Sutton she was used to: affable, fun, solicitous, polite Jason who tended to stay in the corners unnoticed rather than demand attention. Safe Jason. This Jason was cooler, edgier and just a little bit scary. An excited thrill shot through her as reason struggled to retain control. Safe didn't live in the same zip code as this guy. "Stop that."

"Can't." His grip eased, but he kept hold of her. "That would defeat your purpose."

"This is Vince's doing, isn't it?" Kyla tried not to focus on how perfect their fingers twined around one another. "He told you to babysit me after you told him about Julia."

"Vince doesn't need me telling him anything." That tell of his didn't appear, not even in the dim light of the club. "I said I wouldn't tell him and I didn't."

"Yeah, well, he knows."

"He might suspect, but trust me, if he knew you were at a nightclub stalking the owners who are rumored to have serious underworld connections, he'd be here himself to haul you home. Care to wager what Simone would do to you?"

Guilt had her squirming. "Then how did you—"

"Because you're a terrible liar. And because I saw

the website on your computer screen. Plus—" he drew
a finger down her forehead to her nose and over her lips
"—I can tell when you're keeping a secret. Relax," he
said again and moved closer. "Touching is one of the
many things people do here."

She tried to do as he suggested and relax but dealing with Jason touching her wasn't exactly easy. He was
waking up parts of her that had been happily asleep for
months. "I'm not casing the place."

"Honey, you may as well be taking notes like Lois
Lane. You are not good at this. Now take a drink and
laugh as if I'm really entertaining you."

"Don't call me honey." But she did as he suggested
and drank, mainly because it gave her something to do.
All the nerves she'd been quieting the past few minutes clanged back to life. "What do you think you're
helping?"

"Keeping you from getting that job you think you
want."

She stiffened. "I know what I'm doing."

"No," Jason said with a dangerous gleam in his eye.
"You really don't." He tugged hard on her hand, spun
her stool around so her knees knocked into his. "Colin
O'Callaghan got here about ten minutes ago. He's been
watching you while he and his brother have been talking upstairs. No, don't look." He reached up, caught her
chin with his free hand and peered deep into her eyes.

Kyla licked her suddenly dry lips. Then jolted when
Jason's gaze dropped to her mouth. For a long, awe-
struck moment, she thought he was going to kiss her.

"You have his attention, Kyla," he whispered.

A pinprick of fear stabbed her in the heart. "How long have you been coming here?"

"A few nights. I wanted to be ready when you turned up." His voice was a breeze against her skin.

"If you've been here, what have you learned? Did you ask about Julia?"

"Indirectly." He moved in, kept his lips close to her ear. "Things like this don't happen at warp speed. Information and trust take time and patience."

Warp speed? What? Were they taking the Enterprise out of the space dock?

"I had to readjust my plans," he added. "Stop trying so hard. The disguise is good." He raised an appreciative brow, drew a finger down the dark strand of hair by her cheek. "Definitely not you. I much prefer those beautiful curls of yours. But you should know the only reason I'm not asking you to leave is because that would draw attention. And not the kind of attention we want."

When had this become we?

"It could also be because I'd tell you to forget it." She smiled so wide she felt air hit her back teeth. She was so caught up in her own protestation she didn't notice him straighten in his chair and look beyond her. "I don't need anyone's permission or protection, Jason. No one else is interested in finding out what happened to Julia. Besides, I know what I'm doing." Had she ever told such a bald-faced lie in her life?

"And what would that be?" The baritone voice that drifted over Kyla's almost bare shoulder sent shivers down her spine. She started to turn, but Jason's fingers tightened around hers and had her biting back a gasp. "Good to see you again, Jace."

*Jace?* Kyla blinked. Colin knew Jason? What was happening here?

"You, too, Colin." After another quick squeeze, Jason released Kyla and stood to shake Colin's hand. "This is Darlene. It's her first time here." He tugged his tailored jacket closed and reminded Kyla how handsome he looked. Dark navy suit and a shirt in nearly the same hue. The black narrow tie finished the image as perfectly as a master painter signing his name. With his beard and bright blue eyes, Kyla was surprised he hadn't turned half the population of the room, male or female, into a molten puddle of goo. "I'm hoping that means I get first shot."

"That you do. For now." Colin signaled to Lola. "His drinks are on the house until further notice."

"You got it, boss." Lola arched an approving look at Kyla before she refilled Jason's glass.

"So. Darlene." Colin shifted as if to place himself between Kyla and Jason, but Jason remained where he was. As irritated as she was at having Jason attempt to dictate her next move, she couldn't help but feel a bit of relief at having him as a buffer. "How do you like what you see?"

*Oh, ick.* "I'm taking it all in." The words felt thick on her tongue. From a distance the O'Callaghan brothers had been intimidating. There was something about the pair of them, with their stark red hair and ruddy, thin faces that reminded her of the old photographs her grandfather used to show her of the bootleggers he ran with back east growing up. With her half Cajun, half-Irish heritage, she had a wide range of exposure to both aspects of her bloodlines.

But it wasn't the visual resemblance that stopped her cold; it was the cool detachment in both brothers' eyes.

A barely concealed promise of cruelty that had Kyla instinctively shifting closer to Jason.

She inclined her chin toward the dance floor. "I heard you might be in the market for a new Temptress." The second the words were out of her mouth she wanted to take them back. The point of no return. She thought of racing up the stairs, running back to her car, and getting back to her normal life as a junior prosecutor.

But she couldn't do that. Not as long as she had questions about Julia's death. And now, looking Colin O'Callaghan right in his suddenly flat green eyes, she had no doubt he held at least some of the answers she was looking for.

Colin reached out a finger and trailed it down her hair. She barely resisted the shudder of revulsion.

Kyla felt Jason tense beside her, his entire body poised to strike.

"You are a stunner, aren't you?" Colin said without flicking his gaze from her face. "Normally I prefer to make the approach, but I like your spirit, Darlene. Judging by Jace's reaction here, I think my clientele would find you most...tempting."

"I'm flattered you think so." Kyla was amazed the words actually emerged. Inside she felt as if she was shaking from head to toe.

A more distinguished version of Colin approached him and tapped him on the shoulder. After a quick flash of annoyance, Colin apologized and joined his brother at the end of the bar.

"You've been here enough to make an impression

yourself, *Jace*." Kyla faced Jason, but this time she continued to play up the role of Temptress and danced her fingers up his arm. "What's going on?"

"I don't believe in coincidences." He settled a hand on her hip and tugged her closer. She gasped, bit her lip and told herself he couldn't see the flush in her cheeks. "Our cases have lined up. Night Crawler's a common denominator with both Bess and Julia. It made sense to check it out."

He had her attention. She lifted her hands to his shoulders, clung to him. "How long ago was Bess here?"

"Almost two weeks." Jason always seemed to be moving, but Kyla realized that was his way of trying to keep Colin O'Callaghan in sight so he didn't sneak up on them again.

"Perhaps too long ago to be connected to Julia then," Kyla said.

"Maybe." Jason didn't sound sure.

"Maybe?" she echoed.

"I'm not ruling anything out at this point and we don't have time to discuss it here." He shifted his gaze to the private rooms. "I've gotten the layout of the place down well enough. Liam doesn't keep an office at the club, but Colin does. It's behind the private rooms. If I can get into his computer, I might have time to clone his system, and if they're networked with his brother's, ride into his."

Kyla gripped his arm so hard her fingers went numb. The way he spoke so easily about breaking the law reminded her he was a convicted criminal. A man who had served his time but had still lived on the other side of the law she'd dedicated her life to. The hole she'd leapt into to help her dead friend apparently didn't have a bottom. "Confessing to a felony before the fact—"

"Yeah." He leaned in, his warm breath caressing her cheek. "We can discuss my approach to undercover work when you've ditched the wig and push-up bra."

"Shows what you know." Kyla tilted her head so she could look at him. "I'm not wearing a push-up bra."

"You don't say?" His hand drifted to her hip again and had her shivering. "This isn't a game, Kyla."

"No, it's not." Far from it. "And I'm betting you won't have much opportunity to get into Colin's office without a distraction." She had to admit, she felt better having an ally nearby. And if he could use her help to find a missing girl... "I can take care of that part of things if you agree not to tell Vince or Simone you saw me here."

"Afraid they'll ground you?"

"Ha ha." He wasn't too far off, though. "What are you doing?" She shivered as she felt his fingers trail up her side, then down her arm. If his fingers elicited this much of a reaction from her, she could only imagine what the rest of him could do to her.

"Keeping up appearances."

"Let's make a deal." Kyla leaned into him, felt her breasts brush against his chest. She hid her grin as his eyes darkened. Two could definitely play at this game.

Jason cleared his throat, his brow furrowing as if he couldn't think.

"I'll play distraction for say, fifteen minutes. Enough for you to get in and out of Colin's office. And in exchange, if you find anything, even the smallest scintilla of information about Julia, you give it to me."

Jason narrowed his eyes. "Distract how?"

"Let's leave a little to the imagination." She tried to play it light, but he clearly didn't find any amusement in her teasing. "Relax, *Jace*. I'll keep him on the dance floor where there are hundreds of witnesses. What?"

He shook his head, lifted his hand to her face. "I don't like you being here."

She wanted to say she didn't like the possessive gleam in his eye, but she couldn't. The Jason standing so close to her, the Jason who hadn't stopped touching her for the past few minutes, was a Jason who overwhelmed her senses. And quite possibly her reason. "We both need to find answers. You have your strengths. I have mine. Unless you'd rather ask me to access private records or use my connections at the DA's office to help with your case again."

"No." The word came out with enough force to effectively slam the door closed on that option. "I didn't ask you to do that in the first place. I asked what the odds were I could get access to them." His eyes sharpened and his jaw tensed. "I'm an *ex*-con, Kyla. Not a current one. I'd never ask you to compromise your ethics or career."

"Said the man about to break into a private office." But she got his point. Throwing his past in his face certainly wasn't going to get either of them what they wanted. "You'd better get moving."

"Why?"

"Because Colin and his brother are done arguing and Colin looks as if he's ready for a distraction." She reached up and stroked her hands down the side of his face. "I like this, by the way. The beard. Super sexy."

"Careful, Kyla." He caught her wrist in his hand

and turned his lips to brush against the sensitive skin. "Mixing business with pleasure is never a good idea."

"Right." She seemed to be having a lot of bad ideas lately. And they were multiplying in her mind the longer she looked at him. "Speaking of bad ideas." Kyla turned out of Jason's arms and faced Colin, who looked as sour as if he'd been sucking on a lemon. "You look like you could use a drink, Mr. O'Callaghan." She shifted close enough to be the focus of all his attention without touching him. "And maybe we can discuss that job opening?"

"Uh, sure." Colin blinked out of a stupor and found that creepy, come-hither grin. "A drink sounds good. Lola!" He snapped his fingers over his head.

Jason turned away from the bar, his phone up to his ear. "I've got to take this. Can I use one of the private rooms?"

"Sure." Liam gestured toward the back of the club. "One or two should be empty. When you get back, I want to discuss that deal you were talking about. Sounds like a good investment."

"Oh, it is. Believe me." Jason nodded. "I'll be back in a few."

Kyla watched Jason move through the dance crowd that had come to a mass stop as the band began to tune their instruments and adjust the speakers.

"Have you known him long?" Kyla asked, avoiding Lola's warning look as the bartender served Colin his drink.

"He's been coming in for about a week." Colin slid onto the stool Jason had abandoned. "Don't tell me you've decided to ditch your career plans at Night Crawler for some rich tech guy."

"Is that what he is?" Kyla blinked over-innocent eyes and added a smile. Being alone with Colin shoved her right back into anxiety mode; her heart pounded so hard she almost couldn't breathe. "Does my interview include a few minutes on the dance floor?" She looked longingly toward the crowd. "I wouldn't mind earning one of those armbands."

Colin trailed a solitary finger down Kyla's bare arm. "I think we might be able to come to an understanding about your future with Night Crawler. On and off the dance floor."

"Well, let's start with on." She found the beat—a techno-salsa tempo that had her mama's Cajun blood pumping. Crooking a finger in Colin's direction, she swayed her hips and drew him into the crowd, even as she kept one eye on the private rooms.

# Chapter 4

Jason chose the private room closest to the hall leading to the offices and storage area. By the time he got out of this club, he was going to have a headache painful enough to fell a rhino, and not just because of the ear-blasting, spine-throbbing, over-tuned speaker system.

The silence landed on him when he closed the door behind him. His head spun as his ears readjusted to the dull pounding kept mostly at bay by the sound-proofed walls. One-way glass allowed him to get his bearings, seemingly to focus on the next few minutes, but instead he found himself distracted by the image of Kyla dancing with Colin O'Callaghan at the edge of the sprawling crowd.

A primal, protective urge surged through him. Tonight proved a couple of things. One: she was just as stubborn as he thought, and two: it was only a matter of time before she got into trouble she'd have no way out of.

How she thought she was fooling anyone in that costume of hers he'd never know. Kyla had a presence he could always, *always* spot in a crowd. A presence he wished he didn't feel to the marrow of his bones. Sometimes it felt as if she had a homing beacon only he had the frequency to. She tempted him in ways no woman ever had. It was a gravitational pull he couldn't find a way to avoid.

She'd been hanging around with Simone too much, he decided, and was no doubt trying on a pair of Simone's Avenging Angel wings. The women's ability to focus their attention and risk everything for the people they cared about, up to and including their professional careers, was both inspiring and terrifying. The sooner he got Kyla out of this situation completely, the better. For both of them.

Jason looked away from the dance floor, the seconds ticking loudly in his head. He had a job to do and, contrary to Jason's desire to play hero where Kyla was concerned, she knew what she was doing when it came to distracting men. She'd been doing it unintentionally with him for long enough.

Double checking that the flash drive containing the most recent password decoder program available on the dark web was securely in his pocket—maybe he hadn't given up all his ex-con habits—Jason grasped the door handle and waited as Liam O'Callaghan made his way up to the second floor landing.

Before the older O'Callaghan brother could exit, however, he was stopped by a young man that captured every bit of Jason's attention.

"Well, well." Jason muttered, eyes narrowing. "Welcome home, Tristan Wainwright." Seventeen, wealthy, privileged and, up until the time she'd disappeared, Bess Carmody's boyfriend, Tristan had been on the top of Jason's "need to talk to" list from the start. His attempts had led him to a locked down rehab facility in Napa where Tristan had been since Bess vanished.

Jason's blood pumped heavy in his veins. The coincidences were piling up. Tristan turning up at Night Crawler connected even more dots. Obviously the kid and Liam O'Callaghan knew each other; how else would an underage boy gain entrance? Jason snapped a couple of pictures to add to his file, then stood to the side as they finished their short, but clearly tense conversation. Liam's expression had gradually shifted from irritated to one of barely restrained rage before he'd shoved by the kid, pushing him aside as if Tristan wasn't worth his attention.

When the two of them were gone, Jason breathed a sigh of relief. He didn't have any trouble handling Colin. Tell the guy a couple of good stories, flash around a hefty stack of hundred dollar bills that were mostly ones and fives in the middle and throw in a few spontaneous promises of investment wealth, and Colin was clay any toddler could mold.

Liam on the other hand?

Liam was as cold-blooded as they came. All the more reason for himself and Kyla to steer as clear as possible.

With Liam gone and Colin occupied on the dance floor with Kyla, Jason casually headed back to the restrooms. He made a sharp detour around the corner and toward the fire exit. He stopped just out of camera range, remembering Colin's ego-driven tour of the security system the club owner had recently installed. One thing Jason had learned both as a criminal and as a PI: there was little that people liked more than bragging about their expensive hobbies. Tech was definitely Colin's catnip.

A few taps of his phone and Jason looked up to see the small red light on the camera monitor blink off. Seconds later he was through the locked door, lamenting the fact that Colin had spent a small fortune on the security monitoring service and hadn't bothered to spend fifty bucks on a good handle.

Jason closed the door behind him, relocked it and took an extra beat to scan the room to ensure he didn't see any other cameras inside. The decor wasn't anything spectacular. Nothing but never opened books on the shelves; framed photos of Colin and Liam along with some of their more impressive clientele—politicians and their kids, actors, directors and a disgraced movie producer who had reignited the women's rights movement into the stratosphere. One picture in particular seemed to be a favorite. With a thick gilded frame, the image showed Colin and Liam, still in their teens, bookending a pretty redhead with stunning, sharp green eyes. He'd dug deep enough into the brothers' past to know the young woman was their older sister, Caitlin, who had died ten years ago in the same fire that had killed their parents.

The computer beeped, pushing him back on track.

The one piece of artwork in the room—a garish painting by an artist Jason probably should have recognized, sat poorly framed in the center of the wall across from the desk.

The rest of the office boasted the same colors as the

club outside, with minimal furniture and office supplies, probably because Colin wasn't overly fond of work. It was the entertainment portion of club ownership that appealed most to him. The women. The money. The women.

Speaking of women, he needed to make this quick. Not just for practicality's sake. He didn't like the idea of Kyla spending any more alone time with Colin than necessary.

He moved in behind the desk, avoiding the chair, and popped the flash drive into the monitor CPU. The program ran without prompting and Jason watched the progress through the app on his phone. It would take a few minutes to clone the drive. Long enough for Jason to get a look through the employee files he found in the solitary cabinet against the far wall, above which hung a bank of four small flat screens showing the security camera feed.

While the program did its thing, Jason snapped pictures of the files, so he could get a look at the names later on. Of course there was no file for Bess Carmody, nor did he find one for a Julia Summerton, but he did find one for Kevin Dowell, the other person who had been found with Julia. Interesting. Since he had a few minutes to spare, Jason opened the file, scanned the pages and, after replacing the folder, stepped back and snapped a shot of the entire collection of files.

His phone beeped, alerting him to the download completing. He straightened the files, closed the drawer and returned to the desk where he popped out the flash drive.

He started toward the door but found himself distracted by the painting. The splotches of red and green reminded Jason of a Christmas tree gone awry rather than anything of artistic value. And that frame didn't sit flush against the wall.

"Probably," Jason muttered, "because it's got something behind it." His pulse jumped. His palms itched. Sure enough, when Jason strode over and lifted one of the corners of the painting, he found it was hinged to the wall like a door. He pulled it open and smiled at the safe there, hiding not-so-discreetly.

He'd gotten smarter with more than books in prison.

He glanced at his watch. He had maybe five minutes before he needed to get gone. Could be long enough just to take a little look inside. If he could get inside. The digital keypad meant the combination was programmed and personal. Colin wasn't exactly a genius and Jason didn't give him much credit for having a reliable memory, especially given Colin's reputation for using his own product. He'd have to have left a clue around the office.

Jason did another quick walk around and ended up standing in front of the bookshelves displaying the photographs. Lots of people. Lots of places. But only one animal. A bulldog. Jason bent down and searched the picture. And saw the ID tag around the dog's neck. "It couldn't be that simple."

Jason keyed in the dog's ID number. "My brother's right again," Jason told the empty room when the lock clicked open. "Not very bright people definitely make our job easier."

Inside the safe he found stacks of cash, passports, foreign currency. Various baggies filled with colorful pills—not enough to sell, but plenty for personal use.

A box filled with DVDs with dates on them, a solitary flash drive and a beaten up cell phone.

Jason's heart skipped a beat.

The screen was cracked and the edges looked as if they'd been filed with sandpaper. The make, model and description fit the one Bess's parents had told him about.

"But I thought we were going to dance some more!" Jason swore.

He pocketed the cell along with one of the flash drives and closed the safe, replaced the painting and searched for somewhere, anywhere to hide. He raced back to the desk and ducked under it just as the door opened.

"I need to check something." Colin's tense voice echoed through the room. "My computer has an alert on it when it's been accessed."

Jason gritted his teeth.

"Wow." Kyla followed him inside. "That sounds fancy. You sure you didn't just leave it on? Mine does that sometimes. Just wakes up for no reason." She snapped her fingers.

Jason wasn't sure what was going to pop first. His knees or his spine. In the past two years he'd put on more than twenty pounds of muscle and right now he could feel every ounce of them. He squished himself back as Colin's feet appeared in front of him.

"It's never done that before," Colin said. "Hang on. I'm going to check the security feed."

"This is boring." Kyla sighed so dramatically Jason could have given her an acting award. He heard a dull thunk on top of the desk as if she'd set down her purse. "Let's go back out and dance."

"We will in a minute." Colin sounded completely distracted as he moved away.

Carefully, slowly, Jason reached out and tapped the side of Kyla's ankle. She jumped and nearly kicked him when her foot shot back.

"Colin?" she called before she hopped up to sit on the desk. Her feet swung back and forth, those glittery skyscraper shoes of hers sending all kinds of thoughts through his head. Her fingers curling over the edge of the desktop.

"What?"

"I think you're just using this computer thing as an excuse to be alone with me."

Jason rolled his eyes. No one was going to fall for that.

"Huh?" Colin said. Jason watched Colin's feet shift. Then again…

"It's okay if you are," Kyla said. "I think it's cute. Like computers just turn on all by themselves." She giggled. Jason bit back a snort. Kyla was not the giggling sort.

"Computers don't turn on by themselves," Colin said slowly. "That's the point. What's going on with the monitors?"

"Now you're just being silly," Kyla said. "I'm sure it's nothing to worry—"

Careful not to make a sound, Jason twisted so he could pull out his phone then tapped the app to restore the feed to the monitors. He could hear the screens buzz to life and the computer began to hum.

"See?" Kyla announced. "They're all fixed. Maybe it was a power glitch."

"Hmm." Colin didn't sound convinced. "Maybe."

"So maybe we go back to dancing now?" Kyla asked and Jason could all but see the pout on her pretty, full lips. Lips that he might have begged to kiss not so long before. He squeezed his eyes shut. *Not for you. She is so far out of your league you're not even playing the same game. She's not for you.*

"Or maybe we do what you said and have some alone time." Colin's feet moved back into view, right in front of Kyla, whose knuckles went white.

A knock sounded on the door.

"What?" Colin yelled.

"Sorry." Lola, the bartender's voice called through the door. "Boss, you need to come out. I think we're being raided. Clyde called from the front door. We've got police cars all over the place."

"You've got to be—" The rest of Colin's statement was lost amidst the flood of cries and screams echoing above the blaring music.

Kyla ducked down, the hem of her dress inching up to barely there status. Jason couldn't pull his gaze away from those amazing legs of hers.

"He's gone," she whispered. "Did you get what you needed?"

"Along with a few spinal fractures." Jason unfolded himself from under the desk and followed her to the door. The second she opened it they were nearly trampled by the dozen or so patrons streaming down the back hall toward the emergency alley exit. He reached back for Kyla's hand, murmured "stay close," then, deciding to take the chance, merged them into the crowd. Kyla's fingers tensed around his. He glanced back, scanned the crowd before he found her slightly confused gaze.

"I'm fine," she said as if reading his mind. "Adrenaline rush." She fanned her glistening face as they were jostled by their fellow customers. "Kinda fun." The smile she flashed him almost lit up her eyes. "Should only take two or three showers to clean off the feel of his hands on me."

Once outside, the chilly night air did nothing other than send a shiver of dread down his spine. Whatever direction they went would put them right in the sights of the patrol cars parked at either end. Given the amount of people, potential suspects in what he assumed was an unfortunately timed narcotics raid, everyone's panic was about to mount tenfold. He looked for another way out. Not good. For either of them, but especially Jason, who had stolen evidence in his pocket.

"Where are you parked?" he asked her.

Kyla stumbled into him as a young woman ran past and knocked her into Jason. "A few blocks back there. You?"

"Opposite direction." He scanned the alley and spotted an old-fashioned mail slot in the front of the abandoned building next door. He shifted direction, shoving through the growing crowd. Without stopping, he pushed Bess Carmody's cell phone and the stolen jump drive into the rusted metal slot.

"Act natural," he ordered. "Don't be in any rush." He released her hand and drew her close, looped an arm over her shoulders. Out of the corner of his eye, the stark blond head of Tristan Wainwright caught his attention. The kid was trying to blend, trying to find a way out, but the only way out was through the cops. And they didn't appear to be letting anyone pass unchecked. "The less concerned we appear, the better."

"All right." Kyla snaked her arm around his waist. "It wasn't you who called the raid, was it?"

"Didn't even cross my mind. The police have never and will never be my first choice."

"Don't let Cole and Jack hear you say that," Kyla said with a strained laugh. "They'd probably be offended."

"Cole and Jack are…exceptions." That he considered two detectives with Sacramento's Major Crimes division friends was more evidence of how much someone's life could change. "For now, let's keep them out of our playbook."

"Agreed," Kyla whispered as her arm tightened around his waist.

He flipped a mental coin and headed right. The crowd was a bit more dense in this direction. More people meant a better chance of staying under the radar. The closer they got to the street, the more Jason realized how large a police presence was on scene.

The nerves he'd kept under control surged to life. This was far more than some ordinary nightclub raid. His pulse thundered in his ears. They'd no sooner reached the front of the crowd when a line of officers moved in, holding up their arms to stop the free flow of escapees.

Jason did a quick assessment of their options, none of them good.

Behind them, he felt the tension mounting in the crowd and heard the desperate, panicked cries of uncertainty and fear. "Get out your ID," he murmured even as he tucked Kyla into his side.

"But it's—"

"Whoever's name is on that card, that's who you are until we get you out of this." Jason, on the other hand, was going to have a difficult time explaining two sets of IDs should the police search him.

"I made that ID to fool a bouncer, not the police." Kyla's protest was barely out of her mouth before he spotted two deputies out of the corner of his eye heading toward them.

"Play this like you did before." Jason leaned his head down to murmur into her ear. When she glanced up, he saw the fear leap in her eyes. "What?"

"I know them," she said. "And so do you."

Before Jason had a chance to think, Deputy Scott "Bowie" Bowman, along with who he now recognized as a very out of uniform Deputy Serena Clarke were pushing through their fellow officers. He'd seen her inside earlier, at the bar, chatting up a few of the customers.

Now, however, she was wearing an SMPD windbreaker and vest. "Sir? Ma'am? IDs please." Her voice was clipped, formal and left no room for protest.

Surprised at not being called by name, Jason kept his mouth shut, pulled out his wallet and handed his over. Kyla did the same.

"These are fake." Deputy Clarke, dark hair spilling over her shoulders, barely glanced at the information. "Come with us, please."

"But—"

Bowie, his normally easygoing and jovial expression locked down tight, sent Kyla a look that Jason felt certain could freeze boiling water. The instant they were out of the crowd, Bowie grabbed Jason's arm while Serena pried Kyla away and headed around the corner toward the front entrance.

"Not a word," Bowie muttered out of the corner of his mouth as he and Jason followed the women. "Trust me on this, Jason. Just keep your mouth shut." Any chance Jason might have had to respond evaporated the second Bowie shoved him over the hood of a patrol car and, using a ruthless efficiency Jason was all too familiar with, cuffed him with a click of metal.

Jason peered over his shoulder just as Lola the bartender, Clyde the bouncer and Colin O'Callaghan were being questioned by detectives. Jason glanced away just as Colin looked in his direction, then toward Kyla, who had gone a bit ashen as she was pushed into the back of a separate patrol car, hands cuffed behind her.

The last thing Jason saw before he was put into his own car was Kyla's stricken expression aimed straight at him as she was driven away.

## Chapter 5

Of all the ways Kyla anticipated ending her night, finding herself in an interrogation room at the Major Crimes division hadn't even cracked the top ten. What on earth was going on? She'd been cuffed and driven away sans Miranda warning, something she'd reminded Serena Clarke of multiple times during the drive to the Sacramento Police Department. In the few hours since, she hadn't seen a sign of Jason, who, although he wasn't on parole, couldn't afford another arrest on his record.

Guilt lodged in her throat. If she hadn't been at the club tonight, he might have found another way out of Night Crawler. Instead he'd been concerned about getting her to safety. Even her perennial rose colored glasses weren't so opaque that she didn't see the potential danger for his future despite her own tilting on shaky ground.

Pacing, as she had been since she'd been placed in the isolated, stale smelling interrogation room, she tried to stop chewing on her thumbnail, a bad habit she thought she'd kicked back in law school. This whole thing was so TV crime drama. All that was missing were files on the table and a cigar-chomping detective interrogating her. She wasn't supposed to be waiting to be questioned and certainly not for hours on end. She should be standing on the other side of the two-way mirror watching someone in this room sweat buckets.

Deputy Clarke had brought her a cup of coffee, a now cold brew of something resembling swamp sludge, but instead of answering Kyla's questions, Clarke had merely said someone would be in to speak with her soon and to just wait.

"Just wait." Kyla's pacing picked up speed, the gold flecked walls blurring in her vision as she tried to work out exactly what had happened in the club tonight. "Just wait for what?" Something weird was definitely going on. She hadn't been questioned yet, nor had she been booked or processed. They had taken her purse, along with her cell, which meant she'd start going through withdrawal at any moment. Maybe it was time to ask for her phone call. But who would she call? And what would she tell them? She hadn't been charged with anything.

Yet.

It was closing in on four o'clock in the morning. Plenty of time for that to change. Jason on the other hand… Kyla's stomach took another sour turn. One thing she had learned tonight—Jason Sutton wasn't above bending or even breaking the law.

Maybe it was true what so many of her fellow prosecutors believed: once a criminal, always a criminal.

She swallowed a hard lump of regret. Had she risked her entire career—her future—for nothing?

When the door finally opened, Kyla jumped, bracing herself for whoever would enter. To her surprise and relief, she watched Jason be escorted in by an all too familiar—and clearly irritated—major crimes detective.

"Jack, thank goodness." An odd relief swept through her at the sight of Detective Jack McTavish. "Jason, are you okay?"

"I'm fine." Clearly more at ease in this situation than she was, Jason took a seat as Jack closed the door behind him. "Apparently we've landed on someone's naughty list."

"Now's really not the time for your comedy routine." Jack set a cardboard tray of coffee cups on the table. "Mocha. Decaf," he added when he handed Kyla one of the tall coffee cups. At her scrunched up face, he added, "Deal with it."

"Thank you," she mumbled before sipping. What was the purpose of coffee without caffeine, anyway?

"Triple shot macchiato with caramel. I cannot believe I actually knew that about you," Jack muttered at Jason's smirk.

"How come he gets full shots?" Kyla demanded.

"Because I want him alert when Vince gets his hands on him."

Kyla panicked. "Tell me you did not call Vince. Or Simone. Jack, they're on vacation—"

"Relax. We haven't called them." Jack hesitated. "But we might. Whether we do or not is going to depend on how your next conversation goes."

The foreboding those words evoked nearly stole the breath from Kyla's lungs. "Jack, this was all me. I went to the club on my own. Jason just happened to be there. In fact if it wasn't for him—"

"Jason never happens to just be anywhere. Forget about Night Crawler being dangerous, Kyla. That's literally the least of your problems right now."

"Stop hedging, Jack. What's going on?" Jason asked.

Jack swore and glanced over his shoulder before he lowered his voice. "Night Crawler's been under investigation for months."

"And?" Jason asked.

"*And*—" Jack glared "—you two going in there with your own agendas may very well have blown us out of the water."

"What was I supposed to do?" Kyla asked. "No one seems interested in finding out what happened to my friend. Not Detective Peterson, and not you. I don't recall anyone giving Eden this much grief when she went after the Ice Man. Or you, when Greta was being gaslighted or when Ashley was kidnapped by those escaped convicts a few months ago. Why do you all get free rein when it's someone you care about but I get stomped back?"

Jack opened his mouth and glanced at Jason who, out of the corner of her eye, Kyla saw shrug in agreement. The fear and resentment she'd felt bubbling up dropped back down to where she hoped it would stay. Why was the only person on her side the convicted criminal?

"All right." Jack's eyes filled with concern. "Let's forget the fact you've jeopardized our case. You scared us, Kyla. You and Jason. It's difficult enough keeping tabs on our own people. We don't have the manpower to add civilians to the list." Jack pushed to his feet. "You two sit tight. You'll be briefed in a few."

"Jack, wait—" Kyla's request came too late as Jack left. "What is going on around here?" So much for thinking she was in friendly territory.

"Damage control and protecting their backs." Jason toasted her with his coffee.

"Gee, really?" Kyla batted her lashes. "That much I got." She started pacing again, this time grateful for digestible coffee. She really didn't need the added distraction of being locked in a room with Jason Sutton.

"You're a good dancer."

"What?" She almost stumbled.

"I said you're a good dancer. It's called small talk." Jason sipped his own drink. "What else do we have to do? Oh, I've got sudoku on my phone." He reached into his pocket, then sighed. "Cops took it."

"How can you be so relaxed?" She faced him, arms crossed over her chest.

Jason smirked, but no humor reached his eyes. "This place is like coming home."

"Not funny," she snapped. "You're just sitting there as if nothing's happened."

"Oh, plenty happened." Jason's tone didn't change. "More importantly, plenty of people saw it happen, including Colin O'Callaghan. That should kill any interest or suspicion he has in you."

Kyla dropped into the chair on her side of the table. "They saw you get arrested, too."

"A classic double standard, I'm afraid. That'll only bolster my rep with them." Jason shrugged. "I'm a potential investment opportunity for the O'Callaghans, not a distracting woman who shows up just before their club is busted. FYI," he added when her eyes went wide, "If you don't believe the O'Callaghans will zero in on you as more than a coincidence, you're not nearly as smart as I thought. Might I suggest—" he leaned his arms on the table and lowered his voice "—we get back to the small talk, unless you'd like whoever is watching on the other side of that glass to hear about the rest of our evening?"

Kyla's mouth twisted and her eyes narrowed.

"Start thinking like a DA, Kyla, because dinky office aside, that's what you are. Believe it or not, it gives you some power in this situation."

The door clicked open and a curvy, dark-haired woman stepped inside followed by Jack, who didn't look anymore pleased to see them than he had a few minutes ago. At first it was Jack who had all her attention, as he set a bulky manila envelope on the table. Then she noticed Jason lean back in his chair and cross his arms over his chest. When Kyla turned her gaze to the woman, her mouth went dry. "Lola?"

"Marcella, actually." The bartender from the club tucked a couple of file folders under her arm. "Detective Marcella Alvarez. Narcotics Division. Undercover."

The red leather was gone, replaced by a simple black pantsuit and shirt the color of the ocean. The garish, attention-grabbing club makeup was also no more and her hair was clipped severely against the back of her head. Talk about night to day.

Jason let out a whistle. "Jack wasn't kidding."

"About what?" Kyla asked.

"You two just blew six months of undercover narcotics work off the rails." Detective Alvarez held her thumb and forefinger less than an inch apart. "Some-

thing I personally don't appreciate considering the out-
fits I have to wear and the nonsense I have to put up with
in that place."

"We didn't—" Kyla started.

Alvarez's hand shot up. "I had seven team members
working that club. Good cops who have been putting
in long hours, time spent away from their families as
we try to shut down a major drug distribution ring."
She tossed her own files onto the table, leaned her back
against the wall and crossed her arms. "Now tell me
why I shouldn't lock you two up in a cell until I wrap
up this case."

"Because we haven't broken any laws." Kyla sat up
straighter. Jason was right. She had neglected to use
one of the best weapons she had at her disposal: her job.
"I had every right to be there, as did Jason. You can't
stop me from looking for information on my friend."

Detective Alvarez's gaze shifted to Jason.

"I was working. Looking for a client's missing
daughter," Jason added as easily as if they'd rehearsed it.

"Your client's name?" Detective Alvarez asked.

"Is confidential."

"Of course it is," Detective Alvarez sneered.

Jason's smile made Kyla shiver.

"Ms. Bertrand," Detective Alvarez said, "Kyla, do
you mind if I call you Kyla?"

"Junior Prosecutor Bertrand might work all right,"
Jason suggested.

Kyla reached over and touched Jason's arm. Having
Jason in a room with cops really was like splashing
gasoline on a lit match.

"Kyla." Alvarez nodded. "What happened to your
friend was a tragedy. I am so sorry for your loss."

Until this moment, Kyla hadn't understood how empty those words sounded. Or how frustrated they made her.

"I spoke with Detective Peterson," Alvarez continued. "She did not sound surprised to learn you were looking into Julia Summerton's death. Irritated, maybe, but not surprised. Not a good way to start your time as a prosecutor, by alienating detectives you'll be working with."

"Now why does that sound like a threat?" Jason asked.

"Shut it, Jason," Jack ordered.

Jason smirked.

"It wasn't my intention to alienate anyone." Kyla wasn't about to apologize. She was not going to let Julia down. Not again. "The second Detective Peterson decided Julia's death was a drug overdose, there wasn't going to be any further investigation. It didn't matter she'd been beaten to the point of being almost unrecognizable." She inched her chin up. "I heard it in the detective's voice. She's already moved on."

"We can't treat every drug overdose suspiciously that hits the city, Kyla," Jack said. "You know that."

"What do I have to do to get people to hear me?" Kyla demanded. "Julia did not do drugs."

Detective Alvarez looked to Jack who, after a long moment, shrugged, then nodded. Kyla's stomach dropped as Alvarez flipped open her tablet, tapped the screen and flipped it around for Kyla and Jason to see.

"This is surveillance footage from two nights before Julia Summerton was murdered."

Kyla sat still, her eyes scanning the crowd on the screen. She recognized the area as one behind the dance floor, near the DJ. Crowded with lights spinning and strobing. Julia appeared, drink in hand, stumbling a bit as she approached a young blond male. Young enough Kyla couldn't imagine he was legal.

The bank of deep purple sofa-like seats lining the back wall were filled, but the young man stood to greet Julia. It was clear they knew each other, the way she placed her hand on his arm, the way he shifted his grip when he took hold of her hand. They looked…familiar. Julia pulled something out of her bag, moved in close to him.

"He just passed something to her," Jason murmured. "She paid for something."

"Not necessarily drugs." Kyla's chest tightened. For the first time, Kyla had doubts.

"Addicts can fool their closest friends and family, Kyla." Detective Alvarez's tone gentled, but instead of giving Kyla some comfort, she found the condescending sympathy scraped against her nerves. "Addiction is insidious and most times inescapable. I know this is difficult to see." Alvarez closed the tablet as if that ended the discussion. "But maybe now you can start to move on."

Kyla opened her mouth, but shut it again when Jason shifted and stretched an arm out along the back of her chair. His fingers brushed her shoulder in a way that had her shifting tactics.

"Who was that boy? It's not Kevin Dowell." Kyla struggled to put the pieces together into a puzzle she could understand.

"No," Jason murmured. "It's definitely not."

"How do you know that?" Jack asked. "We purposely

asked Detective Peterson not to release either Julia's or Kevin's photo to the media."

"Because this kid was at the club tonight." Jason caught the exchange of looks. "What? Don't tell me you guys missed him?" His eyes widened with fake innocence. "Last I saw he was headed straight for one of your patrol vehicles."

"Clearly our attention was elsewhere," Alvarez said.

Kyla watched Jason reach for the file with the autopsy reports. He flipped it open to read.

"We'll go back through our tapes," Alvarez said. "Kyla, Dowell was a small-time dealer and on-again, off-again addict. My people tailed him for a few days, but nothing came of it. I know you don't want to believe this, but chances are he was Julia's dealer. Maybe they were doing another deal and someone tried to rob Dowell, or both of them, and then everything went south."

Whatever doubts had been materializing vanished. They'd almost had her convinced she was wrong about her friend. But she knew Julia, they didn't.

"No one's judging anyone, Kyla," Jack said.

"Clearly." Kyla's throat was so tight she could barely breathe.

"I see the tox results came back," Jason said, pointing to a folder.

Jack nodded, and Jason opened it and read.

Kyla glanced away and closed her eyes.

"The results came back positive for a substance identified as PoWWer?" Jason glanced up at the detectives. "I've never heard of it."

"There have been reported cases back east, in Florida. Some overseas. It's an ecstasy hybrid with the addictive quality of meth," Jack explained. "It's very nasty, frequently lethal and is popping up slowly in larger cities around the US. Sacramento alone has seen more than a few overdoses of the stuff in the past month."

"What's being done about it?" Kyla asked, still reeling from the news about Julia and unable to grasp it all.

"What we can for now," Alvarez replied, "We know PoWWer is being produced somewhere in the northern region of the state, and given the cluster of overdoses, it, or at least its main distribution hub, has to be near the city. We were this close to being able to get hold of a sample and at least start our lab people on dissecting its chemical code before all hell broke loose."

"This close meaning they're selling it at the club."

"Whatever shot we had of proving that just went out the window thanks to you two," Alvarez told them.

"Your investigation wasn't very tight if it could be so easily derailed," Jason said.

"We covered by putting the raid under Vice's purview," Jack said. "As far as anyone knows, we went in to bust up a prostitution ring."

"The Temptresses," Kyla murmured.

"It was a way in," Alvarez confirmed, "without completely blowing our investigation."

"If the rumors about the drug going into wide distribution are true, that tells us they're getting ready to move," Jack added. "The O'Callaghans are the main point of distribution. We've spooked them which means they'll change tactics after tonight. No telling what they'll do, but we'll be watching."

Kyla's stomach dropped straight to the floor as grief blanketed her heart. "So that's it then. The official ruling of Julia's death is a drug overdose."

"Kyla—" It was Jack who spoke.

Kyla snapped. "You can show me all the videos and test results in the world. I will never believe Julia did drugs." Which begged the question: if Julia wasn't at the club for drugs, what had she been doing there? What had she gotten from that kid? And who was the kid in the first place?

"Hang on. Let's go back." Jack leaned his arms on the table. "How did you even tie Julia to the club to start with?"

"Other than her body was found a block away from Night Crawler? This." Kyla pulled the second file folder free, the one she'd noted was Julia's case file, and, blanking her mind to the photograph of her dead friend, pointed to the notation on the diagram showing the armband welt. "All the Temptresses at Night Crawler have this tattoo. While they're testing out new ones, they wear removable bands."

"I would think as a junior prosecutor you'd know a welt on a dead woman's arm isn't enough evidence for a warrant, let alone a reason to blow apart a six month undercover operation." Alvarez inclined her head. "It's purely circumstantial, Kyla. Observant. But circumstantial. Not to mention plenty of the Temptresses are paid with narcotics. Getting them hooked on PoWWer would ignite an instant customer base."

Arguing was useless. The more she tried, the deeper Alvarez dug into her beliefs.

When all was said and done, her friend was dead and the police had no intention of following through on finding out who had killed her.

"Let's say you're right and Julia was using." Kyla felt sick saying the words. "And she was using this PoWWer stuff. Doesn't that automatically link her death to the club? You said that drug is in the beginnings of distribution, so there are limited places it can be bought. That connects Julia's death to Night Crawler, right?"

"Nice," Jason muttered under his breath.

Alvarez didn't look nearly as convinced. "That's still not enough to change the ruling of her death."

"I'm not asking you to change it." But they would. As soon as Kyla found Julia's killer. "I am asking you to lessen the blow to her mother and hold off revealing the results."

"I can do that," Alvarez said slowly as she gathered up her files and tablet. "I'll even go one further and say I'll keep all options open where Julia is concerned."

"Why does it sound as if there's a really big 'but' coming," Jason said, even as Kyla silently agreed.

"You really are a smart guy, aren't you?" Alvarez smirked. "Your involvement with all of this ends. Right here, right now. Both of you. I don't want to see or even hear about you snooping around the club or into Julia's death. Understood?" She stared daggers at Kyla.

Kyla stared back.

"I see even the hint of either of you at the club," Alvarez continued. "I will file a complaint with the DA and your career with the DA's office will be over. And you?" She shifted her attention onto Jason. "It wouldn't take more than a call to put you back inside."

Kyla glanced at Jason and almost gasped at the deadened, hostile look in his eyes.

"I don't appreciate being threatened, Detective."

"And I don't appreciate you interfering with my case," Alvarez said, waving Jack back when he leaned forward to intervene. "The O'Callaghans are on the verge of going global and we almost found out who their main supplier is. I am not going to risk blowing this investigation because of someone's personal vendetta."

"That's not what this is." Kyla's ears roared at the prospect of losing the job she'd worked so long and hard to get.

Alvarez planted her hands on the table and stared her right in the eye. "Look in the mirror and tell yourself that, Kyla. Whatever happened with Julia, if it was something other than drugs, it'll reveal itself eventually. One point in your favor is that stunt you pulled tonight gives us cause for a warrant." She turned toward Jason. "I don't suppose you'd like to share what we can expect to find in Colin's office?"

"And just like that I'm useful again."

"Jason," Jack warned as Kyla's lips twitched.

Jason sat back, folded his arms across his chest in indifference, but Kyla could swear she saw the wheels turning in his head. "His security is all flash and no substance. He's got a safe behind that hideous painting. If you're looking to make an arrest and hold him for a few days, you might find some recreational drugs inside."

"What else might we find?" Alvarez asked.

"DVDs. Cash. Jewelry. Nothing out of the norm," Jason said. "And before you ask, the combination is his dog's ID number. There's a picture—"

"On the shelves. Yeah, that's Doxie. The mutt's his pride and joy and eats better than I do. All right. Both of you can go." Alvarez stood up.

Kyla didn't have to be told twice. "What about...?"

"No charges are being pressed, but we did file an arrest record using your false ID, just in case the O'Callaghans get curious. Only me, my team and our COs know the truth. This is bigger than either of you." Alvarez's tone finally gentled. "And it's bigger than either Julia or your missing girl. I'm sorry but that's the truth," she added when Kyla let out a huff. "This drug could be the most deadly substance to hit this country in decades. I have to put that consideration first. But I promise we'll keep our eyes and ears open in regard to your friend."

"I'll take your word on that." It was, Kyla thought, the biggest lie she'd told yet. "One more thing?"

"If it's a favor—" Alvarez said.

"I'd like Julia's personal effects that were brought in with her body. I need her keys. Mrs. Summerton asked me to check on the house. And since I'll need something to keep me occupied." She plastered on a smile. "Unless the police have it closed as part of a continuing investigation?"

Alvarez considered, then nodded. "I'll have her effects waiting at the front desk for you. Jack? How about you show them out? I've got a case to try and save." Alvarez left the interview room at what seemed like warp speed.

"These are yours." Jack set an oversize plastic bag on the table.

Jason pulled out their cells, her purse and his car keys. "Thanks. Now what's the bad news?"

"Could it get worse?" Kyla muttered.

"Alvarez has blinders on," Jack said. "Julia's autopsy showed no—"

"Long term drug abuse traces," Jason finished. "I can speed read. Kevin Dowell also didn't have any bruises on his knuckles and hands so obviously he didn't hit her."

"Pinning the killing on a drug dealer was an easy way out," Kyla said. "But dealers don't kill potential profit makers."

"Agreed," Jack said.

"Then what was all this?" Jason demanded. Anger was radiating off him in waves. "Show and tell?"

"I'm saying that as your friend, and as a cop with decades behind me," Jack said slowly. "We aren't your enemy on this. We just have to choose our priorities."

Kyla couldn't muster another smile to save her life. "Julia's my priority. Did the police even search her home?"

"No." Jack riffled through his files.

"If they had, maybe they'd have found her drug stuff." If Julia had been an addict as suggested, she'd have a kit with needles and such somewhere. "But since she doesn't really matter, why bother, right?"

Jack, looking more than exhausted, shook his head. "I am sorry about your friend, Kyla."

Because she knew him, she knew he meant it. But that didn't make the situation any easier. Or her any less upset about her friend's death being discarded into the "we have more important things" pile. "Tell Greta I'll call her next week, okay?"

"Will do."

"I'll call for a Lyft for us." Jason pulled out his phone.

"No need. I had Bowie pick up Kyla's car and bring it here," Jack told them. "It's just outside in visitor parking."

"Thank you," Kyla said.

"I guess we know who rates around here," Jason said with his usual humor. "Don't suppose you had them grab mine?"

"Sorry, bro. You're on your own." Jack clapped his hand on Jason's back. "Plus I'm a lot more scared of Simone than I am of Vince. She'd never let me forget it if she found out I left Kyla car-less."

"Noted for future reference."

Kyla pushed the down button for the elevator, but saw Jason bypass it for the stairs.

She looked down at her shoes, but the irritated expression she'd planned to shoot him didn't have time to appear as she hurried after him. "Hang on. Let me get these off." She pulled off one shoe, hopped and grabbed for the other. "You have an issue with elevators?" Her bare and very sore feet hit the grimy floor and made her wince. "Oh, ick. First Colin, now this. I'm going to need to bathe in sanitizer when I get home."

"Stairs are faster." Jason's comment didn't even hit the atmosphere of truth, but she followed him down to the lobby where she put her shoes back on, then lined up at the front desk to sign for Julia's possessions. Large manila envelope tucked under her arm, she exited the building and found Jason standing at the foot of the stairs, taking long, deep breaths.

He dropped his head back.

"Are you all right?" She touched his arm, felt him tense before he relaxed.

"Police stations aren't my favorite places for meet and greets. And I don't appreciate being threatened with a return trip to prison."

"I get it. I'm sorry about that." Of everything that had transpired, she thought that had gone too far. "Come on. I'll give you a ride back to your car." And then she'd go home and take a long shower and drop into bed until the turn of the century.

"Thanks."

Once ensconced in her mini SUV, she wanted to breathe a sigh of relief. But she couldn't. There wasn't any arguing that if she continued down this path, she'd be in trouble again. Trouble that could very well sever her from the future she'd worked so hard for. Jason was frowning, looking in his side view mirror. "What's wrong?"

"Looks like we weren't the only ones to get sprung early. Recognize him?"

"Who?" Kyla shifted around in her seat and watched a familiar face emerge from the station. "That's the kid from the club. The one Julia was talking to in the video."

"His name is Tristan Wainwright," Jason told her. "Kid's got a record longer than mine. Interesting. Detective Alvarez didn't know he'd been swept up in the club raid."

"Maybe he had a fake ID like I did. But that is a strange miss for someone supposedly so dedicated to her case," Kyla mused. They watched as Tristan, cell phone up to his ear, was approached by an older man carrying a satchel. "Must be his lawyer. That suit costs more than the down payment on my condo." The older man also looked seriously put out yet resigned at the same time. "How do you know the boy's name?"

"Because he's been Bess Carmody's on-again, off-again boyfriend for the past two years. He was talking to Liam O'Callaghan before I went into Colin's office. And it did not look like a friendly conversation. Kid's in this up to his beady little eyeballs."

Kyla pinched her lips together. "I guess we really haven't had a chance to talk about what we both saw and heard back there. Wait. Wainwright?" She tested the name on her tongue. "I know that name. Is Tristan any relation to Dr. Forrest Wainwright, the plastic surgeon?" No one in the valley could turn on a cable station without seeing his commercials.

"Tristan's his son."

Now it was Kyla's turn to frown. Forrest Wainwright was one of the DA's biggest campaign contributors. Something uneasy roiled through Kyla's stomach. She pressed a hand against her belly.

"I've been wanting to talk to Tristan ever since I took this case, but he's been in a locked down rehab facility since Bess disappeared."

"I'd suggest you try now, but I don't think his lawyer would approve."

"Agreed," Jason muttered. "Besides, I don't think there's time." A black Lincoln Continental pulled up and seconds later, Tristan disappeared inside while his attorney headed to his own vehicle.

Kyla started the car, hit reverse and pulled out in the direction of the Lincoln.

"What are you doing?" Jason asked. "There's an exit right there."

"But Tristan Wainwright's going this way," Kyla said with a quick smile. "I've always wanted to tail someone." She pulled off her wig, tossed it into the backseat and gave her head a good shake to loosen her curls. "Let's see where he goes."

# Chapter 6

"And so the prince returns to the castle." Kyla bypassed the turnoff for Faustus Estates, an exclusive gated community in Rancho Murieta—one of Sacramento's wealthier suburbs.

"You've got that right," Jason said. "At least I know he's back home with his father. The same father who stuck him in rehab." Whether Dr. Forrest Wainwright had done so because of his son's drug issues or to put him somewhere he couldn't be reached was the question.

"Faustus." Kyla made a U-turn at the dead-ended road and pulled to a stop across the street. She turned off the engine and killed her headlights. "Why do I know that name?"

"Other than being a major contributor to politics?" Jason typed Faustus into the search engine on his phone. "Barnaby Faustus is one of the biggest real estate de-

velopers in the state. He was under investigation a few
years back for tax evasion. His name's come up a few
times on jobs Vince and I have worked. Vince calls him
gangster light. He talks a big game, and takes chances
he shouldn't, but he's not what anyone would call vi-
cious. Most people who know him actually like him."

"No." Kyla shook her head. "That's not what I mean."

"You probably just came across his name at work.
This is a new community," Jason mused as he scanned
his phone. "The third one he's built in the valley. Multiple houses up for sale. More than fifty percent of them.
Not a great investment rate."

"Not surprised considering those places make mini
mansions look like tiny houses." She leaned over to
look at his screen.

"Word is Barnaby is one of those bigger is better kind
of guys." With the sun just beginning to peek over the
horizon, Jason was getting a clearer vision of the property. The guard gate was made of shiny cobblestone and
had space for two security guards, one for entrance, the
other for exiting vehicles. Jason angled his cell phone
and zoomed in. "No golf cart guards for this place. That
SUV has Faustus Estates painted on the side. And that
metal protrusion right there." He pointed to the top corner of the guard house. "That's a state of the art scanning system. Residents must have some kind of barcode
in the front window of their cars."

"Guess that means taking a lookie-loo drive-through
isn't an option."

"Not without an appointment."

"Or an escort," Kyla added.

One of the guards stepped out of the guardhouse and

looked in their direction. "Just our luck," Jason muttered. "Competent employees. Let's go."

"But—"

"Kyla, trust me. Drive."

"Fine." She turned the car back on and headed down the winding hill. "We could have just told the guard we got lost and were looking up directions."

"People don't get lost around here. Cheap cars bring attention."

"Hey!" Kyla frowned at him. "Don't be mean to my car. She's paid for." She leaned over and patted the dashboard. "Don't you listen to him, sweetheart. You do just fine."

"I meant cheaper by comparison," Jason said by way of apology. "And besides, having them see our faces now means we can't come back later if we find a way in. If Tristan's wrapped up with the O'Callaghans and he's just been arrested again, his father might send him out of the country this time."

"I'm open to suggestions."

"Yeah." Jason frowned. "It's going to take some thought."

"Sounds like the poor kid's a trouble magnet."

"Happens to the best of us." Jason flinched and looked out his window. "I need to do some digging into the family, maybe get a look at Dr. Wainwright's financials."

"Lalalalala."

"What?" Jason glanced at Kyla.

"As an officer of the court who has taken an oath to uphold the law, I'd appreciate it if you wouldn't tell me when you're going to break the law."

"Didn't say I was going to break it." Jason's lips

twitched. He shouldn't find her irritation entertaining, but he did. "There's plenty of public information out there for me to find." And plenty of additional information just waiting for him to dig up.

"Uh-huh." Kyla rolled her eyes. "I thought all you wanted to do was talk to Tristan about Bess."

"Well, that's going to be a little difficult without a plan." He clicked his phone off and shoved it into his back pocket as she gunned it down the freeway back into town. "Interesting timing on this whole thing, don't you think?"

"How so?"

"Tristan disappears into rehab a day after Bess Carmody was last seen. Now he's back and one of his first stops was Night Crawler to talk to Liam O'Callaghan, who owns the club Bess was last seen in. Now we have video of him selling drugs to Ju—"

Kyla let out an angry breath.

"Kyla, we both saw that tape. Whatever he sold her, it wasn't ice cream."

Instead of responding, she pressed her lips into that tight line he just wanted to kiss away.

"I don't know why you didn't just call Tristan's father or lawyer to see if you could interview the kid about Bess."

"Did that on day one," Jason said. "I called both of them, in fact. No go."

Kyla cringed. "Forrest Wainwright has every right to refuse the request."

"I hate it when those pesky rights get in the way."

"Especially for minors," Kyla said in a warning tone.

"He turns eighteen next April."

"Really?" Kyla arched a brow. "That changes things.

As a minor we don't have a lot of options, but as an adult…he'd be looking at a serious sentence after he turns eighteen."

"You're forgetting the privilege of wealth."

"Not necessarily. The system works," Kyla said, but at Jason's doubtful snort, added, "Most of the time. What we need to do is find a way into Tristan's life that he isn't expecting. Maybe make a connection so he'll let his guard down. He could let something about Bess or even Julia slip."

"*We*?" An unfamiliar chill raced down his spine. "You heard what Detective Alvarez said. You get caught investigating anything connected to her case—"

"I'm not going to get caught," Kyla said. "You didn't really believe her when she said she'd keep an open mind where Julia was concerned, did you?"

"Of course not." There was no point in lying. "Just like I don't think she believes you're going to keep your nose out of this case. She's just waiting for you to break your word, Kyla. And I doubt she'll regret following through on her threats." He caught himself before he uttered his next thought; that he'd die before he went back to prison.

Kyla would no doubt call him an alarmist, but it was the truth. He'd barely made it out the first time with his sanity and humanity in place. But he also knew Alvarez had uttered that threat because she knew how powerful it was. What the detective didn't know was that Jason was never, ever, going to let someone have that much power over him.

"Julia didn't deserve to die." In the early morning twilight, he saw Kyla's hands tighten on the wheel. "I'm not letting it go unanswered. I'm not walking away."

"Neither am I."

"As long as you know what's at stake. I guess we're in this together then."

"I guess we are."

Jason took a deep breath, then let it out slowly. The time had come to admit that being in the vicinity of Kyla for any length of time wreaked havoc on him. She made him want things he could never have: a marriage, family, a place to belong like Vince had with Simone. Like a lot of their friends had found. But some wishes, some desires, were futile.

In small doses he could convince himself that being friends was enough. Maybe it was the residual adrenaline from last night, but after being so close to her, touching her, being within a hairbreadth of kissing her, he had to accept that his feelings for Kyla were not only inconvenient; they were dangerous.

It had been a long time since he'd knowingly walked into danger.

Maybe this time, the risk would be worth it.

"So." Kyla slipped the car into Park and faced him as he unhooked his seatbelt. "What now?"

"Now this."

He didn't think. He moved. His hand came up to cup the back of her neck, his brain short-circuiting at the sensation of her curls brushing against the backs of his fingers. Jason leaned in, his eyes boring into her surprised ones, as he waited for her to push him away. To say no. Relief and desire crashed through him as her hand came up, brushed against his shoulder, then curled into the fabric of his shirt to the point her nails scraped his skin. She drew him closer.

He brushed his mouth, lightly, so lightly, over hers.

The soft escape of air from her mouth when she gasped sent his nerves tingling. There wasn't a cell of his being that hadn't been wanting this, dreaming of this, and as he settled his lips on hers, the powerful surge of want he'd been keeping at bay for what felt like forever took over.

Jason tasted, he tempted, he invaded, claimed her mouth with an urgency he could barely control; afraid the moment would break apart should he think too much. He could smell blooming flowers even as he tasted the promise of summer and heat on her lips. That she met every move he made with one of her own had him melting into her, wanting nothing more than to transport them somewhere, anywhere, other than where they were.

When he broke the kiss, he barely moved, keeping his mouth on hers, his other hand brushing against the soft skin of her cheek. He squeezed his eyes shut, wishing he hadn't given in to the temptation because now he knew, he *knew,* it wasn't just him.

"Jason?" Her hand clenched in his shirt, pulsing like the beat throbbing in his throat.

"Yeah?"

"I think I know the answer already, but—" she drew back, licked her lips and nearly sent him spinning into the afterlife "—is this a good idea?"

"Definitely not." And because he feared it would be the only opportunity he had, he kissed her again. "I needed to get that out of my system." He pressed his forehead against hers, released his hold on her, sat back, and pushed open the door. "Get some sleep. I'll call you tomorrow at work and we'll figure out where to go from here."

When he faced her, when he looked at her, and saw

the dazed, sort of giddy expression on her face, he nearly climbed back into the car.

"Did it work?" she asked before he closed the door.

"Did what work?"

"The kiss?" Her eyes glinted with arousal and more than a hint of amusement. "Am I out of your system?"

It would be easy, so easy, to lie. "Not even a little bit."

# Chapter 7

The incessant ringing of her phone dragged Kyla out of the depths of an exhausted sleep late that morning. Without opening her eyes, she felt around the top of the mattress and nearly knocked her cell to the floor. She flipped it over, pried open her eyes, and groaned. Ten thirty.

She started to roll over, but found she couldn't. Not with the familiar, yet inconvenient weight settled on her backside.

"I am immune to your powers of persuasion, Ninja." Far from it. The Chiweenie had won her heart at a rescue shelter event last year. The two year old pup hadn't had the best life, but she was determined to change that. Unable to resist the adorable face and huge personality, she'd surrendered herself immediately. He was definitely the quietest and stealthiest roommate she'd ever had.

She'd barely had the brainpower to strip down to her underwear and drop face first onto her mattress when she got home last night. She reached back, and Ninja took that as his sign to shove his wet nose into her palm. She smiled into her pillow even as she accepted he wasn't going to let her get back to sleep. Neither, it seemed, was her phone.

When she saw who was calling, she frowned, synapses beginning to fire as she answered. "Darcy." She licked her dry lips. "What's up?"

"About time." The relief in Darcy's voice had Kyla patting the mattress in an effort to get Ninja to relocate. "I've been calling since ten. Are you all right? Where are you?"

"Home." Kyla rubbed her eyes, then pulled her sleeping scarf off her hair. "Why? Where are you? What's going on?"

"You asked me to come over today to help you finish unpacking. You forgot, didn't you?"

"I did." Kyla groaned and sat up. "I'm sorry. I was out late last night—" The hours flew back at her with the force of a tornado. Her time at Night Crawler, first with Jason, then with Colin O'Callaghan. The raid, her near miss of an arrest… Jason's kiss.

She groaned, unable to process.

"Tell me about it when you let me in," Darcy ordered as the doorbell chimed. "I've got coffee. And strawberry pastries from Mahoroba."

Kyla's stomach rumbled at the magic word and she made her way to the front door, Ninja, all six pounds of dark brown fur and frivolity, nipping at her heels. She still had her phone up to her ear when she looked Darcy in the amused, undeterred eye. "You're my hero." She hung up and sagged against the door, blinded by the radiant, always in place smile offered by her friend. "But you're going to have to give me some time to wake up."

The two had met a few years prior when Darcy, a water rescue diver and consultant, had been brought in to assist in the recovery of a missing trial witness of Simone's. Shorter than Kyla, rounder than Kyla, and definitely more entertaining than Kyla, Darcy had the kind of open, freckled face that was incapable of hiding anything. She was also one of the funniest, most reliable people Kyla had ever met in her life. "Come on in."

"You sure?" Darcy scooted around her. "You don't look so great."

"Thanks." Her head was spinning with too much information, too little sleep, and more than a hint of unease. "Do me a favor," she said as she led Darcy and Ninja into the kitchen. "Grab Ninja's food out of the fridge?"

"Doggie food or human?"

Ninja hopped up on his back feet and offered his answer.

"I think he's earned a human treat this morning." Kyla would have been down to give him a good scrubbing pat, but she was afraid she might tip over.

"You hear that, Ninja?" Darcy earned several hops and a barely there bark. "You get salmon and rice this morning. Mama's being nice to you."

"Awesome, thanks," Kyla said around a yawn as Darcy scraped a generous portion of food into Ninja's spotted food bowl and refilled his water dish.

"So." Darcy gave an approving look at Ninja as he

dived nose deep into his breakfast. "Long night, huh?" She popped a large paper coffee cup out of the tray and handed it over. "Who with?"

*Oh, just a couple of drug dealers and half the Sac Metro PD.* "Jason Sutton."

Darcy stared. "I'm sorry. You spent the night with Jason Sutton and this is how I hear about it?"

Kyla laughed at Darcy's expression. "It wasn't that kind of night." It could have been, though. So very easily. She turned away as her cheeks warmed before Darcy called her on it. It would take some time to accept that her fantasies about Jason—and yes, she'd had her share of them—hadn't come close to matching reality. Hooboy, that man could start a fire on an iceberg. Kyla made a show of retrieving paper plates from next to the microwave. "I was working on a case and we crossed paths."

"Must have been some path if you unpacked those glitter shoes you bought for Halloween a few years back." Darcy opened the paper bag and pulled out a selection of pastries.

"It was definitely an unexpected one," Kyla confirmed. "I can't really talk about it."

"You mean you can't talk about the case," Darcy clarified with a meaningful glare. "Doesn't mean you can't talk about the private time you must have spent with Jason. Come on. Spill. It might be enough to re-ignite my faith in love and romance."

"Dating apps not working out so well?" Kyla grabbed hold of the change of subject as if it were a life pre-server. "I thought you had a bunch of swipe rights."

"The only thing I've gotten from swiping is carpal tunnel and the potential for restraining orders," Darcy grumbled. "And don't think I don't know what you did just there." She circled a finger in front of Kyla's nose. "If you don't want to talk about him—"

"I don't." Because she could still feel traces of Jason's mouth on hers. She bit into the crispy, strawberry and cream-filled pastry and did her best not to swoon as the sugar hit her system. When she swallowed, she asked, "You want me to try to fix you up again?"

"Absolutely not." Darcy held up a hand and shook her head. "No, thank you. I'm still recovering from lawyer boy's affinity for Victorian death masks and funeral rituals."

Kyla laughed. "I had no idea his interests were so… unique. Simone and I both thought he'd be a great catch for you."

"Catch. Ha. Funny. The man had stuffed fish all over his living room. I don't know what your excuse is, but Simone's got her head stuck in the cloud of marital bliss, which means reality no longer exists for her."

Kyla's smile slipped. Oh, reality existed for Simone. With all its razor sharp irony. Kyla glanced at her phone. Why was it when she got a late start, the day seemed to fly by even faster? "Thanks for picking up breakfast. Well, lunch."

"My pleasure. Not like there was anything else on my schedule this morning after I hit the pool. Where do you want to start? Unpacking," Darcy added at Kyla's blank look. "Wow. You really are still foggy, aren't you?"

She was and until she got all these details out of her head, she would be. "I'm sorry. I've got a million things running through my brain. I need some time to get it all in order."

"So go do it." Darcy brushed her hands off on the

back of her jeans and cleaned up. "I'll unload boxes and when you're ready to take a break, we'll go from there."

"You mean it?" Kyla didn't like the idea of unloading her unpacking on her friend. "But it's Sunday."

"What else do I have to do? Stay at home and stare at my goldfish?"

"I thought Harvey died last month."

"Exactly." Darcy sighed. "Which is where this handsome guy comes in." Darcy bent down to scoop Ninja into her arms. "Go do what you have to do. Ninja and I will keep down the chatter."

"You do know he doesn't talk back," Kyla reminded her.

"Maybe to you he doesn't." Darcy's smile rivaled the sun streaming through the breakfast nook windows. "I've got a training week ahead with some new recruits. This will be relaxing by comparison."

Kyla wondered if Darcy had something she wanted to talk about. Her job as a rescue diver could be a stressful one, especially in the summer months. Watching Darcy in the water was tantamount to witnessing a mermaid at peak season; she moved so fluidly she made the laws of physics quake. She also didn't take anything about the water for granted and made sure that her trainees walked away not only with the ability to do their jobs, but also left with a healthy if not fearsome respect for the element's power. The fact Darcy was one of the first calls made when a crisis was at hand spoke to both her talent and her reputation. She was definitely the kind of woman anyone would want in their corner come crunch time.

"All right," Kyla said. "I owe you big-time for this." She gathered up a stack of notepads and her laptop. "Oh, hey, if I said the name Barnaby Faustus, what would you say?" She couldn't shake the feeling the real estate developer was ringing more than one bell.

Darcy shook her head. "Sounds like a character from the Flintstones."

Answers like that, Kyla thought as she chuckled to herself, were only one reason she loved Darcy Ford. She took her coffee and another pastry with her, got settled at the small desk in her bedroom and began to work.

She fell into her routine easily, making and organizing notes as she scribbled all over the legal pads in between internet searches. Time slipped away as she shifted between her upcoming case and trying to figure out where she'd come across Barnaby Faustus's name before. She dropped her pen, lowered her face into her hands and, because it was always her memory trigger of last resort, recited the alphabet.

"A, B, C…" She frowned. "Why do I know his name? Where have I heard… D, E, F, G… E!" Kyla dug around on her cluttered desk, found her phone and dialed.

"Happy central," Eden St. Claire—she hadn't taken her detective husband's last name—answered, the ear-splitting yet oddly melodious sound of a wailing toddler echoing in the background. "What's up, Kyla? You finally come to your senses and decide to come work for me? Better yet? I've got a soon to be toddler I might be willing to pass off if you're up for it. She's little. Doesn't take up much room."

"Just bandwidth!" Eden's husband, Cole, yelled.

Kyla's lips twitched. "I'll have to pass, sorry."

Eden's next words were muttered, no doubt because her daughter, Chloe Ann had taken to repeating everything. And by everything, Kyla meant *everything*. Considering Eden's inability to censor herself, Kyla could only imagine what little Chloe Ann was picking up and tossing out. "Seriously, what's up?" Eden asked. "This have to do with your little trip to the pokey last night?"

Pokey? And here Kyla thought Jack's wife was the one with the old movie obsession. Still, Eden's question posed a problem. "Ah, it might?" She hadn't thought this through. Asking what she wanted to meant revealing she wasn't walking away from looking into Julia's death; Eden's husband definitely wouldn't want to know about that.

"Well, that's good news," Eden said a little too loudly. "Cole will be relieved to know you're staying out of it." She lowered her voice. "Cole's taking Chloe Ann to the playground around four. That's code, by the way, for he's going upstairs to Jack's to watch football with the guys. He'll be gone for hours so come on by and we'll talk."

"Wouldn't you rather have that time to yourself?"

"I was just going to watch the game myself. Besides, you wouldn't be calling me if this wasn't important and that means you're doing something you shouldn't," Eden said nonchalantly. "Naughty Kyla gives me life, especially since Simone won't be around to hear about it. See you in a bit." She hung up before Kyla could argue.

She checked the time, cringed at the hours that had passed and hurried in for a quick shower. In record time, she was returning to the kitchen in jeans and an oversize, orange tank. She stopped short in the arched doorframe, shock mingling with guilt and gratitude. "Darcy! What have you done?"

"Drats." Darcy, perched on the top of the counter and stretching a length of the bronze contact paper Kyla had picked out into one of the cabinets, looked over her shoulder. "I was almost finished."

Kyla stared at the pile of empty boxes stacked by the door and Ninja, who was curled up in his cushy little dog bed across the room. "Where'd everything go?"

"It's put away. I found a diagram over by the refrigerator. Hang on. Let me just get...this...here. Man, corner cabinets are the worst. That's where you stick the stuff you don't need but couldn't bear to part with."

"Right." Kyla retrieved the nearly illegible paper. "I forgot I made this." She opened the cabinet closest to her and found her glasses—on top of the shelving paper—perfectly lined up. "Darcy, you're a miracle worker."

"I can work a plan. Besides, now it's done and you don't have to worry about it." She turned and slid off the counter. "Not sure that's really where you'll want your plates. Personally? I'd put them down here—top shelf of the center island. But that's me. You're more of a cook than I am."

"I'm sure my mother will have her ideas as well. This is great. Thank you." It would be so nice to come home and not be faced with an enormous to-do list.

"Help me break down the boxes and we'll call it even?" she asked and grabbed the box cutter. "This case you're working on, is it about Julia Summerton?"

Kyla stared. "How did you—"

"I found these." She picked up the extra photos Kyla had come across when she'd been looking for pictures to give Detective Peterson. "I recognize her name from the news." She indicated Kyla's writing on the back. "It's terrible what happened to her."

"Yes," Kyla murmured, not wanting to look at the

smiling face of her friend. Not when she still had the image of Julia's dead body in her head. "Quite terrible."

"I'm so sorry." Darcy's eyes widened in sympathy. "Are you doing okay?"

"I'm fine." Kyla managed a quick smile. "We hadn't seen each other in a while. It came as a shock of course." She set the photos aside. "I've been in touch with her mother, trying to help where I can."

"In other words, yes, you are looking into it." Darcy tossed a collapsed box onto the floor, then reached for another one.

"Darcy…"

Darcy shrugged. "I know, I know. You can't talk about it. That is the case you can't talk about, right?"

"If it was, I couldn't talk about it, Darcy."

"Yeah, yeah, okay. I get it." Darcy waggled a finger at her. "You're doing something you aren't supposed to, aren't you?"

Kyla pinched her lips together.

"All right, I'll stop." But Darcy looked far from deterred. "I am dying to ask a ton of questions, but you've gone into stealth mode. Will you tell me about it when you can? Or, at the very least, when it's over?"

"I'll tell you what I can when I can. Just, for now…" Kyla tried to find the right words. "Pretend like we didn't have this conversation, all right? It could really mess things up for me at work if anyone found out what I'm doing."

"No problem." Darcy pretended to lock her lips with an invisible key. "This is going to make one of the best stories ever for girls' wine night when you're on the other side of it. It isn't dangerous, is it?"

"Dangerous?" Kyla winced. "No." Not unless defying a senior law enforcement official and wedging her way into a drug-related nightclub counted. And it didn't, not when compared to the damage she could do to her career. "Not really."

"Dangerous enough you're working with Jason, though, right? That's what last night was about? Okay, you're right. Can't ask. Won't ask. Just tell me one thing."

Kyla sighed.

"Have you kissed him yet?" Darcy's eyes sparkled with mischief.

"Darcy!" Kyla ducked her head, but given Darcy's uproarious laughter, not fast enough. "Okay, stop."

"Are you kidding? This is me living vicariously, remember? Jason Sutton is H-O-T hot. Especially since he grew that beard. Who knew facial hair could make that much of a difference? I mean, he was cute before—"

"Darcy." Kyla couldn't help it. She laughed. "How about we table all this until I'm on that other side? Then I promise, I will tell you everything."

"Oh, you're darn right you will. Otherwise I'm not going to show you where I hid your air fryer."

Friends, Kyla thought as she and Darcy finished cleaning up the kitchen.

What would she do without them?

Jason lost most of Sunday, mainly because he'd ended up crashing on his sofa the second he'd gotten home. After grabbing a late lunch down at the bar, he decided to leave his car and take a long walk back to the alley between the club and the abandoned building next door. All before he headed over to Jack's to watch the football game.

Daylight brought with it the promise of a new start

as well as a clear perspective, which is exactly what he strived to find along with the cell phone and jump drive he'd ditched last night.

Sleep had managed to reboot his energy level as well as his thought processes, but not enough that he felt any regret for having kissed Kyla when she'd dropped him off at his car. Nope. No regret. At least not for kissing her. Impulse had driven him most of his life. Often that impulse got him into trouble. For a man who wasn't known for thinking things through, he had thought about this. Until the frustration of it drove him into throwing all caution—and logic—to the wind.

Kissing Kyla had, without a doubt, been worth the risk. What on earth was he supposed to do about it now?

As he walked through the downtown core, past the kitschy, artsy stores, the coffee houses and book shops, he wondered if she was at home. Was she thinking about their kiss? Was she considering what might come of things now that he'd ignited that spark? It could effectively torch their friendship dynamic. Jason rolled his eyes and shook his head. He sounded like a love-sick teenager waiting for someone to pass him a note in homeroom.

As if he'd spent that much time in school.

If ever there was a moment to walk something off, it was now and walking had always helped him think. He needed to come up with a plan; a plan that would put some distance between him and Kyla before the two of them did something they would regret.

He didn't want to live with the knowledge of what it was like to love Kyla Bertrand. And she didn't need the stigma of being involved with a man like him.

This was practicality and realism, not self-pity, he

told himself. He knew the hurdles Vince had to jump over because of him. He couldn't imagine the road-blocks his presence in Kyla's life would put in her way. He wasn't good for her, except now he knew...

Now he had proof of just how good they would be together.

And that was something he needed to push far, far out of his mind. Deep into the recesses where he couldn't hurt her.

"Then solve the case already and move on," he muttered to himself as he made his way down the street. The coffee he'd drunk before leaving his apartment still buzzed through his system.

Finding Bess Carmody seemed like a cakewalk compared to what he and Kyla were facing now. Adding a suspected juvenile drug dealer, a violent double murder, a pair of nasty brothers and a criminal enterprise knocking on this city's back door and their lives were tumbling into one giant snowball of danger. A missing person felt like a simple case, even as the weight of finding Bess pressed down on him. The more he found out about Night Crawler the more he had the horrible feeling that good news would not be waiting for any of them on the other side of this case.

But he was getting ahead of himself. Until he knew otherwise, there was still hope where Bess was concerned.

He stopped at the corner when he saw the crime scene tape stretched across the alley next to Night Crawler. He'd hoped by now the patrol officers had been called off. No such luck.

Jason pulled out his cell phone and pretended to answer a call even as he surveyed the area. The officers in the car were dividing up paper wrapped packages out of a sack. They were parked in front of a sign tacked to a boarded up window announcing the building's pending demolition.

The windows of the patrol car were slightly down to let the warm afternoon air waft through. Jason strode past, turned left and hurried down the street and around the block. He breathed a bit easier when he saw the other end of the alley was clear of police, but the door with the mail slot where he'd dropped the cell phone and jump drive was too far away to get to without being noticed.

He could wait, but another day or two delayed getting whatever evidence was in Bess's phone, not to mention what was on the jump drive. And he needed that information. It was the only way to move forward with the case.

"Time to test just how much luck you have." Jason put his phone away, pulled out a pair of black latex gloves, then a leather case holding his lock picks. He chose the two he used most frequently and tucked them into his hand. Keeping low, he ducked under the tape and inched his way down the alley.

He could only hope he wasn't in sight. He slipped around trash cans and metal bins, stacked boxes and crates as quietly and slowly as he could as he kept the metal door in sight. The stench of vomit and alcohol drifted up from the damp ground. He'd smelled worse in prison. Far worse, but that didn't stop his stomach from churning.

A car door slammed. Jason looked up to see one of the officers climb out of the car to stretch. Jason bent down, waited and forced himself to be patient as the deputy came around the car and stepped into the alley.

Jason tried to ignore the sudden rise of panic. He stayed crouched in the same position he'd held under Colin O'Callaghan's desk. Voices echoed down the alley as the deputies were separated, one heading off on foot, and the other staying in the driver's seat.

Jason pushed forward. Just enough to creep around to the wall and make his way to the door. He made quick work of the padlock, keeping one eye on the patrol car. When the lock snapped free, he left it on the ground. Cringing, he twisted the knob and pulled the door open. The hinges screamed in protest. Without looking back, Jason snuck inside, sending a shaft of light slicing through the darkness. When he pulled the door shut, the world went black.

He heard rustling in the distance. Mice, Jason told himself as he withdrew his phone again and tapped the flashlight app. Or a very determined cat. The air was stale, thick in his nose and mouth, and smelled like time rotting away. The faint hint of chemicals wafted beneath, threatening to choke him.

Thick cobwebs hung from the abandoned tables and chairs, stacked haphazardly in the center of the room. Plywood-covered windows didn't allow for even the hint of light to invade and in the shadows, any promise of a future died. Time stood still in this place, ever since the padlock had been applied.

More rustling. From above. Louder this time with a muted, unfamiliar sound Jason couldn't quite place. *Hearing things*, he told himself. That had happened to him in prison, early on, on those stressed out days when the walls closed in and the fear crept up. He squeezed his eyes shut, determined to set the darkness and fear aside as the past reached up and locked its chilly claws around his throat.

He shifted, searched the floor and quickly located the phone and drive. When he pushed open the door, he did so in increments and poked his head out and around before slipping all the way out. He reveled in the fresh air and the reminder that now he could step out of whatever darkness he found himself in.

A defining squeak coming down the alley had him freezing against the wall and ducking down. Muttering and mumbling, male, sounding somewhat detached from reality, headed right for him. Jason gnashed his teeth together and glanced toward the car. The officer hadn't moved.

When he looked back and up he found a tired face looking back at him from beneath a bedraggled, overgrown beard. Wearing what looked like multiple rain ponchos over tattered sweatpants and laced and looped boots, the man inclined his head and raised a very curious eyebrow. "You new here? This is my alley. Or at least it was." He pointed to the nightclub. "They kicked me out a few weeks back. Says they're gonna tear this place down. Destroyed my house and told me to get gone."

"I'm sorry," Jason said. He could see the pain and anger in the man's eyes. Dignity, Jason knew, was something humans clung to even in the darkest of times. The contents of the man's cart were covered for the most part, but in the far corner, Jason saw a pile of books, worn, yet neatly stacked. "I think you'll be okay for a while. They had a dustup last night. Cops will be sticking around."

"Yeah? Cops around here are pretty good. They don't hassle much."

"Right."

"You setting up house?" The homeless man suddenly looked suspicious. "Don't look like you belong here."

"I did at one time," he told the man. "Right now, I'm looking for something I lost. Trying to avoid unnecessary attention. I'm Jason." He held out his hand and forced himself not to look back at the cop car.

"Edmond Dantès."

Jason's brow creased. "Count Edmond?" As in *the Count of Monte Cristo*?

"It's my secret identity," the man whispered and cackled so loudly his voice echoed in the alley. "No one messes with a count."

"No," Jason said. "I don't suppose they do." He glanced up the alley. "I'm just waiting to make my getaway."

"Go on." Edmond motioned with his hand and pushed his cart out ahead. "I'll keep you safe."

"Thank you." Jason reached for his wallet, removed all the cash he had and held it out, pointing at the cop. "For your trouble, Count."

"I shall put it to good use." The man grinned, saluted, took the money and pushed his overflowing shopping cart down the alley.

Jason moved fast, not wanting to take the time to check if he was seen. He was safely around the corner when he heard the wail and crash.

"My cart! Dang blasted city! Is nothing sacred anymore?"

Jason made his way back around the block, crossed the street and found himself smiling as he saw the cop from the car helping Edmond right his cart and retrieve the belongings that had rolled free. The count looked at Jason and beamed.

"Best hundred bucks I've spent in years," Jason told himself and snapped off his gloves before he headed off to Jack's.

# *Chapter 8*

After stopping by her favorite bakery, Kyla lucked out and found parking right in front of the multistoried building where Eden and Cole now lived. It was a far cry from the cramped yet homey gentleman's cruiser Cole had lived on when they first got married. Kyla estimated not only Cole's boat, but Kyla's apartment and The Brass Eagle could easily fit in the space.

The historic building located in the heart of downtown Sacramento had at one time been a high-end department store, decked out with all the elegant architectural details of its first era. While it had gone through many incarnations since, it had stood empty for years until renowned artist Greta Renault-McTavish, Jack's wife, bought the building and converted it into loft apartments. It had become a bit of a central hub for Kyla's friends, with Greta and Jack living on the top floor while Eden and Cole and their daughter, Chloe Ann, lived on the second. There was talk about turning the lobby and first floor into an art gallery to display Greta's work, but apparently that talk was on hold for the time being.

Kyla reached into her bag, then stopped herself from pulling out her cell and calling Jason. Agreeing to work together didn't mean she had to tell him every single detail of what she was thinking. Besides, she wouldn't really have any information to impart until she talked to Eden, and maybe not even then. She reached again for her phone, but then pulled her hand away. Why was this so difficult?

"Because you don't know what to say to him now that he kissed you." Irritation slid through her. She wasn't frequently at a loss for words. There was always a verbal escape from anything she got herself into. Except now she'd gotten herself into a situation she wasn't entirely sure she wanted to extricate herself from. It didn't help that her imagination had utterly failed to prepare her for the intoxicating power of Jason Sutton's kiss. "He must have short-circuited my logic wires."

She spotted Jason coming around the corner just as she was getting out of the car. She froze. What did she do? Well, first she admired the very nice way those jeans fit him. The stark white of a T-shirt peeked out from under the lightweight jacket. The breeze caught strands of his hair and tossed them away from his forehead, leaving his eyes clear for admiration. Half-out of her car, she knew instantly when he spotted her and, as the smile eased across his mouth, the knots inside her belly loosened.

With one look, he erased all confusion and uncertainty, even as she wished and hoped for a repeat of this morning's intimate vehicular activity.

He picked up his pace just as she closed the door, shifting her purse and the brown bakery bag into one hand. "You coming to watch the game?"

"And here I thought you knew everything about me." She grinned at his sudden confusion. "I don't watch any football game that doesn't include the Saints."

"New Orleans? I thought you were a Northern California girl?"

"Oh, I am. Mama is from New Orleans and, as my father learned early on, New Orleans always wins. Even when they don't. You should see her house come Mardi Gras time." Her lips twitched. "You, ah, get some sleep?" They walked toward the thick, double glass doors.

"Enough that I'm probably wired for a week. You?"

And here they were. Making small talk. "I'm good. I'm keeping Eden company." She pointed up. "Look, about—"

"I was out of line," he said at the same time as he reached over and hit the buzzer for Jack and Greta's apartment. "Sorry." He took a deep breath. "This is all complicated, Kyla. I mean, your job. My past. I don't see it working and I just…don't want things to be strange between us."

"Then let's not make it strange." She chalked it up to her previous short-circuit that she rose up on her toes and pressed her mouth against his. It wasn't nearly the kiss they'd shared that morning—more of a promise of what was to come. She drew her tongue gently across his lower lip, and smiled as he rested his hands on her hips and drew her in. "See?" she murmured and opened her eyes. "It's only as strange as we make it."

"Kyla," he whispered her name as if it were a prayer. Or perhaps a plea.

"Stop over thinking so much. You'll ruin whatever this is."

"I know what it is," Jason said and as the door buzzed, he released her to open it. "It's trouble."

"Maybe it is." Kyla agreed as she walked past him into the lobby. "But for once, I'm not sure I care. I'm taking the stairs. You coming?" She looked behind her as he moved toward the iron-gated elevator.

"No, I think it's best I don't."

"There you go, thinking again." Kyla shook her head as she started to climb, feeling more emboldened by the second. "We really have to do something about that."

It wasn't until she reached the second floor landing that she could breathe again. She pressed her hands against her cheeks and blew out a long breath of air as she laughed. "I can't believe I did that!" But even better? She couldn't wait to do it again. Before she lost herself in too many dreams, she rang the doorbell and, after testing the knob, found it unlocked and opened it.

"LaLa! LaLa up!" The energy ball that was Chloe Ann Delaney flew across the room the second Kyla stepped foot inside.

"Ooooh, hey there, Little Bit." Kyla dropped her shopping bag and her purse on the floor and bent down to scoop the toddler into her arms. She buried her face in the little girl's neck, gave her a rough snuggle and earned an earful of giggles. Tears of joy pooled in the corners of her eyes, but she blinked them away before she pulled her head back to look down into the most innocent expression imaginable. "You are the cure to everything that's wrong in the world, you know that?"

"Ya!" Chloe Ann threw her arms into the air and yelled in triumph. "Ima cure! Treat, LaLa?" Chloe Ann leaned over and nearly toppled out of Kyla's arms as she reached for the now familiar paper bag.

"In a bit. Where are your parents?" Kyla settled Chloe Ann on her hip, grabbed her things and made her way into the kitchen. The second she stepped into the room, Cole and Eden went silent and swung to greet her, their faces far too open and innocent. "What's going on? You still plotting out a way for me to take this one for the next twenty years? What do you think, Chloe Ann?" Kyla planted a loud raspberry on the little girl's cheek, sending her into another fit of giggles. "You want to come live with me and Ninja?"

"Mama treat!"

"One track mind." Kyla sighed and set her bag on the counter. "Whatever it is you're trying not to talk about in front of me takes second place to sugar."

Eden groaned. "What did you bring her?"

"Her, you." Kyla glared at Cole. "Despite your lack of assistance with Detective Alvarez."

"See?" Eden elbowed her husband. "Told you she was ticked."

"I was busy locking down the club," Cole said by way of an apology. "Jack said you did fine."

Kyla smirked and sat Chloe Ann on the counter and pulled out a dedicated little wrapped pink cardboard box. "I heard you're taking Chloe Ann to watch football upstairs."

"I am," Cole said guardedly. "Why?"

"No reason." Kyla shrugged, then untied the box and pulled out the double chocolate mini cupcake and handed it to Chloe Ann. "Eat up, Little Bit."

"Ooooh!" Chloe Ann's eyes went wide as she grabbed the treat with both hands and shoved it into her mouth. She wrinkled her little nose and licked her chocolate covered face and fingers. "Yum!"

"You play mean." Cole walked over and, before he attempted to retrieve his daughter, pulled Kyla into a hug. "I'm glad you're all right." The hug lasted longer than normal and when she looked up at him, she saw the worry in his eyes. "Stay away from the O'Callaghans. You hear me?" He gave her another squeeze.

"I don't have a choice, do I?" Kyla smiled as he picked up Chloe Ann and headed out. "Have fun!"

"Bye bye bye!" Chloe Ann yelled.

"She'll be zooming around like a rocket up there in about ten minutes," Eden said with a chuckle. "Serves him right. So what did you bring me?"

"Double chocolate triple layer torte for you." Kyla pulled out the second box and slid it across the counter. "And a bottle of wine for me. But I'll share," she added at Eden's guarded look.

"I'll get the plates. You get the glasses." Eden pointed to the cabinet across the open-plan kitchen. "Then you can fill me in on your side of what happened last night."

Finally beginning to relax, Kyla settled in. It still amazed her that Eden St. Claire had embraced domestic bliss so easily. The crime blogger had developed her talent for investigating cold cases over the years, and had become a highly sought after specialist. She consulted with dozens of law enforcement agencies all over the country and had assisted in solving multiple murders and kidnappings. She also had the uncanny ability of upsetting pretty much everyone she ever came across, yet managed to find a balance in her home life, with a detective with the Sac Metro PD.

It boggled Kyla's mind. Especially after the conversation she and Jason had just had. How did they balance things? How did they keep things…compartmentalized? She had yet to figure out how to balance her job and investigating her friend's murder…and that was with help from Jason. Of course, maybe Jason was part of the problem.

They retreated into the spacious living room, Eden kicking a number of toys aside on her way to the well-worn sofa. "Sorry it's a mess around here. I've been working on a new case and the place shows it."

"Better than living in a house filled with moving boxes," Kyla laughed and traded Eden a glass of wine for a slice of torte. "You hear from Simone?"

"This morning, actually." Eden frowned. "She and Vince went to this new seafood restaurant last night and she ended up with food poisoning."

"Oh, no!"

"Oh, yeah. I got an earful." Eden nodded, but there was still sympathy in her eyes. "First time in years she and Vince get some alone time and she's spending it like that."

"Word is Allie can probably give her a run for her money in that department."

"Hardly." Eden rolled her eyes. "Not a bout of morning sickness to be had for our brave psychologist. She's sailing through the first trimester without a blip. I, on the other hand, was much less fortunate. So—" Eden forked up a mouthful of chocolate, took a moment to revel in the taste, then sat back "—give me your version of *Nightmare on K Street*."

Kyla did her best to censor, not wanting her friend to feel torn about whether there was something Cole needed to be informed about. By the time she got through all the details, including an abbreviated explanation of her trip to Julia's house, Eden was frowning, eating more chocolate, and had downed half her wine.

"I've met Alvarez," Eden said. "She's tough. Came up hard through the ranks. Good cop," she added. "Don't ever tell her I said that. She's not particularly sympathetic to anyone else's causes but her own."

"That's about where I landed," Kyla said. "She also made it clear I hadn't made any friends by invading their investigation."

Eden shrugged off Kyla's concern. "Please. I might be married to a cop, but I'm well aware of their short-comings sometimes. Nearsighted vision. They only see what they see. Nuance can escape them, as can emotional connections. Unless it's about their own."

"Julia wasn't an addict." She said it with such vehemence, Eden lifted a brow. "Sorry. I swear when I say that no one hears me."

"I hear you," Eden assured her. "And I believe you. You're not an alarmist, Kyla. You never have been. It's one of the reasons I've tried to lure you from the dark side."

"Being a prosecutor isn't the dark side," Kyla said.

"Any profession with that many rules is as far as I'm concerned."

"You sound like Jason."

"Do I?" Eden sent her a knowing, side-eyed look. "Do tell."

Kyla shook her head. "Don't. I already had this non-conversation with Darcy."

"What non-conversation?"

"That wide-eyed innocent look only works for your daughter."

Eden laughed. "I know. Simone, Allie and I all have a bet on how long it'll take for you two to hit the sheets."

Kyla choked on her wine. "You do not."

"Please. You two practically set the building on fire when you're in the same room. Tell me you haven't thought about it."

"Oh, I've thought about it," Kyla admitted out loud for the first time. "He kissed me. This morning. After… everything." She shot her friend a sheepish look. "And then I kissed him just now at the front door."

"This is better than chocolate." Eden set her plate down and jumped up enough to cross her legs and settle in as if she were about to listen to campfire ghost stories. "And?"

"And nothing. I'm here. He's upstairs."

"Oh." Eden frowned. "Not a good kisser?"

"Oh, that part was…exceptional," Kyla confirmed. "He's…uncertain."

"About what?"

"Us. Him. Me." Kyla struggled. "I can't imagine getting involved with a prosecutor is particularly appealing. And knowing Jason, he's probably overthinking the effect of me dating an ex-felon."

"Gah!" Eden slapped her hands over her face. "These men! Why do they have to make things so complicated?"

"He's not entirely wrong," Kyla said. "Dating Jason could create some professional complications." It felt good to talk to someone about this. Normally she'd have waited until Simone pried it out of her, but Eden was a good backup plan.

"He earned a commendation from the governor for the work he did helping to find Ashley when she was kidnapped. He could probably even get his record expunged if he pushed for it."

"He won't." That much Kyla knew for sure. Jason was a man who owned up to his mistakes. Asking to have his conviction overturned or dismissed would go against his natural grain. "But what's really irritating is that he served his time and he's still being punished for it." Especially by himself.

"Time he served because he wouldn't rat out his friends," Eden reminded her. "That's good character right there. Foolish for getting into that situation in the first place, but good character."

"He still has moments of debatable behavior."

"So he skims the edge of the law from time to time," Eden corrected her. "Who doesn't? Well, present company excluded, of course."

"He skims it for the greater good." Funny how she could see more gray than she used to. "And maybe he's right. Maybe we're just asking for trouble if we see where this thing between us goes."

"I know where it should go." Eden picked her plate back up. "If you could make it before Halloween, I can cash in on the after-holiday candy sale."

Kyla chuckled. "It won't happen at all as long as Jason has a clear thought in his head."

"Congratulations." Eden lifted her wine glass in a toast and chuckled. "You're carrying on the fine tradition of finding the one man who's the right guy for you and also somehow emotionally unavailable."

Kyla's gray mood lifted. "Can we talk about why I called earlier?"

"Yeah, sorry. We'll get back to Jason later."

Oh, Kyla really hoped not. "Barnaby Faustus."

"Barnaby?" Eden's eyes widened with surprise. "Wow. Not a name I expected to hear from you. What about him?"

"He's in real estate, yeah?"

"Among other things." Eden's tone slowed and she became fascinated with her torte again.

Clearly getting information out of Eden was going to be like prying a cupcake out of Chloe Ann's hands. "He owns the gated community where a person of interest lives. Tristan Wainwright," Kyla added. "Tristan was at the club last night, and he's the boyfriend of the missing girl Jason's looking for."

"A missing girl?" There was a shift in Eden's expression, as if part of her guard came down. "Interesting. Surprised Vince took the matter on considering his history with those kinds of cases."

"Vince didn't," Kyla clarified. "Jason took it on himself."

"Right." Eden nodded. "So, Barnaby Faustus. The cold case I worked in Arizona last year—the one where, after fifteen years, we finally linked a suspect to one of the dump sites? He was the guy who asked me to look into it."

"He hired you?"

"I would have looked into it, anyway, once I had the information, but he added a substantial financial incentive." Eden sipped her wine. "His niece was one of the missing girls."

"Oh." Kyla blinked. It was hard to think of a man

known for criminal activity as being affected by tragedy. "I take it she wasn't found alive."

"None of them were. I dug into the case, found a connection to a floral delivery service, made nice with the primary investigator." She took a larger drink of wine. "We found Barnaby's niece, along with four other young women buried on the suspect's property."

"I'm sorry." One thing about cold cases, Kyla had learned while working occasionally with Eden, was that while she might get the answers people were looking for, rarely did it come with a happy ending. Or closure. Closure, as Eden often said, was a myth. "And Barnaby still paid you?"

"He did. But I only took half of what he offered and I put it in a dedicated account meant for Chloe Ann's college fund. I asked him to donate the other half to a charity of his choosing. He's a good guy," Eden added. "He might operate outside those laws you're so protective of—"

"Like you said, who doesn't?" Kyla sighed.

"He doesn't hurt people, Kyla. Gambling, counterfeit handbags, smuggling cigarettes and booze, sure. But the dark stuff? If he was involved with crimes like that, I wouldn't have taken his call. Which would have been a mistake," she added. "Because of him, all those families were able to know what happened to their loved ones. I don't care what someone does if it helps find answers for people who are suffering."

And that, right there, spoke to the core of Eden St. Claire.

"Yeah, no, I get it, Eden. When Jason and I left the police station—"

"And back to Jason. Awesome."

"Stop," Kyla chided. "This is serious."

Eden waved her hand and sighed. "Fine."

"We tailed Tristan Wainwright to his house in Faustus Estates."

"You're looking for an in so you can keep tabs on this Wainwright kid?"

"It feels like the only real lead. He knew Julia. He was dating Bess Carmody when she disappeared, then went into rehab when she vanished. He's been frequenting Night Crawler. He's the only common thread we can pull since other avenues have been blocked." Basic principles of deduction dictated this was the right tactic to take. "He's the key to this. I'm sure of it."

"What does Jason think?" Eden asked.

Kyla shrugged. "I haven't really talked to him about it actually."

"Because you were too busy kissing?" Eden fluttered her lashes. "Sorry. Last one, I promise. You think Tristan's involved with the drug dealing?"

Kyla remembered the video of Julia and Tristan in the club. "He's involved in something shady and if this new drug is part of it? The stuff's horrible, Eden."

"I know." Eden sat forward and reached for her phone. "Cole and Jack have been working the case so long that it's keeping them up at night." She scrolled through her contacts. "You know who else detests the drug trade?" She tapped a name, then lifted the phone to her ear. "Barnaby Faustus."

"What does that mean? Who are you calling?"

"It means...hang on, it's his service. Hi. Eden St. Claire for Barnaby Faustus, please. Yes, I'll hold." She tipped her phone down. "It means you're about to get up close and personal with surveillance. Just one thing."

She held up a warning finger. "No way am I letting you do this alone. I suggest you let Jason know the two of you are about to get very cozy as the Wainwrights' new neighbors."

## Chapter 9

The last thing Jason anticipated doing this fine morning was jogging.

Especially on a Monday morning after a long night of watching football with his friends. Friends who had worked in not so thinly veiled references to his and Kyla's "relationship." Hence the need for a brain-cleansing run.

*I blame Max Kellan*, Jason silently grumbled as he dragged himself up the last few steps and back into his apartment. The former firefighter turned part-time PI who, even though he was halfway across the country with his wife mixing business with pleasure, had somehow managed to plant subliminal messages into Jason's psyche that reminded him a run was the best way to clear his head.

"Clear my head and kill the rest of me."

Then again, anything was better than sitting around

waiting for the jump drive he'd "borrowed" from Colin O'Callaghan's safe to decrypt. His optimism that he'd be able to access the stored information had quickly dissipated as it became clear, around ten last night, that the decryption program he'd written wasn't going to get him anywhere. It made his decision to do some exploring on the dark web easier. Obviously, whatever was on the drive was worth protecting beyond the usual encryption. The program was still running, spewing out code and virtual gibberish on his screen as it worked. Patience, he told himself. This was going to take time.

Except time was something he—and Bess Carmody—didn't have much of.

He ducked into the bathroom for a quick shower, then tossed his sheets and towels into the laundry, all the while willing technology to work its magic so he could extricate himself from this case. "Who are you kidding? You need to extricate yourself from Kyla."

He tossed together a quick protein shake, grabbed a bottle of water and headed to his desk. He woke up his laptop, plugged in Bess's cell phone and waited for it to turn on. It's fragmented screen was barely readable as it requested the boot-up password.

Jason initiated the password retrieval program he'd created, checked his voicemails, wrote an update on his search for Bess—Vince was a stickler for paperwork—and had just hit save when the phone beeped.

"Okay, here we go." Jason went into the settings and disabled the face ID and then to be safe, set her music to play in the background to stop the phone from going dark again. He scanned through Bess's call log, starting with the most recent. He recognized Tristan's cell number right off, and her parents', who she'd nicknamed Gomez and Morticia in her address book. Kid definitely had a sense of humor. Every other number he made note of and set the list aside to check later. "Now let's see your photos."

Whatever hope he'd had at finding a new lead, it died instantly.

All the photos had been deleted. Even the "Waiting for deletion" file was empty. Frustrated, he sat back in his chair.

"Okay, this makes no sense. If there's nothing on this thing, why did O'Callaghan have it in his safe?"

He'd have to try another tactic and access any cloud accounts Bess might have. That would take some digging since her parents were clueless and didn't even know the password to her laptop. This was going to be a challenge.

His phone rang just as he was making progress. He tapped the speaker option. "Jason Sutton."

"Mr. Sutton, this is Bernice Yablonski with Sacramento Juvenile Probation Services. I understand you were trying to get in touch with me regarding Bess Carmody?"

"Ms. Yablonski, yes." Maybe things were looking up after all. "Thank you for returning my call. I hope your leave went well."

"Couldn't have gone much better." Her voice immediately softened. "My daughter just had a baby, so I was able to spend time with her and my new grandson. Thank you for asking."

Small talk, he'd learned early on while working for Vince, broke through a lot of barriers in his business. Small talk that took an interest in people's lives worked its own special magic. "The fact you're returning my call on a Sunday tells me I definitely reached out to the right person." And that his impressions of professionalism and altruism about the woman were dead on.

"Well, I certainly hope that's the case."

"I'm sure you're swamped, catching up with work now that you're back." Jason forced himself to look away from the computer and grab a new notepad. "I wasn't sure if you'd been made aware of the situation with Bess."

"Yes, I was just catching up on the notes my assistant left for me. How long has she been missing?" Jason heard the distinct rustle of files over the line.

"A little over three weeks." It took effort to keep the dread out of his voice. The realist inside of him kept trying to break free of his hope. "From what I understand, this isn't the first time something like this has happened."

"No, I'm afraid it's not. Mr. Sutton—"

"Jason, please." One of the benefits to running his own case was establishing his own string of contacts. Vince had his share of them within various agencies and departments, but Jason was determined to do the same. Information was often the key in this business. "I know officially you're unable to help," Jason said. "But I was hoping there might be something you could share with me? Something to point me in the right direction?"

"I'm not sure what might help, but I'll try." He heard resistance in her voice—a tinge of regret, perhaps? "I met with Bess once a month for the past eighteen months. You've no doubt had extensive conversations with her parents—"

"Parents don't always see the truth," Jason said. "They don't always want to." In Jason's case, his father simply hadn't cared. "As far as Mr. and Mrs. Carmody are concerned, Bess is just going through a phase." And it was far easier to pay someone else to see her through that phase than deal with it themselves. "I'd like your take on her. Your personal take." The silence that followed made him wonder if the call had dropped. "Ms. Yablonski?"

"I'm still here. Mr... Jason," she corrected herself. "If we're discussing my personal impressions of Bess, which would be based on more than twenty years' experience in the juvenile justice system, I'd say that Bess's actions have nothing to do with growing pains and everything to do with addiction. Rather than have her face up to the consequences though, the court was convinced the Carmodys could see to Bess themselves."

Jason cringed. He'd thought as much.

"I recommended recovery programs on multiple occasions, both to Bess and her parents. Her parents dismissed the idea outright, declared there was no way their daughter was an addict. But Bess seemed somewhat intrigued. She even attended a few sessions at a youth center. Not that it did any good. At least it hadn't the last time we spoke."

Listening to what wasn't being said gave him even more insight. "You drug test your charges, don't you?"

"Yes. Especially when one of the dismissed charges has to do with narcotics. She didn't seem to care whether she passed or not."

"I don't suppose it would be possible for me to see those test results?"

"I'm afraid not."

Jason's mind raced. "All right. Can I ask if she passed or failed those tests?"

"You cannot. However." Bernice paused. "I can tell

you that she was in danger of having her oversight revoked, if that gives you an indication."

"It does." And it wasn't the answer he was hoping for. "Can you tell me, hypothetically of course, that if she did test positive for narcotics if the drug was identified?"

"Ah." The sound of computer keys clacking had his hope rising again. "Interesting. In previous results, yes. In the past two...the substance came back as unknown. Does that mean something to you?"

"It might."

"I'm not a pessimist by nature, Jason. I couldn't do this job if I was, but I'd be lying if I said I didn't think Bess would end up in the exact situation you're currently investigating."

"What was the name of the youth center Bess went to for meetings?"

"Uh, that was the Dempsey Center, I believe. They've had an above average success rate with younger offenders and addicts."

"Is there someone there you'd suggest I speak to?"

"Yes. Alona Lopez. She's been running the place since it opened. I can give her a call, let her know you'll be reaching out."

"That would be great, thank you." Jason checked his watch. "This number you called is my cell, so you can just forward me any information you can share that way. Thank you for your help, Ms. Yablonski."

"Bernice," she said. "Would you do me a favor, Jason?"

"Of course."

"Would you let me know how this all turns out? As difficult as Bess was, I would be incredibly relieved to see her sitting across this desk from me again."

"Good or bad, I'll let you know."

Jason returned to his computer to address the phone numbers from Bess's cell. His frustration ebbed as he filled in the data. A lot of the numbers were spam and robocalls. "But not this one." He looked at the information on his screen. "Dempsey Youth Center. I wonder..." He dialed the number on his own phone, waited...

*"Hi, this is Julia Summerton. I'm either away from my desk or with one of my charges. Please leave a message and I'll get back to you as soon as I can. Thanks!"*

He clicked end call. Bess had Julia's direct office number. "Now that's not a coincidence."

Reinvigorated, Jason opened each app on Bess's phone. Games. Social media accounts asking for verification—which he'd do later. Banking app. Online payment service... Notes. Empty. Although...he tapped on recently deleted and found one.

A long string of numbers stared back at him. Numbers that had absolutely no context. Too long to be a phone number, even an overseas one. Not a credit card. Maybe a bank account? He shook his head as he wrote them down. This was going to take some time.

Only thing left was to try to find an online cloud storage account she might have used to back the phone up.

"One step at a time." Jason slapped his laptop closed and tossed the phone on top of it. "The answer has to be here."

And he wasn't going to give up until he found it.

Energized after her evening with Eden, Kyla found herself pleasantly surprised to be ahead of the game by the time lunch rolled around on Monday afternoon. She'd finally found her groove with the draft of her opening statement, had declined a plea offer from the defendant's attorney that would have made her laugh if it wasn't so astonishingly arrogant, and she'd gotten her email inbox down to under thirty emails which, she decided, was definitely a reason to celebrate.

Nerves, she told herself as she ran out of things to do. Nervous energy was definitely the cause of her productivity, which allowed her to take the rest of the day off since she was all caught up.

It would have been a perfect fall day were it not for the fact Kyla was going to a dead friend's home. The Fabulous Forties, so named because construction dated back to the WWII era, was one of her favorite neighborhoods, filled with delightful cottage houses in various styles and sizes. The streets were narrow, the yards and lawns lush with color and maintained with precision and care. Dr. Allie Hollister-Kellan and her husband, Max, lived within walking distance, Kyla realized as she got out of her car and walked up the sloping driveway to the front porch of the colonial gray-blue, single-story home on 42nd Street.

A large camellia tree sat in the middle of the raised front yard, clinging to its last pink petals of summer as cool temperatures continued to grab hold.

She stopped and frowned. The garage at the back of the property didn't look large enough for a car and there wasn't one in the driveway. One couldn't get around the valley without a vehicle, at least not easily, so where was Julia's? She pulled out her phone and made a note to follow up.

A line of windows welcomed her when she stepped onto the porch, along with a trio of pumpkins by the front door. Heavy sage green curtains were drawn across, blocking any sight of the interior of the house. The iron railing had been painted the same ivory as the front door, which was accented with a delicate brass knocker. A mail slot was situated in the wall beside the door, one of those details few, if any, modern homes possessed. Kyla slid the key into the deadbolt, but when she turned it she found no resistance.

She froze, frowned and carefully depressed the door handle and pushed the door open. She strained, listening for any hint of movement. Nothing.

"Hello!" Kyla stepped inside, set her bag down and, glancing around, pulled a baseball bat out of the umbrella stand next to the door. She flipped the switch on the wall and the end table lamps flicked to life. Books and belongings were strewn all over the floor. The TV had been knocked over, the stand beneath it emptied of its contents. The piano situated along the wall behind her seemed unmarred, but the stool was open, music sheets and books flipped open and discarded.

Kyla yelped when the antique mantel clock announced the hour, its dull chime almost tinny as it echoed through the empty house.

The hardwood floor squeaked under her feet as she made her way into the dining room, clicked on another light, then went left and down the short hall to peek into the small bedrooms and one bath. She found the same level of disarray everywhere, but the search had clearly been focused on the front bedroom which had served as Julia's office. The closet door in the corner of the room stood open, with the filing cabinet inside spilling its contents. The desk under the window was cluttered, but there was an obvious void in the thin layer of dust.

"No computer."

Something crashed. She spun, bat raised and poised, and she made her way back down the hall, through the dining room and into the galley style kitchen. She looked left, to the laundry area, and found the back door swinging back and forth.

Kyla ran out, stood on the top back stair and caught a flash of blond hair before the side gate swung shut and clicked closed. The same blond hair she'd seen in the video of Julia that Detective Alvarez had shown her. Tristan Wainwright.

She ditched the bat and followed, out the backyard, down the driveway to the street.

Kyla pivoted, looking one way and then the other, her heart pounding. The street was quiet. Empty.

Frustrated, she returned to the house, going in through the still open front door again, and retrieved her purse and phone to call the only person who could help her make sense of things. "Jason, hi. Bad time?"

"No. Just...working. What's going on?"

She bit her lower lip. The second she heard his voice, her entire body warmed. She tried in vain to block out the memory of that kiss, of his kiss. Now wasn't the time, not with drug dealers, dead friends and runaway teens to worry about. "Someone broke into Julia's house." Kyla bent down and examined the front door. "I don't see any damage, either to the lock or the frame." She ran her hand over both. "The door was unlocked when I got here."

"So of course you went inside."

She smirked. "Let's just say I can't complain about those too-naïve-to-live characters in TV or horror movies anymore."

"The what?"

"You know, those people who just have to run up to the attic when they hear a weird noise?" Instead of doing what rational people would do, which would be getting out of the house as fast as possible. Yep, she was rambling.

"What's the address?"

Kyla rattled it off.

"Great. Did you call the police?"

"No." She bit her lower lip again. "If I do that, the place becomes a crime scene and we won't have the chance to look for anything. It could be days, maybe weeks before I get back inside." She'd also bet her next paycheck that Detective Alvarez would love to find an excuse to keep Kyla at bay.

"Seeing things from my perspective for a change. Good call."

"I can't be a hundred percent certain, but I think it was—"

"Wait, you mean whoever broke in was still there?"

Kyla's mouth twisted. "Didn't I mention that?"

"You did not."

"He's gone now so don't break any speed limits to get over here," she told him when she heard the engine of his car rev. "I'm fine, Jason. I had a bat."

"Oh, great. A bat. Good to know. I'll be there in ten, maybe fifteen minutes." He hung up.

Kyla stared down at her phone. "Well, that was rude." She plucked up her bag and set it on the dining room table. Planting her hands on her hips, she turned in a slow circle, taking in the mess. Whoever had been in here certainly wasn't organized. He'd just dumped and ransacked, tossing cushions and knickknacks all over the place. Broken bits of china and porcelain lay strewn about. There wasn't a lot left intact and Kyla hoped for Julia's mother's sake that the woman wasn't overly sentimental.

While she waited for Jason, Kyla went to the front bedroom and sorted through enough paperwork to put a bit of Julia's life into focus. From the broken frame of her diploma, Kyla learned Julia had earned her degree in psychology even after dropping out of Sac State. Julia had rented this house a little over two years ago and was leasing a silver four door sedan, whereabouts currently unknown. Her income was steady and, despite what appeared to be a severe shoe addiction, her credit cards were current and paid up. Checking account was healthy, as were her meager investments—typical of a woman her age in a stable profession. There was no indication of substance abuse or instability. Everything was quite to the contrary.

Her friend had been meticulous with her paperwork. She had files for everything: bank statements, insurance contracts, computer repair warranty, tax records, utility bills.

"Huh." She pulled the remnant of a torn storage unit invoice from under a stack of papers.

She glanced up and out the louvered window when she heard a car door slam. Kyla waited until she heard him step inside before calling. "I'm back here!"

"This place is a mess." Jason shoved his keys into his jacket pocket and strode over, his hand immediately coming to rest on her shoulder. "You okay?"

Her skin warmed where he touched her, and she wondered if and when he might kiss her again. Or when she might kiss him. *Not the time. Not even close to the right time to think about that.* She stepped away. "I'm fine." It didn't occur to her to be anything but. She picked up the wallet she'd found on the floor. "What kind of burglar passes up a wallet filled with cash and credit cards?"

"An inept one," Jason agreed.

"Or someone who was looking for something else. Her laptop's gone." She tossed the papers in her hand onto the desk. "Julia's employment and financial information. The invoice for a garage renovation. Nothing out of the ordinary. She's been working as a youth counselor for about six years."

"At the Dempsey Center."

Kyla frowned. "You knew?"

"I found her number on Bess's phone."

"Were you planning on sharing that bit of information or…?"

"I figured I would at the right time, which appears to be now."

"How did you get Bess's phone?" Kyla asked. "Is that what you ditched outside the club Saturday night?" She turned slightly amused eyes on him. "Yes, I noticed. I might have been frantic, but my vision still worked. So now we can connect Julia and Bess and Tristan."

"Calls between Bess and Julia went both ways. I also spoke with Bess's probation officer this morning. Bess failed at least her last few drug tests."

"What drug was she taking?"

"She wouldn't give me the details, but the last two came back as unidentifiable. They probably chalked that up to a lab mix up. I bet if they run it now looking for PoWWer, they'll get a match. What's the plan with this place?"

"I'm supposed to call Julia's mother when I have an inventory." Kyla sighed. "I'm really not up to starting that today." She walked over to the windows, closed the blinds and headed toward the front door. "I'll come back another time and get started cleaning up this place." Julia was paid up through the month and besides, her body still hadn't been released for cremation. She grabbed her belongings and motioned for him to precede her outside.

"I can help you with it," Jason offered as she locked up. "You want to start tomorrow after work?"

Kyla took a breath to brace herself. "No. I don't think we'll have time for a while." She faced him, saw the puzzled expression on his face. "What about setting up surveillance in Faustus Estates?"

"Surveillance? On who?" Clearly puzzled, he shifted to face her.

"Tristan Wainwright, who else? I think maybe he was the one in here earlier. Even if he wasn't, he's the link to everyone in this thing. To Julia, to Bess, to Night Crawler—"

"Night Crawler is off-limits."

"Yeah, yeah," Kyla waved off his concern as she headed to her car. "But Tristan isn't. Keeping an eye on him might lead you to Bess. Or he could let something slip about Julia."

"To his family? I hardly think—"

"Listen, we have the chance to do something the police can't. They don't have enough evidence to get a warrant—"

"Ah." He nodded, disappointment flashing in his blue eyes. "Okay, now I get it. What's some illegal surveillance for an ex-con, right? I've broken the law before. No reason not to now."

"That is not what this is about," Kyla countered.

"This is about you wanting to close your case and me wanting to find out who killed my friend."

"Right." He shoved his hands into the pockets of his jacket and glanced away.

"Wow." Kyla shook her head. How had she not seen this before? "That's pretty sad, Jason. If you want people to stop treating you like a felon, maybe you should stop clinging to the past like it's an anchor."

"That's not what this is about." He threw her words back at her.

"No?" She arched a brow.

"No. Look, Kyla, this isn't some kind of game where we can set up house and play happy family while we wait for a suspect to incriminate himself. This is real crime we're dealing with, bad guys who will literally do anything to protect their business. I'm not putting you in the line of fire because you think it's going to be fun."

"I can assure you," Kyla said in as frigid a tone as she could manage. "Losing Julia has not been fun."

"No." His gaze softened and he nodded. "Of course, I'm sorry. It's just… I don't think this is a good idea."

"You don't even know what the idea is yet," she reminded him. "Unless the idea isn't what's worrying you."

"I don't know what you're talking about." But he'd hesitated. Just a moment too long.

She smirked. "You're the one who kissed me first, Jason."

"That was a mistake."

"One that seems to still be bothering you." And that gave her more insight into him than he was probably comfortable with. "Is this where you give me the *'it's not you, it's me'* speech?"

"It would be a mistake. You're...you and I'm me and—" he took a deep breath "—getting involved isn't smart. For either of us. You're a prosecutor. You have a reputation to think about, and you need to keep your personal life above board. And. Well, to be honest—"

"Please." She closed the distance between them. "Be honest."

His eyes flashed, as if he hadn't intended to tell her the truth. "I'm not good for you."

She'd always known his past haunted him, but she hadn't thought he'd let it overwhelm him this much. Or scare him off. "Because you're a former convict and you don't want to tarnish my reputation."

If he heard the sarcasm in her voice, he didn't let on. "That's part of it."

What other part could there be? But one thing was for certain: he'd given them some thought. Enough that he was willing to put a stop to whatever was happening between them before it could really get off the ground. "Jason, you are who you are now because of what you've gone through. That's who I like. This man. Not your criminal self."

"They're one and the same, Kyla. And there are plenty of people who will always see me as a criminal first," Jason said. "You saw how Detective Peterson was with me at the morgue. How Alvarez treated me in that interview room. I don't want that coming back on you."

Kyla nodded and dug out her keys. "How nice of you to martyr yourself in an effort to protect my feelings." As she walked past him, she felt irritated he had so little faith in either of them. "It's fine, Jason. Message received. As for the surveillance, I'll figure out a way to do it myself."

"How exactly?"

"Google and YouTube," Kyla snapped.

"Kyla—"

Tires screeched. She'd barely stood up straight and turned toward the sound as a silver sports car barreled right for her. She froze, logic and reason evaporating as her ears roared. She blinked as the world slipped into slow motion.

"Kyla!" From behind, Jason's arm locked around her waist and he spun them toward the sidewalk as the car clipped Kyla's. They landed hard and rolled, arms and legs tangling. The gritty asphalt scraped against her bare arms. She knocked her head against the street hard enough to see stars.

She lay there, Jason sprawled on top of her, his wide, concerned eyes staring at her before he pushed himself up and off to look down the street. She pulled her legs in to stand, but feared they wouldn't support her. Kyla touched a hand to the back of her head to check for blood. Relief swept through her when she didn't find any. The last thing she wanted was a trip to the ER.

"Are you okay?" he demanded, the unfamiliar, intense look on his face sending a new kind of shiver racing along her spine as he bent down. "Kyla?" He grabbed her shoulder and gave her a quick squeeze.

"I'm okay." She was shaking. Whatever warmth had been coursing through her body had disappeared. She shoved her hair out of her face and let him help her up. "Thanks."

She smoothed her hands down her top, tried to get her fuzzy thoughts to focus. Her nerves were exploding like fireworks, tingling her skin. "That wasn't an accident."

"No. It wasn't." Jason grimaced. "It was Tristan Wainwright."

"It was? Why would he have stuck around?" Kyla wondered out loud.

"Good question."

"Jason, I'm fine. You're fine. There's no reason to be—"

"To be what? Angry?" Jason stalked up to Julia's house, chest heaving. "Oh, I'm past that."

She'd never seen Jason in this mood before. And she wasn't sure she ever wanted to again. He radiated rage, but also control, that had her walking toward him and touching his arm. "Jason—"

"Let's go back inside." He shifted out of her grasp and pressed a gentle hand against her back. "I want you to tell me about this plan of yours. Start to finish. Because whatever it is, I'm in."

## Chapter 10

"I can't believe I thought this was a good idea." Jason kept one eye on the road as he scrubbed a hand across his forehead. His knee-jerk reaction to Kyla's nearly being run down two days ago had clearly overridden his determination to control his impulses.

"We are past the time for second thoughts." Kyla, wearing a pair of kill-him-now denim shorts and a flowing tank top the color of a perfectly ripe pineapple, shifted in the passenger seat to face him. Given the excited expression on her face, he'd have thought she was a kid heading out on her first trick-or-treat run rather than moving into the neighborhood of a rumored crime boss. "Given Tristan seems to be our common denominator, it's only logical he's who we should be keeping an eye on."

It made sense. In theory. But theory hadn't included

the reality of bunking with Kyla. Just the two of them. No doubt with endless hours of close quarters ahead of them.

Now, in another ten minutes they'd be pulling up to the front guard gate of Faustus Estates for a meet and greet arranged by Eden St. Claire. Kyla was right.

Too late to turn back now.

"What about your job?" Jason asked. "You have a trial starting on Monday. Shouldn't you be focused on that?"

"I'm a woman. I can focus on a multitude of things at once. And we're given the option of working from home when necessary," she added with a dismissive shrug. "If something comes up at the office, Penny will call me."

Jason shook his head. He couldn't get rid of the feeling that this plan of hers, of *theirs*, was going to end badly.

Maybe there was still time to turn this around. Maybe there was another option Jason hadn't come up with. But other than camping out in his car and following Tristan Wainwright around Sacramento for the next few days, he had zilch. That meant this all-encompassing idea was it. He sat uncomfortably in his seat. Maybe this was just his irritation at the fact that he'd had nothing to do with the plan itself. By the time Kyla told him about it, everything was already in motion, which left Jason to worry about all the things Kyla and Eden probably hadn't considered. "What's going to happen when Tristan recognizes us from Julia's place?"

"A. You're assuming he will," Kyla said dryly. "How clever can he be, given what he's gotten mixed up in?

And even if he does recognize us, it'll just throw him off-kilter and off-kilter people make mistakes."

"Yes," Jason said slowly. "They do, don't they?"

She went on as if he hadn't spoken. "B. Barnaby spoke with Tristan's father—"

"He what?" Why was he just hearing about this now?

"Yesterday. They're friends," Kyla explained as if his IQ had suddenly tanked. "Their kids attend the same private school. Well, did. Tristan's younger sister Alicia still goes there but—"

"Tristan got booted last Christmas for selling pot to three members of the faculty," Jason said. "I read his file."

Kyla narrowed her eyes. "Tristan's school file is private."

"His file's stored on the school's server." A very unsecure server. Jason hit the turn signal and glanced in the mirror before changing lanes. "Don't worry. I followed up my hack with an email recommending a new security program. And you're changing the subject."

"I didn't think you were listening that closely."

Jason felt his patience strain. He took a long, deep breath, and let it out. "Finish telling me what option B is, please."

"Barnaby spoke with Dr. Wainwright and found out that Tristan's been rejected by at least two other private schools, so he'll be doing at-home study. Said schooling is mandatory for his staying out of juvenile detention. If he leaves the house for more than a few hours at a time, he must do so in the company of an adult," Kyla added in a rather self-satisfied tone. "That's new since he was picked up at Night Crawler. It's also his last chance to keep his freedom."

"Meaning he might actually be motivated to stay home and not bolt." His doubt and reluctance faded. "Is there a C?"

"Oh, sure. C." She nibbled on her bottom lip. "I know! C can be us getting each other out of our systems."

"Okay, Kyla." His hands tightened around the steering wheel. "That's not something you say while I'm driving a two-ton machine."

"On the contrary—" she uncurled her leg from under her and arched up her hips, digging into her pocket "—It makes it harder for you to argue with me. Eden suggested these. Just to bolster our story." She held out her hand and when Jason glanced down at her open palm, he saw two gold bands and a rather stunning diamond engagement ring.

Every synapse in his brain short-circuited. "You have got to be kidding me." It was going to be difficult enough to live in close quarters with Kyla for the next few days. Very close quarters. And sure, he figured they'd be feigning an intimate relationship when in any neighbors' line of sight, but pretending to be married? That opened up a whole can of unwanted worms he didn't want to even think about. Didn't dare let himself think about. "Kyla, we don't need—" He trailed off as she reached over and tugged his left hand off the wheel. Before he could form another thought, she slid the one gold band onto his finger. Something inside of him jumped, shifted, then settled, even as his pulse kicked into overdrive. "This is such a bad idea."

"Maybe." She shrugged, slipped the other rings on her own finger and looked down, fluttering her lashes in an expression so atypical of Kyla, his lips twitched.

"Not exactly your style." Jason didn't realize he'd said the words out loud until Kyla responded.

"Hmm?" She examined the ring more closely. "It's gorgeous."

And so was she. Jason cringed, grateful that sentiment hadn't escaped his lips. It was also seriously over the top. Kyla was more elegant. Sophisticated. With a hint of practicality. She'd appreciate history, family connections. A ring passed down would be more fitting for her. Definitely something with a little less…glare. "Where did Eden get it?"

"Oh, it's Greta's. It belonged to her mother."

"Ah." Jason nodded. Greta Renault-McTavish, was the daughter of a former screen siren; a siren who definitely would have worn a ring like that. "So we're going in as Faustus family members?"

"Barnaby's got tons of family all over the country, very few of whom have ever visited him here which means an unfamiliar face—or two of them—won't be suspect. Also in our favor, one of Barnaby's nieces, who happens to be about my age, recently got married." Kyla explained. "We are Kyla and Josh Cooper, although I'm still on the fence about taking your name. We're at the end of a cross-country trip from South Carolina before we settle down. My Uncle Barnaby suggested we house sit for him while he and his family are away."

"I assume this house we're sitting is in close proximity to the Wainwrights?"

"Luckily enough, yes, it is. Right across the street. We're considering relocating to California, but haven't reached a decision yet," Kyla added as if she were telling Chloe Ann a bedtime story. "We're exploring our options. I've just graduated from law school and you're in the tech industry. Eden suggested keeping things as close to the truth as possible."

Jason scowled. "I guess you two thought of everything then."

"Hopefully. I thought about bringing Ninja for authenticity—"

"Ninja?"

"My dog. But he gets stressed around strangers and new places. Plus, I don't think we'd have brought a dog on our honeymoon." She beamed at him. "The rest we'll just make up as we go along. Oh, did you pack a swimsuit? I hear there's a wicked pool in the backyard."

"This isn't a vacation, Kyla." Just the idea of Kyla in a swimsuit threatened to erode his resolve. "We'll be doing a job." A job he needed over and done. Fast. "We're trying to find out who murdered your friend. And I still have a missing girl to find. Speaking of which, I rescheduled my meeting with Alona Lopez to tomorrow."

"The Dempsey Center's administrator?" Kyla scowled. "I thought we were going to talk to her together."

"That's still the plan. But first we need to move into this supposed dream house." He made the final turn onto Wingate Road. "Okay, here we go." Another left and he drove up the hill to the gate he and Kyla had parked across the street from a few nights earlier. He powered down his window.

"Afternoon," he called to the uniformed female. "Kyla and Josh Cooper."

"We're meeting my Uncle Barnaby at his house," Kyla declared as she leaned over Jason to beam at the guard.

The thirty-something woman, with her hair pulled so

tight Jason was surprised she could blink, eyed them for a moment before consulting her clipboard. "Welcome to Faustus Estates." She was all business as she retrieved an envelope and handed it to Jason. "This contains a list of the HOA rules and regulations. There's a page for each of you to sign, acknowledging you're aware of them. We'll expect you to turn it in when you next leave the premises."

"Got it." Jason nodded even as he wondered what overly uptight community they were joining.

"Please keep the included parking permit visible if you park outside the garage. There's a gate scanner label for your dashboard." She pointed to the camera just over her head. "It will trigger the gate automatically for both entry and exit. If you have any security issues or concerns, please don't hesitate to dial eight-one-eight. That'll put you straight through to us." She stepped back and pushed a button.

The enormous iron gates swung open.

"Enjoy the rest of your day." If the woman tried to smile any harder she might hurt something.

"Appreciate it." Jason gave her a wave as he drove through the gate.

"You're really not thrilled with any of this, are you?" Kyla asked.

"No."

"Because it wasn't your idea?"

"No." Because he didn't know how to be around Kyla 24/7 without wanting to take her to bed. It would be one thing if he knew she wasn't interested, but the way she'd kissed him back, the way she'd kissed him on Sunday afternoon, the anger she'd displayed when he'd declared there shouldn't—couldn't—be anything between them, only made resisting temptation more difficult.

Distance was the best strategy for him. Except Kyla had gone and erased every single inch of distance. "I'm not thrilled because this feels reckless."

"You're saying that as if you aren't an act-now-and-think-later kind of person," Kyla pushed back. "We both know that isn't true so try again."

He really didn't appreciate her being right.

"If this is about us kissing—"

"We're done talking about that," he said. He could feel a headache starting, throbbing in the back of his neck.

"All right."

Investigating Julia's death and Bess's disappearance was one thing. Doing so while locked up with Kyla was something else entirely. It was evident their conversation the other day about their kiss being a mistake hadn't done anything to deter her. To the contrary, she'd been emboldened. Now?

He glanced down at his hand.

Now they were married for crying out loud.

Kyla Bertrand was officially the quicksand of women. The harder he tried to resist her, the deeper he sank.

The houses were what would usually be called mini-mansions, although personally he'd remove the descriptor. Houses like this—with their elegant lines and tiled roofs, as well as shuttered windows that offset the natural earth tones of the paint—made it seem as if they'd driven into some picturesque area of the south of France or Spain. The trees were beginning to turn, embracing fall with leaves of gold and orange dotting the lawns and drifting onto the sidewalk. And the sky around and above them was as clear and blue as the eye could see.

"According to the GPS, we should be right up here." Jason made a slight left and headed toward the house with the black town car parked in the driveway.

"I don't know why I expect Barnaby Faustus to look like Marlon Brando from *The Godfather*."

"Maybe because you watch a lot of crime movies."

But Jason had to agree when he caught sight of the man. He definitely gave off the same kind of vibes—powerful, direct, knowing. Barnaby Faustus shifted from his conversation with his neighbors and offered them a brilliant "I can charm you out of anything" smile. The man was tall and dressed in an elegantly tailored suit that cost more than Jason's truck. "We won't have to wait for introductions to the Wainwrights. That's Forrest, Tristan's dad, and his wife, Lynn."

"The little girl's name is Alicia, right?"

"Yes. Both kids are from Forrest's first marriage. Alicia's eight." He shoved the SUV into park. "Go ahead," he told Kyla. "This is your show. Take the lead. Just be careful."

Kyla shoved open her door, hopped out and confidently walked up to greet Barnaby just as if he really was her uncle.

"There's my girl." Barnaby caught Kyla in a big hug and, glancing over her head, offered Jason a sly smile as Jason approached. "You guys made excellent time." He motioned to the fake license plate Jason had switched out before leaving The Brass Eagle.

"I made him drive all the way through," Kyla said. "I was so excited to get here. Thank you for letting us try out California for a few weeks."

"I'm grateful you and Josh could help us out by house sitting. Josh...good drive?"

Jason had to give the guy props. He knew how to sell a story. "Yes, sir. Long, but good. Nice to see you."

"You, too. Forrest, Lynn—" Barnaby kept his arm around Kyla and faced his neighbor "—this beautiful sight is my sister Kardea's middle girl, Kyla, and her new husband, Josh. I say new just in case you don't see them very much," Barnaby chuckled as Jason's face went hot. "They're still in the honeymoon phase."

"Uncle, stop." Kyla laughed and patted a hand on the older man's chest.

*Yes, Uncle. Please stop.* Jason resisted the urge to glare.

"Kyla, this is Dr. Forrest Wainwright and his wife, Lynn. Forrest is a plastic surgeon—"

"Semiretired," Forrest added with a slight smile. "I keep my toes in to make sure Lynn's happy."

Lynn gave a playful shrug. "I keep telling Forrest this won't feel like home until we have some actual neighbors and now we do!" Lynn reached over to draw Alicia close to her side. With jet black hair, but as sharp as obsidian, the woman's green eyes sparkled against her pale, freckled complexion. "Sorry I'm a mess." She gestured to her yoga pants, oversize, damp green T-shirt and fingerless gloved hands. "I just got back from my boxing cardio workout. This is our girl, Alicia. Isn't she just beautiful?"

"Lynn, don't." Alicia rolled her eyes as she gave them a quick wave and smile. "Hi. Do you have a pool?"

"I believe we do," Kyla told her.

"Aw, man. You're lucky." Alicia pouted as only an eight-year-old can.

"Ours is being redone," Lynn sighed dramatically. "After I saw the paradise Barnaby built in his backyard, I've been obsessed." She gave Alicia an affectionate squeeze. "It'll just be another few weeks."

"Barnaby's been telling us about his big moving plans." Dr. Wainwright, dressed as if he'd just come off the golf course in his khaki slacks and green and white polo shirt, deftly changed the subject. He was average height, beginning to show a little extra weight that claimed many in the over-forty crowd and had hints of silver threading through his blond hair.

He blinked tired, dark-circled eyes.

"And here we thought you detested San Francisco," Lynn teased.

"Elsie's getting restless again," Barnaby explained without batting an eye. "Chances are in a few months my wife will change her mind and we'll be on the move again. We still have to break it to the kids, but in the meantime, she deserves to be happy." He winked at Jason. "That's how it is with wives, right, Josh?"

Given Jason's current situation, he couldn't very well argue. "Hasn't taken me long to learn that, sir."

"Only one in the family to call me sir. Gotta love him." Barnaby chuckled.

"You ready for Halloween, Alicia?" Jason asked Forrest's daughter.

"She's had her costume picked out for weeks." Lynn's enthusiasm came across as a bit over the top. Stepmother overcompensation, Jason supposed. "She's going to be Boudicca, the ancient Irish warrior."

"I wanted to be a space princess," Alicia grumbled.

"But then we decided on Boudicca." Lynn's smile

looked forced and strained, the expression sharpening her gaze.

"That's a pretty fantastic Halloween display you've got," Jason said, admiring the plastic tombstones and a large black coffin spilling its contents of skeletal remains onto the front yard.

"We have lights up for nighttime," Alicia said. "Tristan's supposed to set up a fog machine so it's extra creepy."

"Awesome," Kyla muttered in a way that made Jason grin.

"Tristan's our oldest. Seventeen," Forrest explained. "And about as reliable as a broken clock."

"He said he'd do it." Alicia glanced down at her feet.

"Tristan says a lot of things," her father said.

"Teenagers," Lynn said with a forced laugh. "The main cause of family drama. We should let you get settled."

"Please let us know if you need anything," Forrest said as a goodbye as he and his family crossed the street. No sooner had they reached the house than the familiar silver sports car pulled around the corner and screeched to a crooked halt in their driveway. Jason's blood pressure spiked when he caught sight of the broken right headlight and scraped bumper.

"Okay," Jason murmured and moved closer to Kyla. "Now we find out if this is over before it begins."

Tristan emerged from his car and cast a quick glance in their general direction. For a moment, Jason thought they were in the clear until Tristan tripped over his own feet and nearly hit the ground face first. Alarm, even from a distance, was still alarm, Jason thought, but the kid covered pretty quickly and disappeared inside when called.

When the garage door came down, the knots filling Jason's stomach loosened.

"You think he…?"

"Oh, yeah," Jason said. The question was… What was the kid going to do about it?

"Agreed," Barnaby said. "Let's get you two inside, shall we?"

"Sounds great, Uncle."

Jason shook his head. "You're enjoying this far too much," he muttered to Kyla as Barnaby walked away.

"And you're not enjoying it at all. You need to loosen up or no one around here is going to trust us with anything, let alone information."

"There aren't enough neighbors around that it'll matter." That, along with his and Kyla's "honeymoon" status would make their observation of Tristan Wainwright fairly straightforward.

"For the record—" Kyla caught his arm when he turned around "—this was Eden's idea. I just ran with it."

"Refresh my memory." Jason glanced down to where she held onto him. "It was Eden who ended up chained to the ceiling of a meat locker because she taunted a serial killer online, right?"

Kyla's mouth twisted. "Her judgment has improved since then."

"It couldn't get much worse."

"It would help if you'd remember bad moods are contagious and while you might be fine moping your way through what could be a career-defining case for you,

I'm not." Kyla gently patted his chest. "Well, we're in this together now whether you like it or not."

He grinned after she turned her back. Seeing Kyla even mildly irritated was turning out to be one of his greatest pleasures.

The house they'd be occupying was, for want of a better word, stunning. Two stories and painted in a sandy tone of yellow. Cobblestones came up and around to the base of the enormous, wood trimmed windows. Not overly ostentatious, which Jason found surprising. It was just over the limit of practical and offered a tasteful, welcoming entry through hand-carved wooden doors depicting trees shedding their leaves in the perfect representation of fall.

The foyer's gold and silver flecked marble floors melded in nicely with the high archway doors and open air space of the interior. Jason watched as Barnaby keyed in the security code to deactivate the system. Then, when the front door closed behind him, Barnaby offered them a wide smile.

"You two couldn't have pulled that off better if you'd really been family." He looked at Kyla. "Pretty as a picture. Just like my nieces."

"Thank you for your help, Mr. Faustus," Kyla said. "When Eden called you, I had no idea—"

"It's Barnaby. Eden brought my sister's baby home." The light dimmed in his eyes. "There's nothing your friend could ask that I'd refuse. Come in, please." He led them down the long hall into a large chef's kitchen that Jason swore could have fit his entire apartment. Twice. "We've had the kitchen stocked for you. Basic furniture, both downstairs and up. You need anything else, we have an account with the local market. You just call and they'll deliver."

"Sir, that's not necessary," Jason told him. "Your house is more than—"

"If that kid is dealing drugs in my development, this is the very least I can do." Barnaby's voice went razor sharp and reminded Jason just how dangerous a man he could be. "Eden says you consider him a suspect in other crimes?"

Kyla glanced to Jason, who nodded. He'd done enough background on Faustus to know where he drew the line.

"We believe he's connected to his girlfriend's disappearance as well as a murder that's currently under investigation." He shot Kyla a warning look that reminded her Barnaby didn't have to be given all the details. While Jason was more than happy to cultivate him as a go-to for information, when all was said and done, whether she wanted to admit it or not, this was a man who could do massive damage to Kyla's career.

"Sounds like trouble I definitely don't want anywhere near my communities." Barnaby gave them an approving nod. "I'll give you a quick tour before I take off. I've left the upstairs front bedroom that overlooks the street mostly empty. I think it'll give you the best vantage. That out there—" he pointed behind Jason to the sliding glass doors around the other side of a substantial table "—that's the best part of the place."

Jason wasn't a man who was easily surprised, but finding an oasis of a backyard in the middle of the Sacramento Valley knocked him speechless. A three-tiered waterfall trickled into a large stone-encased swimming pool. The hot tub connected to the other end was bubbling and steaming away, looking to cook whoever dared dip a toe in. Jason could just imagine Kyla taking a swim and as he did, wished he hadn't formed that image in his head.

"Gardeners come by twice a week, one of whom maintains the rose trellises my wife insisted on installing on the back of every house." He shook his head. "They're gorgeous for sure, but they take a ton of work. The pool's heated. Spa's on a timer. Lights, too with motion detectors. Security floodlights all around the exterior. Also, security cameras. I've got all the server password information so you can hook into whatever you need to with your equipment. I won't insult you by asking you not to get caught hacking into the system."

Jason smiled. Who would have thought Barnaby Faustus had such an interesting sense of humor.

It didn't take long to get the lay of the land—including five bedrooms, four baths—nor to see that Barnaby was correct in choosing which room was best for Jason to set up his surveillance and computer equipment. He was already mapping out his setup when Barnaby led them downstairs.

"Tell me something," Barnaby said.

"If we can," Kyla said in a far more guarded tone than before.

"Eden mentioned this connects to an investigation of Liam and Colin O'Callaghan." The way he said the brothers' names definitely had Jason thinking he wouldn't ever want to be on Barnaby Faustus's bad side. "Is that true?"

"Yes," Jason confirmed and avoided Kyla's arched brow. Some things Barnaby needed to be aware of.

"I see." Barnaby's eyes narrowed. "Come with me,

please." He led them around the staircase to the door on the other side. It was obvious this was meant to be a study. Not a large room, Jason thought, but the built in shelving would definitely house enough books to compete with the best collections. A surprisingly small desk was situated in the corner of the room; an elegant burgundy upholstered sofa took up the central space.

"Cozy," Jason said as Barnaby walked over to the shelving unit and ran his hand alongside the third panel. A slight click sounded before the unit shifted forward and to the side, exposing a large metal door. Jason's eyes went saucer wide. He'd never seen a safe room in person before and his techie heart was going pitter-patter.

Barnaby tapped in a code on the dial pad, making sure that Jason could see. "I reset the code to the default. You have to know it to open it from the inside."

"Got it." Jason nodded as the door popped open with a hiss of air.

Barnaby pushed it open the rest of the way, then stepped back. "I'm one who believes you can never be too safe. It's stocked with enough supplies for up to two weeks. There's also a dedicated landline separate from the main one in the house. There's also a SAT phone in case that one's compromised, emergency medical supplies, as well as security cameras that cycle through various feeds in the house. Don't worry," he added at Jason's raised brow. "They only work when someone's locked inside."

"I can't imagine why we'd need this," Kyla said with a sense of awe in her voice.

"You're dealing with the O'Callaghans," Barnaby warned. "Be ready for anything."

"You don't like them," Kyla observed.

"Like doesn't come into it. The O'Callaghan brothers are why rooms like this exist." He closed up the room. Then he motioned for them to precede him. "The house is yours for as long as you need it. My wife's out of town with some friends so you don't have to worry about her dropping in unexpectedly."

"Is there anything else you can tell us about the Wainwrights?" Kyla asked.

"I got a good feel for them thanks to the financial check I ran when they submitted the offer for their home. He and Lynn married shortly after his first wife died in a boating accident. Lynn makes a good show of being wealthy even though Forrest's net worth has dropped significantly since the marriage. She likes people to think she's as sharp as a golf ball. Don't let her fool you. She's got more control in that house than she lets on. She and Tristan pretty much ignore each other, but she dotes on Alicia—drives her to school every day, picks her up, makes sure the little girl has music lessons, ballet, whatever catches the kid's interest. Oh, Kyla. Maybe you should take a quick tour of the bathrooms upstairs. Make sure there's enough towels and such?"

Clearly Kyla wasn't buying the suggestion and didn't seem to appreciate being shuffled out of the room, especially on a bathroom check. Jason could see her biting the inside of her cheek as she left the room.

Jason shook his head. "Not very slick, Barnaby."

"Slick doesn't concern me." Barnaby motioned him into the office. "She's a DA. Some things she doesn't need to know about."

Jason's stomach took a giant dip to his toes.

"Not sure what you brought with you, but you're free to use anything here." Barnaby clicked a button on the underside of his desk. A secret drawer popped out displaying a terrifying array of firearms. "You use one, it'll come back untraceable." He flashed a quick smile. "Promise."

"I don't use guns." Not only because they were the fastest track back to prison. With guns came consequences, most of which Jason didn't want to even think about dealing with.

"Your choice. Just wanted you to be aware. I wouldn't leave anything off the table where the O'Callaghans are concerned."

Jason nodded. He followed Barnaby out to his town car where a driver jumped out from behind the wheel and came around to open the back door. "Would it be possible to get a look at the file you have on Forrest? And don't give me the song and dance about only knowing their financial information. A person like you wouldn't rely solely on provided details."

"I like you, Jason." Barnaby gave him an approving grin. "You get it. I'll have my assistant send the whole file over in the morning. You're sure about Tristan being mixed up with the O'Callaghans?"

"No doubt about it."

"Nasty buggers." Barnaby's eyes flickered. "Nasty and remorseless. They won't hesitate to hurt anyone who gets in their way or jeopardizes their profit margin. Not you. And not Kyla. You be careful with her." The concern in Barnaby's hard gaze was unmistakable. "Watch out for her."

"I will." Jason sighed as Barnaby drove away. "I already am."

# Chapter 11

Reality, when it hit, at least in Kyla's experience, tended to do so with unmistakable force.

She wasn't feeling quite in unmistakable territory yet; but it was coming up pretty darn fast.

Unloading Jason's SUV didn't take nearly as long as she'd thought—or hoped—and the fact they'd done so mostly in silence meant either Jason was trying to pretend she was invisible, or he was planning something she wasn't going to like.

"I think this is the last of yours." She hefted the box up and onto the queen-size canopy bed. "Can I help you unpack? I can take this into the master." She reached for his duffel bag just as he shifted it out of reach.

"No, thanks." Jason gave her a quick, if not dismissive, glance. "I'll bunk in here. I'm hoping that jump drive I liberated from Night Crawler will be finished decrypting soon. I want to stay close for when it does."

Close to it and away from her. "You've definitely made yourself at home."

"Doesn't take me long to settle."

The bedroom had gone from pristine and nearly empty to looking as if this was where old electronics had come to die. Computers and speakers and tripods and cameras—along with an obnoxiously long padded microphone aimed out the window. Luckily, it was hidden by hanging vines and greenery. The equipment cluttered the area that not so long before had been a simple but delightful bedroom. It even had its own full bath that included a shower-sauna combo.

"Since we're in for the night, I thought I'd fix us dinner. See what's in the fridge. Try out the kitchen." And she was resorting to small talk again. When was this going to get easier?

"Have at it. Oh, Barnaby said he'd be fine if we decorated for Halloween. Thought maybe we could pick up some stuff before the weekend."

"Uh, sure. I guess."

"You guess?" He blinked disbelievingly. "Don't tell me you're one of those people."

Her lips twitched. It was interesting what offended him. "Which people are those?"

"The ones who turn their noses up at the best night of the year. Come on, Kyla. The spooky lights and shadows, the pranks. The dripping blood and chain jangling ghosts. The creepy crawlies—"

"That last bit has a lot to do with it." She wrinkled her nose. "And the masks." Granted they weren't as bad as some of the masks that people wore in their everyday lives. She shuddered. "Those weird rubbery masks are freaky. And don't get me started on clowns."

Jason chuckled. "I'll give you that one. This is my first year to really celebrate since I got out. I was on a case last year and wasn't home. But I've saved my costume. And no, I won't tell you what it is. It's a surprise."

Kyla sat on the edge of the bed. The fact his gaze flickered down when she crossed her legs told her he wasn't quite as detached as he appeared. "You really like Halloween, don't you?"

"Sure." For a moment, she saw a hint of the Jason she'd known the last couple of years. The fun, flirty, funny Jason. The BK—before kiss—Jason.

"Why?"

He stopped fiddling with his toys and seemed to consider her words. "I guess because it was always the one night a year I could be anything and anyone I wanted. Anyone other than who I was. It was, I don't know." He shrugged. "An escape."

"It was bad for you." She'd never imagined his explanation would make her see the one holiday she disliked in a different light. "Growing up, it was bad."

"Not as rough as it gets for some. Worse than it is for others."

She couldn't fathom what Jason had gone through as a child. She wished her parents were here, so she could hug and thank them for giving her the encouraging, accepting, caring upbringing they had.

Jason reached for a different electrical contraption.

"Okay, what is that thing?" Determined to get them back on track, she changed the subject. "It looks like a cross between a lie detector and a deluxe blender."

"You're not far off." Jason held it up as if raising a

certain newborn lion prince. "It's a voice analyzer. New to the market. Picks up stress levels in a person's tone. I was kind of throwing everything in. Not entirely sure what we might need."

"Sorry you had to wing it."

"What?" He glanced up. "No, that's not what I meant. So far it looks like you—and Eden—were right. Being here puts us in a decent place to potentially see what Tristan's really up to."

Right. Tristan. She looked out the window, then at the screen on Jason's desk displaying the activity in the living room of the Wainwright house.

"Line of sight won't be very extensive," Jason said when he saw where she was looking. "It'll be more audio than anything, once I get this system set up. This baby can pick up a fly farting a quarter mile away." His hand patted the large microphone he had aimed out the window.

"Charming." Kyla snorted. "So, you…um, dinner? You'll come down?"

"Just need to get the recording system going. Shouldn't take me more than an hour."

"Great. Okay then. I'll just…" She stood, smoothed her hands down her bare legs and felt a spark of triumph when Jason's eyes narrowed. "You need to stop doing that."

"Doing what?" It took him a moment to drag his gaze from her legs to her face.

"Looking at me like that." She took a step toward him. "It's dangerous. Especially for a man who keeps telling me he's not interested."

"I never said I wasn't interested. I said we weren't

a good idea. But you're right." He ducked his head. "I guess I'm just finding you a little difficult to ignore."

If it were up to her she'd make it downright impossible. "You know…" She moved closer. "This surveillance thing could go on for a while. Days. Maybe even weeks."

"It won't. Ow!" He jumped to his feet, the gadget in his hand screeching and sparking before it let out a thin line of acrid smelling smoke. "Well, that's toast."

"Sorry." No, she wasn't. There was only one thing she was at the moment and that was determined. She didn't want to be practical. Or reasonable. She didn't want to think about her future or the supposed threat Jason believed he posed to it. Smart or not, she just wanted him. "Jason?"

"Uh-huh." He tossed the device onto the desk just as she moved in.

His eyes went wide in the moment before she reached up, caught his face between her hands and pulled his mouth down to hers.

With nothing to lose, she poured every bit of desire, every bit of frustration, every bit of pent-up longing she'd been feeling for him into their kiss. His mouth seemed frozen, as if her touch had turned him to ice. Then, suddenly, he let out a groan and melted into her.

She dived in when his lips opened, shivered at the feel of his beard against her skin. She took everything she wanted as his hands slid down her back to cup her bottom and haul her against him. There was no mistaking his attraction, no denying his hunger for her. She could feel it coursing through every inch of his body. Need, she thought as her desire for him increased. It wasn't just want she was feeling. It was need. The idea of having him in her bed sent her system into overdrive.

Kyla pressed her breasts against his chest, her nipples tightened to the point of aching. She groaned, low and deep, and dropped her head back, clinging to him as his mouth left a trail of kisses down the side of her neck. It was everything, *everything*, she imagined being touched by him would feel like. Everything and more.

Even as her own want kicked reason to the curb, she felt his return. His hands left her; his stance stiffened. She could feel him thinking himself out of what was happening even as she held onto him.

"Jason, don't stop," she breathed, lifting her head and gazing into the eyes she'd fallen hopelessly into only moments before. "Please, stop thinking. Just feel." She pressed her lips to his jaw, inhaled the intoxicating woodsy scent of his skin.

Her fingers skimmed along the waistband of his jeans, poised to unhook the button and make that final move of release. He shook his head and stepped back, while grabbing for her hands.

"Stop." He pressed his forehead against hers, squeezed his eyes shut as she tried to catch his gaze. "Kyla, we have to stop."

"Do we?" It wouldn't take much; she could feel him—hard, strong—beneath her hands. She was so curious about him, every inch of him. She could see the battle raging within him. He was breathing in long, controlled breaths, clearly attempting to regain rational thought. Disappointment swept through her. Along with an odd sense of grief. "I want you, and you want me, right?"

"It doesn't matter what we want. We need to..." He licked his lips and she wondered if he could taste her on them. He turned away from her, yet he sensed her when she attempted to close the distance once more. "Please, Kyla."

His plea dragged her exposed heart through the fire of his rejection.

"You're just not willing to take the chance, are you?" she pushed.

"I'm poison, Kyla," he said, his back still to her. "Not just to your career. I'm poisonous to you."

"And I don't see it that way." She took a deep breath, steeled herself. "I care about you, Jason. I think I'm even falling in—"

"Don't!" He spun around and an odd, unfamiliar, heart-pinging panic was lodged in his gaze. "Kyla, please. What you want, what you need, I can't give you. The sooner you accept that, the better off we'll both be." He moved past her toward the bathroom. "Don't worry about me and dinner. I'll grab something later."

"Jason—"

"Go, Kyla." His hand tightened on the doorknob as he paused before leaving the room. "Just go."

The determination that had been like stone only seconds before crumbled into sadness as he closed the bathroom door behind him. Was he so broken he couldn't see the good that was possible? That not everything in his life had to be mired in darkness?

She stood there, almost shaking. There it was. The moment she'd been dreading.

She'd never uttered those words to a man before. She'd never come close. But even as the sentiment had slipped free of her swollen lips, she knew it was true.

She was falling in love with him.

And there was nothing she—or Jason—could do about it.

Forced politeness, Jason learned the next morning, was tantamount to emotional pain.

Who knew Kyla could be such an expert at it.

On the one hand, it was as if their close encounter in his bedroom had never happened. On the other, it was as if their close encounter in his bedroom had never happened.

Due to a number of closed doors between them, he had no idea how she'd spent her evening and excruciatingly long night.

He knew how he'd spent his, though. Wishing he'd been reckless enough to take what she'd been offering. Wishing he had the strength and courage to take a chance on them.

Instead, he'd spent the hours listening to the toxic back and forth between Tristan and Dr. Forrest Wainwright. The latter definitely solidified Jason's resolve to keep Kyla—and her intoxicating self—at arms' length. Listening to the father and son was like replaying some of his childhood's greatest hits, without the level of violence he'd endured.

Belongings, rather than bones, had been broken. Shouts, rather than slaps, had echoed through the headphones situated on Jason's ears. He'd felt sick and nearly threw up the veggie wrap he'd made for himself once he was certain Kyla was in her room for the night.

By the time their neighbors' house went dark and quiet, it was clear that the Wainwrights had some serious issues to deal with and a tinge, just a tinge, of sympathy had crept into Jason's heart. Living with that much misunderstanding and hostility was bound to change a kid, and it made Jason wonder who Tristan Wainwright might have been had his situation been different.

It was a less disturbing topic to think about than Kyla's utterance that had nearly driven him to his knees. What he wouldn't give to be the man who could accept the gift of her love without thinking about all the ways he could hurt her.

What he wouldn't give to tell her he felt the same.

Kyla had been drinking her coffee and eating a bagel when he emerged from his room. Her murmur "good morning" and a gesture to the kitchen counter let him know she'd relinquished control over the kitchen. He couldn't have cut the tension in the room with a laser it was so thick, but he gave it a shot by blending a smoothie for himself and telling her he'd be ready to go in five.

Minutes later, they were in his car. "How's your opening statement coming along?" It was, Jason told himself, the safest topic of conversation he could come up with as they drove into town to meet with Alona Lopez at the Dempsey Youth Center.

"I think I've finally got it." Kyla didn't look up from her phone. "There's a little something missing, but I'll figure it out."

"It's a big deal—this case—yeah?"

Kyla glanced up. "It could be. You can stop worrying, Jason," she said with barely a flicker in her dark eyes. "From now on we'll keep things professional only and focus on finding Bess and who killed Julia."

"Right." Maybe she wasn't angry, but that look in

her eye threatened to freeze his bone marrow. "Look, Kyla, it's not that I don't want—"

Her cell phone rang. "Feel free to never finish that thought." She shot him a look before she answered the call. "Hey, Penny. What's up?"

Jason tried not to listen and instead focused on the drive. One of the things he'd always admired about Kyla was her ability to compartmentalize and do whatever she set her mind to doing. Obviously she'd taken what he'd said to heart and pushed through to the other side.

Kyla hung up just as he took the exit off the freeway. She shoved her cell into the small purse decorated with flowers that she had crossed over her chest. "I take it Tristan didn't leave the house last night?"

"No."

"Anything interesting happen at all or is this a giant waste of time?"

Far be it from him to remind her this scheme was her idea. "Tristan and his father make oil and water look like best friends."

"That bad?"

"Worse."

"What were they fighting about?"

"A lot of things. Mostly? Stepmommy dearest."

"Predictable," Kyla murmured. "I suppose it might be more unusual if Tristan did get along with Lynn."

"I can tell you Lynn didn't seem particularly interested or offended." But something niggled at him. Something unexpected. "Tristan's taking particular exception to Lynn chaperoning Alicia's upcoming class trip to New York."

"He's probably jealous. Seventeen's a hard age for

anyone," Kyla said. "Lynn's an easy target. She probably picks her battles."

"Didn't sound like jealousy to me. And she won in the end, didn't she? About Alicia's Halloween costume anyway. Maybe I'm reading too much into things." He scrubbed a hand across his forehead. Family dynamics were not his forte. How could they be when his were clouded in darkness? But it was a good reminder that there was always, always, something more going on beneath the surface for everyone, maybe especially for a kid like Tristan.

"You all right?" she asked him.

"Fine. Didn't sleep well."

"Oh." She glanced out her window, but not before he caught the smirk on her lips that may as well have screamed *good.* "The argument between them, Forrest and Tristan's, did it get physical?"

"No." Jason wasn't entirely sure what he'd have done if it had. "Kid has other reasons for acting out, I guess. Happens to the best of us."

"I didn't think about how this could open old wounds for you." She paused, as if about to say something more.

The conversation could end there. She'd let the unspoken question dangle long enough for him to pick it up. As difficult as those years were to talk about, maybe if he laid out more details of his past, just maybe she'd finally understand why he wouldn't allow himself to give in to what they shared.

"Vince took the brunt of it."

Kyla glanced at him. "Your father's abuse?"

"Yeah. He was my shield. It wasn't until Vince could hit back that the old man shifted his attention."

She didn't have to say anything for Jason to know

what she was thinking and feeling. But the last thing he wanted from anyone, especially this woman, was sympathy. Or pity.

"Did you know Vince almost didn't join the marines because he didn't want to leave me alone with Pop?"

"I had no idea."

"It took me forever to convince him to go. It was his way out and his way up. A chance to make something of himself, despite our situation." He didn't want to think what might have happened between Vince and their dad if Jason hadn't been successful. "No way was I going to let him give that up, especially after he'd worked so hard to get there."

"How old were you when Vince went in?"

"I'd just turned fifteen." But he'd felt a thousand years old. "I managed to change Vince's mind, convince him I could take care of myself where our father was concerned. Pop was sick by then. Cirrhosis. He was always mean, but the illness made it worse. Messed with his aim, though." He forced a smile. "And I was a lot faster than he was. By then, it was safer to live on the street or get myself sent to juvie than it was to stay at home. So while Vince was moving up the ranks, I was building myself an arrest record as a warped kind of way to protect myself. One of my counselors pointed that out," he added.

"Counseling helped?"

"Therapy taught me to accept responsibility for what I'd done. And how things turned out. Just because I had an explanation for my actions, it didn't mean they were okay. Vince never gave up on me. Not even after I was convicted of armed robbery."

Unwitting accomplice, his lawyer had argued. He'd

just been driving his friends around looking for trouble. He should have realized those so-called friends had guns. And planned to use them.

"You don't have to explain, Jason."

He glanced at her.

"I've read your file."

"Yeah?" He grinned. Was she teasing him?

"I like to run background checks on all the men I want to sleep with." Her smile broke the last of their tension. "And you're being vague about your conviction. You refused to squeal on your friends and someone had to take the hit, so you decided it would be you."

"Close." A bit too close. "More like I had an attitude problem and wanted to make things hard for the detective investigating the case." Jason had never told anyone that before, but for whatever reason, when it came to Kyla, his impulse control was nil. "He reminded me so much of my father. I could feel the temper just bubbling below the surface, as if he was looking to break loose. My bad luck he kept to himself and I ended up inside." Where he never wanted to be again. It was only because of Simone's reevaluating the case a few years ago that he'd gotten an early release. One of the many reasons he'd fight to the death for his sister-in-law. Some debts could never be repaid.

"You turned it all around, though. You're not who you were then." The gentleness in her voice gnawed at him.

But it was the opening he needed to finally make her understand. "Don't do that, Kyla."

"Don't do what?"

"Don't make me into some tortured romantic hero.

Believe me, who I was then is still very much a part of who I am now."

"That's not true."

"Yes," he said. "I am. It's there." There were days he could feel it percolating under the surface, days he had to pray he could ignore it. "It's always there." Vince had learned to channel his anger in productive ways; it's what the military had given him. It's what Simone and the life he'd built for himself continued to give him. But Jason?

Jason gripped the steering wheel hard. He feared what his anger would do to him one day It would happen. It was inevitable. And he didn't want Kyla anywhere around when it did.

"Jason—"

The GPS came on and told him to turn left, thankfully ending the conversation before Jason confessed anything else. He turned into a small parking lot on V and 20th. The Dempsey Youth Center was perfectly placed, situated near the long-established local Y in an area that was central and easy to get to on public transit. "There was one thing I learned listening to Tristan last night."

"What's that?"

"Alicia. When she walked into the room, he changed. Reminded me of Vince when we were kids. It was like a switch flipped in Tristan and he calmed down." Was even worried about her, Jason thought at the time. Something bad was going on in that house.

"Everyone has something or someone that grounds them," Kyla said. "Alicia must be Tristan's. Just like Vince was yours."

"I guess." He parked, turned off the engine and, when

Kyla started to climb out of the car, caught her arm. "I am sorry about last night."

"Me, too. Not about kissing you." She gave him a sad but understanding smile when he let go of her. "Just about how it ended." She climbed out and when he walked around the back of the car, she was waiting for him. "For the record, the next move is yours. My feelings haven't changed. I don't anticipate they will. I have no trouble waiting for you to come to your senses."

He couldn't help it. He chuckled. "Good to know." That determination of hers, that quality he'd found so appealing, was now focused on him, which meant it was just a matter of time before he caved. There was little Jason wanted more in this world than to finish what Kyla had started last night in his bedroom. But he'd already made enough mistakes in his life, mistakes that hurt far too many people. He couldn't let himself make another.

They headed toward the two-story brick building.

"I came here the weekend they opened this place," Kyla told him. "Simone and I, along with our boss."

"Ward Lawson's on the board of directors, isn't he?"

Kyla nodded. "Ward's been working with law enforcement and local charities to try to bring some solutions to the issues teens face. Back when he was a kid, his older sister ran away, lived on the streets for a while."

Jason recalled hearing something about that during various online and news coverage of the DA "That didn't end well, did it?"

"No." Kyla readjusted her purse. "She died just before her eighteenth birthday. He's never forgotten it."

"Just like Julia didn't forget her brother," Jason observed.

"When you can't save the one you lost, you do everything you can to save the lost ones," Kyla said. "I've heard Ward say that many times and it's always stuck with me."

He noticed it again. That optimism. That clear-headed hope that shimmered around Kyla like an aura. "There's something else that should stick with you."

"What's that?"

"You can't save everyone."

"I know. Up here." She tapped her temple, then her heart. "It's in here that forgets."

Because she carried too much in that heart of hers, Jason thought. "Who else is on the board of the youth center?"

"A variety of people. A few politicians of course. Community organizers, social workers, child psychologists along with a few teachers and business owners. Jack's wife Greta was appointed a few months ago at the mayor's request after the whole scandal with Doyle Fremont. She's a great choice and, considering her position as one of the premier artists in the country, she can work with the city to expand access for teens to art and music programs across school districts."

"But?" Jason could hear her reservations.

"No 'but.' Not really. I love Greta and she's a perfect choice. Just seems more like a political move on the mayor's part considering Greta was one of Fremont's victims." She shivered, no doubt remembering the night Freemont had almost killed Greta as a final attempt to get his hands on her inherited estate. An attempt that had left two other people dead.

"It was completely political," Jason agreed. "But it was Greta's idea."

"Really?" Kyla looked at him. "I didn't know that."

"It's not public knowledge. Seeing as Fremont's company and new office complex were set to provide hundreds of jobs in this city, she felt partially responsible for those plans nearly collapsing."

"Greta felt guilty because Fremont tried to kill her?"

Jason's lips twitched. The word eccentric didn't come close to describing Greta Renault-McTavish. He shrugged. "If there's something Greta can do to make people's lives better, she'll attack it head on."

"All this time I thought it was the mayor, or even the governor, doing damage control." She gaped for a moment. "So it was Greta who called in those investors to save all the jobs?"

"She got the ball rolling. It helped that her paintings are hanging in so many prestigious galleries and buildings around the world." Now, the multistory complex was under the new ownership of a group of progressive businesses with plans to continue to expand its presence in Northern California. Jason had to admit, the women he'd met since moving to Sacramento were formidable and had taught him to never underestimate the power of determination.

The anxiety knotting in his chest eased upon entering through the glass double doors. He'd lost count of the number of places like this he'd been sent to as a kid—each one holding the unspoken promise of safety, help and guidance. None of which he found. Probably, Jason thought, because it was easier for him to stay hurt and resentful than to actually work through his issues.

Then again, what did a kid know about managing conflicting emotions?

Jason checked in at the front desk, asking to speak with the facility's administrator, Alona Lopez. After being told it would be a few minutes' wait, Jason took a seat on one of the padded chairs in the reception area while Kyla strolled around, reading the flyers, brochures and announcements pinned to several bulletin boards.

In the distance, he could hear the echo of bouncing basketballs, of shouts and cries and laughter, ricocheting off the walls. The colors were bright, cool tones of greens and blues, evoking an odd sense of peace that in some ways set Jason even more on edge.

A group of teenagers—a good mix of kids of varying ages, sizes and ethnicities—emerged from a closed door, spiral notebooks in their hands as they made their way along the main hallway.

"You look like you'd rather be anywhere else than here." Kyla took a seat next to him and tucked a couple of pamphlets into her purse.

He didn't respond. What could he say to that? That she was right? How…privileged that made him sound. How completely detached from the reality the current occupants of this place existed in. Every kid, every last one, had their own story—their own truth—and while one solution did not fit all, it was clear the Dempsey Center was at least attempting to make a difference.

"Mr. Sutton?" A woman came around the corner, a hand stretched out and a welcoming, if not guarded, smile on her face. She was young, far younger than Jason would have assumed, in worn jeans and a bright yellow T-shirt. "I'm Alona Lopez. Sorry it's taken so long to meet with you." Her dark hair was tied back in a high ponytail and as Jason looked at her fresh face, he realized he might have mistaken her for one of the teens had she not introduced herself. "You wanted to talk to me about Bess Carmody?"

"Yes. Thanks for taking the time." Jason got to his feet and returned the handshake. "This is Kyla Bertrand."

"Yes, of course. Kyla." Alona nodded as if she recognized her. "You came to the opening celebration. Ward told me you were an up-and-comer in his office."

"It's nice to see you again," Kyla said. "I wasn't sure you'd remember me."

Jason couldn't fathom how anyone could forget her.

"Are you no longer with the DA's office?" Alona asked.

"Jason and I have a similar purpose here, so we've joined forces." The way she explained without a moment's hesitation made Jason relax a bit.

"Similar purpose?" Alona motioned for them to follow and as they headed down the hallway, she held out her hands and gave a sharp whistle to the rowdy group of teens playing keep-away with a younger boy's school bag. The kids came to an instant halt. "Excuse me," Alona murmured to him and Kyla as she detoured to her charges.

Jason watched, intrigued, as the administrator bent down and rested a gentle hand on the younger boy's shoulder. Moments later, the tallest teen picked up the bag and handed it back. Alona nodded, made a motion with her hands and the group moved on. "Sorry. I'm constantly playing peacemaker. We can talk in my office." She led them into a room a few feet away.

Jason hesitated, watching the group as they shifted

out of sight. The older boy, the one who had picked up the bag, had seemed familiar. Maybe it was the hostility he'd felt radiating under the surface of the boy's blue-eyed stare. Or maybe it was the clenched jaw that had loosened briefly under Alona's gentle treatment of the situation.

"Jason?" Kyla stepped out of the office and touched his arm.

"Sorry." Memories he thought he'd locked away for good threatened to surge back and drag him under. Why did he feel as if he'd never break free of them? "How many kids do you have here?" he asked as he and Kyla joined Alona.

"Sixty-four in residence," the administrator answered. She took a seat behind a desk that was piled with files, textbooks and a desktop computer. "We often have more than double that, including day-visitors. There's room for a hundred and six, but that space will be gone come the colder months." She folded her hands on top of her desk. "How exactly can I help you two?"

Jason waited for Kyla to respond, but when he glanced at her he saw she was staring at a framed photo on the filing cabinet behind Alona's desk. Alona glanced back, a wave of sadness twisting her expression. She picked up the picture, then handed it to Kyla who accepted it almost reverently. "You knew Julia." She sighed. "Not only was it devastating news to lose her, having a detective come by to clean out her office didn't go over well with my kids."

Jason had no doubt. "When did the detective come by?"

"Yesterday afternoon."

"Must have been Detective Delaney," Jason said.

"No, it wasn't Cole," Alona said. "He and his partner have come in to talk to the kids from time to time. No, this was someone I didn't recognize. A Detective Monahan." She shifted her attention back to Kyla. "Are you all right?"

"Kyla and Julia knew each other in college," Jason explained when it was clear Kyla couldn't. "She doesn't believe the coroner's findings."

"I believe the test results," Kyla countered and set the frame down on the edge of the desk. "But I don't agree with the conclusion that it's an accidental overdose."

"Overdose?" Alona's eyes narrowed. "Of drugs? That's not possible."

Kyla sent Jason an "I told you so" stare and sat forward in her chair. "Julia and I lost touch after she dropped out of college. I was glad to see she was able to finish her degree."

"She had plans to work in the juvenile courts, get a hold of kids before they were too far gone."

"Unlikely she'd have done that and been on drugs then." Jason's comment earned a withering look from both women. He held up his hands in surrender. "Just clarifying. We understand Julia worked with Bess?"

"Yes, somewhat." Alona nodded. "Bess was what I call a bouncer. She came and went. No rhyme or reason. She was looking not great the last time I saw her. Julia told me they were making progress."

"Would you say they were friends?" Jason asked.

"More like Bess saw Julia as an irritating older sister. Julia was good with her. She didn't judge, but definitely let Bess know she wasn't impressed with her behavior or activities. At one point, Julia and I discussed confronting Bess's dealer to see if that would make a difference."

"Any idea who that was?" Jason asked, although he already had an idea.

Alona sat back in her chair, folded her hands and looked at the two of them. "We're drifting into some sketchy private information I'm not sure I'm comfortable sharing."

Jason opened his mouth to press, but Kyla beat him to it. "Not if we speak hypothetically. For instance, if I were to suggest Bess's boyfriend, Tristan Wainwright, might have been a topic of conversation regarding Bess's buying habits, you could either argue the point or remain quiet. As an unofficial comment, of course."

Alona pinched her lips together and remained silent.

"Did you or Julia ever talk about the club Night Crawler?"

"Frequently," Alona ground out. "But not in regards to Bess. Liam O'Callaghan offered a rather substantial donation to the youth center about six months ago."

"Oh?" Jason's eyebrow quirked. "How substantial?"

"Enough that I have moments of regret for declining his offer. As much as we can do with more cash, I don't take donations with strings."

"What strings did he attach?" Kyla asked.

"He wouldn't say up front. That told me all I needed to know."

Jason nodded. Smart. "Ms. Yablonski said Bess had attended a few support-group meetings?"

"She did. We hold numerous recovery sessions each week. We also offer private counseling, but Bess was only interested in the group meet-ups. Not that she ever said anything. So if you were thinking I'd just hand you information that she—"

"We weren't expecting anything like that," Kyla said.

"Our addiction counselor wasn't disappointed when she stopped coming a few weeks back," Alona told them. "He felt Bess was a disruptive force in the room. Said he thought a number of the other kids felt intimidated and even scared by her presence. Quite a few stopped coming during that time."

Interesting, Jason thought. "When was the last time Bess was here?"

"About three weeks ago. She was in bad shape. Julia took care of her. Even took her home with her for a couple of days. We thought maybe Bess would turn a corner, but then she was gone. I haven't seen her since."

"Did she leave anything behind in her locker?"

Alona inclined her head at Jason's question. "How did you know we give our kids lockers?"

"Most places like this do," he said. "You use it to gauge a kid's trust, don't you? They tend to only leave what they care about in that locker once they feel they're safe."

He ignored Kyla's probing stare. "If it helps, I can get her parents' permission—"

Alona waved his concern aside. "I'll get what's inside and bring it to you. I don't want my kids seeing me handing belongings over to outsiders. Give me a few minutes." She walked to the door, but then slowed and without turning around, she said, "She's dead, isn't she? Bess."

Jason could have lied. It would have been a kindness. But Alona didn't need kindness. She deserved the truth. "As long as she's out there, there's hope." Even as he said the words, he knew his was slipping away.

"Then I'd say the right person's looking for her." Alona gave a slight nod of approval before she left.

"She's right." Kyla rested a hand on his arm. "You are the right person."

Jason wasn't convinced.

But he liked the faith.

# Chapter 12

"Anything interesting in there?"

"I don't know yet." Before they pulled out of the parking lot, Kyla dug through the plastic bag containing the items from Bess Carmody's locker. "You know her better than I do at this point." She started handing stuff to him. "It's typical teenage girl stuff. Notebooks, a few books, a pencil pouch filled with tampons and Tylenol. Looks like she's a science fiction fan. And a collector of hippos." She waved a small stuffed animal at him before dropping it into his lap. "Hang on."

She pulled out a painted purple wooden box with a small combo lock. It rattled when she shook it. A rudimentary heart had been carved into the top with the initials *BC* and *TW*. "Ah. This should be something. Girls always hide things in their hearts. Okay, PI guy, any idea what she'd use as a combination?"

"Just break the box."

Kyla glared at him. "This matters to her. It should matter to us." She flipped the box around and felt the hinges. "Maybe I could pry it open from the back... hang on. What's Bess's birthday?"

"February 2, 2005."

She spun the numbers, tugged on the lock. "No good. How about her parents?"

"If this matters, it wouldn't be them. Trust me," he added when she looked up. "Try Tristan's. April 6, 2004."

"Annnnd..." Kyla held her breath and tried again. "Bingo!" She popped the lock and opened the box. "Eesh. Here we go." She lifted out a plastic Baggie filled with joints and a selection of brightly colored pills. "I wonder if any of these are PoWWer."

"It's possible. Not sure how we get it to Alvarez or even Cole or Jack without admitting we were still working the case."

She scrunched her nose as if she could come up with an answer. "Maybe we hold onto it for now."

"And wait for the right time." When turning it over wouldn't cost her her job. "Anything else?" He pressed.

"This looks promising." She lifted a thin stack of photographs. "When was the last time you printed out photos?"

"Couldn't tell you. But this could explain why there were so few pictures on her phone." Jason said.

"She didn't print these herself. They were processed. They're dated. Here on the back." Excitement surged through her system. "Oh, man. Check this out." She flipped through them and handed them off. "Tristan with the O'Callaghans. Colin and Liam." She handed the pictures off to him. "Meeting in a parking lot. A few at the club. Definitely doing some kind of a transaction." She pointed to the small satchel Liam was passing to Tristan in one photo. She looked closer. "The kid looks terrified."

"Can't imagine why." Jason's sarcasm didn't make her feel any better.

"I mean it. He's not showing that teenage bravado so many of these kids do, like they're untouchable or invincible. He knows he's not." She handed Jason another picture.

"Or he's worried because in a few months he turns eighteen and that protection he has as a juvenile disappears."

"Even for you that's cynical," Kyla said. "And cold."

"It's realistic. These pictures go back months, Kyla. That means he's been in this for a while."

"And he's about to age out of being an asset and straight into being a liability." She angled her head. "Instead of a few months in JD, he'd be facing serious prison time. Is this Bess?"

Jason leaned over. "Yeah. The purple streaks are gone apparently. Her mom said she dyed her hair blue the week before she disappeared."

"She's pretty." Long hair, heavily outlined hazel eyes, pale skin. The multiple piercings in her ears, the illegal tattoo on the side of her neck. "It's such a shame that she's doing drugs."

"She's not doing them according to her parents," Jason told her.

"I guess I shouldn't assume. I didn't appreciate it when others said the same about Julia. Though, we did find the pills and stuff. Are her parents naive or selectively unobservant?"

"Or it could be option number three," Jason's voice dropped. "I'm beginning to think they're hoping I either don't find her at all or that she's already gone. Why else wouldn't they report her missing to the cops?"

"Keeping up appearances. That has to be one of the worst reasons to do anything." Kyla's stomach rolled. "This picture's the most recent. Just a few weeks old. Oh." Tears burned her throat. This Bess was happier; her eyes were brighter, her hair more tamed and smooth. Even the liner around her eyes was more subtle and the smile... "She's laughing. And she's with Julia." Kyla touched a finger to her friend's face. The affection between them was evident.

"If Bess had these pictures," Jason said. "She knows more than just about Tristan's dealing. She knows who he works for. Kid's smarter than I gave her credit for. Those are insurance."

"Insurance for what?"

"We'd have to ask her. These pictures are very deliberately framed to include as much as possible."

"Who's that?" She leaned over, felt Jason's warm breath on her cheek as she tapped a finger against the barely there image behind a car window. "Inside. Someone's in the backseat. Someone else the O'Callaghans are working with?"

"Maybe." Jason shook his head. "I have a scanning program that can work magic with photos." He slipped the pictures he had into his inside jacket pocket. "I should be able to lighten things up, get an idea who it might be. Maybe even find something out about the car."

"What about that jump drive you stole from—"

"Borrowed."

Kyla snorted. "Did you find anything on it?"

"The thing is still decrypting." He pointed at the pictures in Kyla's hand. "These kids actually look happy." She passed them over to him. Tristan and Bess together at Fairytale Land. At the Tower Café. Outside the Delta King in Old Sac.

"They care about each other," Kyla said. "They love each other. It's all over their faces."

"Think so?"

"It would explain why she took the pictures of him with the O'Callaghan brothers." Kyla met his gaze. "People will do just about anything for the ones they love."

It was as if both of them forgot to breathe. She could hear their heartbeats echo in the confines of the car as she shifted her legs.

"What's rattling in the box?" Jason's question broke the silence.

Kyla lifted a small cloth bag free. She pried it open, then pulled out a metal key painted bright green. She smiled. "I wonder if this is how Indiana Jones feels when he finds a clue."

"What clue? That key could go to anything, anywhere."

"Or it could go to a storage locker at the Foxworm Storage Facility in West Sac." She turned the key over. "Unit three twenty-four."

"How do you know?"

"Julia." She smiled. "I found a torn receipt for a storage unit in her papers. Wanna go see what's inside?"

Jason started the car. "Definitely."

\* \* \*

"Why on earth would Julia have come all the way out here to rent a unit?" Jason asked. "There are tons of storage facilities around her house, not to mention that detached garage of hers."

"I'm assuming whatever she has inside will answer that question." Kyla frowned at him. "For a PI, you don't seem very curious."

"I'm not." But he was very, very anxious. That internal alarm he possessed, the one that had been honed by years of questionable activity and additional years in prison, was clanging loudly. "Might have to think this through. We need a code to get through that gate." He pulled his SUV into a spot across the street and under a tree. The storage facility's front office had two doors, one on the outside of the gate, the other on the interior of the property.

"Or we wait until someone goes in and follow."

"I think the odds of anyone coming to visit their stuff in the next few minutes is seriously negligible." The Foxworm Storage Facility was definitely off the beaten track. Dead weeds and neglected fence were in more abundance than freshly paved asphalt. The layout contained smallish to larger metal outdoor storage units with rising garage-like doors painted the same bright green as the key they'd found in Bess's belongings. Some of those doors were secured with padlocks. Others were unlocked and presumably empty.

On the bright side, he didn't see any video cameras or any sophisticated security equipment. Getting in would be easier than getting out unless…he made a mental guess as to how high the brick wall was that surrounded the facility.

"Maybe no one's going to go in, but someone's coming out. Look." Kyla pointed as a dark paneled van pulled up to the gate and the driver keyed in a code to get out. "Let's go."

"Just give me the key," Jason demanded and held out his hand. "I'm going alone."

"Absolutely not." She held onto the key. "We don't have time to argue about this. Start the car—"

"We barrel in there in this vehicle they'll call the cops. We don't want attention, remember? Kyla give me the—Kyla!"

She was already out of the car and headed across the street. With the gate nearly all the way open, Jason knew he didn't have a choice but to follow. He grabbed his cell, shoved it in his back pocket and locked the car before he hustled to catch up. He did so just as the van exited through the gate.

"Easy does it," Jason murmured and took hold of her hand, keeping his eyes open for any cameras he may have missed. "Go slow and..." He gave the driver of the van a quick wave and kept them moving so they would still be hidden by the van when they walked through the still open gate.

"Easy peasy." Kyla squeezed his hand when he tried to let go.

"Space three-two-four, right?"

"Yep. Should be..." Kyla pointed to the numbers on the doors. "Should be down this aisle. Probably all the way at the end."

"Good." The farther they were from the office, the better. "So. You come up with a Halloween costume yet?"

"What?" Kyla shielded her eyes against the sun. "No. Why?"

"I was wondering if Eden mentioned the party at The Brass Eagle on Halloween."

"She did not. Wait." She stopped and caught his arm. "Are you asking me on another one of your non-dates?"

"No." *Yes.* "Not really." He resumed walking. "I'm working the bar that night. Hosting, so to speak. Kind of have to since the party was my idea. I just thought it would be fun if you wanted to come hang out. Maybe change your mind about Halloween."

"Trust me. That is not going to happen."

"Ah. Well. Never mind then. I bet Chloe Ann's costume is going to be super cute."

"No fair using the baby as a lure," Kyla chided. "This is it. Looks like someone was here before us." She leaned over, hands on her knees, and looked at the battered padlock. "It's broken."

"Don't touch it." Jason gently pushed her aside and looked for himself. She was right. Someone had bumped the lock, then hooked it back on to make it appear as if it was still in place. He pulled his jacket sleeve down over his hand, covered his fingers as he worked the lock free and tossed it to the ground. Keeping the material in place, he grasped the handle and lifted the door up.

"What's that smell?" Kyla cupped her hands around her nose and mouth, her eyes watering. "It smells like industrial cleaning fluid."

That's because that's exactly what it was. Bottles of the stuff, along with cardboard boxes and debris that were piled in the center of the unit. "Back away. We should call... Kyla!" He grabbed for her as she darted around him, but he missed. She ducked out of sight, yelled for him to follow. "Kyla, what the…?"

He found her crouched over a body with her fingers pressed against the person's throat. Varying shades of blue streaked the girl's hair. "It's Bess." Kyla turned to Jason. "I can feel a pulse. Barely, but it's there."

Had Kyla not said otherwise, he would have thought Bess dead. Her face was covered in so much blood that he was instantly reminded of the photographs of Julia Summerton's body.

"Call 911." He coughed against the swirling fumes as he leaned down. "Kyla, go! I've got her."

"But—" She backed up and knocked over a stack of boxes.

"Go!" He stooped down, grabbed Bess's arm and threw her over his shoulder. He turned to follow Kyla, but she hadn't left. She'd come to a halt in the middle of the room. "Kyla?" He stepped closer, looked down and felt his entire body go cold.

A solid gray square was wrapped in transparent tape and attached to a blinking red countdown clock and flip-style cell phone with bright yellow coated wires. Even as he realized what he was looking at, the phone rang.

The countdown began.

*Five…four…*

"Bomb." Kyla lifted terror filled eyes to his. "Jason, I think that's a bomb."

"Run!"

Time slowed. Kyla ran. Jason followed, one arm locked tightly around Bess's prone form.

Fresh air hit his face. His lungs burned, choking off his voice when he called after Kyla, who was racing down the narrow path between units. The explosion, when it came, erupted in one horrific whoosh of heat and noise, and sent him flying off his feet.

He tried to hold onto Bess as he landed face first on the ground, but she fell out of his grasp. He scrambled forward, tried to shield her from the chunks of metal and wood framing that rained down.

He covered his head, pushed his feet under him and lunged forward, bringing Bess with him as he heard Kyla's muffled voice shouting his name.

Jason watched as fire arced into the sky. Thick tendrils of gray and black smoke twined their way into the sky, staining the pure-white clouds. He coughed, barely able to catch his breath. "Kyla?" His voice broke.

"Here!" She burst through the smoke and dropped down beside him, her hands framing his face as she looked into his eyes. "Are you all right? Jason?" Her lips were moving, but her voice sounded as if she were speaking underwater. "Can you hear me?"

He shook his head.

"You're bleeding." She traced her finger across his hairline, making him wince.

He could barely hear her. He could barely hear himself think. Tendrils of flame licked at the unit. He blinked, bringing Kyla into focus.

Her face was dirty, the ends of the scarf she wore in her hair singed and smoking. Her bare legs were scraped and cut, but she was alive.

Alive.

He hauled her against him and, because he needed to, crushed his mouth to hers.

She clung to him. Sobbed. As much as he hated the feel of her tears on his skin, he welcomed them. They were proof, incontrovertible evidence, that she—that they—were alive. "That was close," he murmured against her lips.

"Too close." She looked over her shoulder as two uniformed workers came racing around the corner, one of them yelling into his cell phone. "I don't think we're going to get out of here unnoticed."

"No." Dread coated his words. "Check on Bess." He reached behind him, wincing as his entire body protested, and pulled his cell out of his back pocket. He had to blink a few times to clear his vision, then found the number he needed. "Jack. Yeah, hey, it's Jason. I'm at the, um…" He struggled to think. "Foxworm Storage Facility in West Sac." He cleared his throat. Once, twice. His mind raced as he tried to fathom what to tell the detective. In the end, all he could manage was, "We found Bess Carmody."

# Chapter 13

Kyla, stripped down to her underwear and final bit of strength, slid off the gurney in the emergency room cubicle and reached for her smoke-saturated clothes. "I'll never barbecue again." She held out her shirt only to find it torn. No sooner had she dragged on her slacks than the cubicle's curtain was ripped open.

"Good grief, Eden," Kyla snapped. "Have some decorum."

"Not in this lifetime." Eden St. Claire rolled her eyes and pulled the curtain closed behind her. "Seriously, Kyla, when I said you and Jason set the building on fire, I didn't mean for you to take it as a challenge."

"Ha ha."

"Here." Eden tossed a tote on the bed. "I stopped by your place to grab some things. If you wear that shirt home, Cole might have to arrest you for indecent exposure."

"Thanks." Kyla ditched what was left of her smelly attire and put on the clean clothes. She sniffed her hair. "I still stink."

"Not surprising. Cole said that fire went to two alarms. Are you sure you should be getting dressed?"

"I've been lying here for more than four hours. They're just keeping me until my blood work comes back." Kyla sat on the edge of the bed and tugged on the sneakers from the bag. "Have you seen Jason? Did they tell you anything?"

"I did, yes, and I spent five minutes convincing him that *you* were okay. The doctors were in with him when I left. In the meantime, Cole, Jack and I drew straws for who gets to supervise whom." Eden leaned back against the gurney, folding her arms across her chest. "You were designated the short straw."

Kyla glared. "Why was I short?"

"Because you get testy when you don't know what's going on with someone you care about." Eden's tone softened. "He's going to be fine, Kyla."

A breath she didn't realize she'd been holding escaped. Her shoulders slumped. The band of tension around her chest loosened. "Yeah?"

"Yeah. Looks like a bruised eardrum is the worst of it. They were worried about a concussion, but his tests came back clear. Now they're just waiting on the same tox results you are."

The relief that surged through her nearly drove her to her knees. "I want to see him."

"Figured." Eden started walking when Kyla stood to gather her things. Eden suddenly turned and wrapped her in a hug so tight Kyla almost lost her air again. "That's twice you've scared us."

"I know." Kyla only fought the comfort for a moment before she surrendered. "I didn't mean to."

"Now I know why Cole gets so upset whenever I say that." Eden gave her another squeeze. "I called Simone as soon as Cole called me. She and Vince are on their way back."

"What?" Kyla let go of her friend. "Eden, no. There was no reason—"

"You nearly getting blown sky-high is reason enough." The determined glint in Eden's eyes was tempered only by the unfamiliar flicker of fear. "It's amazing you two are alive. That's a quote, not an exaggeration, from the on-scene investigators. If I hadn't called Simone, she'd never have forgiven me. Besides, it was Vince's brother you were with and the hospital asked for a next of kin contact when they checked him in. If I hadn't called them, the admitting nurse would have and then an exploding storage unit would have been the least of your worries."

She could only imagine how much she and Jason were going to have to explain. "What about Bess?"

"She's alive. Jack's currently working on convincing the doctors he can be given her medical status since her parents are still out of the country."

"Having her listed as a missing person could have helped with that," Kyla murmured as disgust choked her. "How do parents leave the country when their kid is missing?"

"That's a question only the Carmodys can answer." But it was evident by the disgust in Eden's voice she agreed with Kyla. "You got everything?"

Before Kyla could answer, the curtain was pulled back again. "Ms. Bertrand, you haven't been discharged." Catherine, the nurse who had been put in charge of Kyla when she'd first arrived, glared at Eden.

Eden smirked. "And I told you she wouldn't care."

"I'm not leaving the hospital." Yet. Kyla did her best to sound contrite as she shoved her purse and destroyed shirt into the bag Eden had brought. "I feel fine."

"If you were fine, then you would have been discharged."

"I'm going to sit next to another patient's bed and wait for both our results."

"She'll be with Jason Sutton," Eden explained when Kyla used her as a distraction to make her escape. Eden caught up to her, grabbed her arm and steered her toward the right corridor off the waiting room. "Move it!"

Kyla nearly tripped over her own feet. "What's the rush?"

"Kyla!"

Eden skidded to a halt. "So close."

DA Wade Lawson approached, a steely expression on his normally stoic face. Kyla had worked for a handful of district attorneys over the years. Some she liked more than others. She'd always considered Wade one of the good ones and not just because he'd been encouraging as she'd moved up the ladder. He knew people's names, knew their families; he heaped praise as equally as he did criticism. He was ambitious to be sure, but he was also conscious of the fact that he counted on the people who worked in his office. He was also good-looking, amiable and really, really terrific at his job. His easygoing manner made living up to his expectations easier. But when he was disappointed…

A tight smile crossed his lips. "Nice to see you're up and around."

"Yes, sir." Kyla gave a curt nod. "I was just on my way—"

"I need a word," Ward said. "Now, please. With me."

"Bed nineteen," Eden muttered as Kyla walked away. "When you're done."

Kyla followed her boss, who made a quick stop at the nurse's station and was directed to a particular room. Then he motioned to Kyla.

The small space reminded her of the one hospital staff had brought her and her parents to when her grandmother had a stroke. Minimally furnished with a few chairs, a low coffee table and a vase filled with dusty, artificial flowers, Kyla was fairly certain good news was rarely imparted within the beige walls.

"Please." He gestured to one of the chairs. "Sit down." He paced a moment—not an easy task in such a tiny room. "I received a call from Detective Marcella Alvarez a few hours ago."

Kyla bit the inside of her cheek.

"Would you like to guess what she and I talked about?" He stopped pacing, leaned his back against the wall and pushed his hands into his pockets.

About the fact that the Sac Metro PD wrote off Julia's death as nothing more than an annoyance? That Kyla had been warned off a case no one was interested in until it interfered with Detective Alvarez's closure rate?

She swallowed what would surely be a career-ending snark and said simply, "Since she's an ambitious detective, I imagine you and she could talk about a great many things." Her arms tightened around the tote bag in her lap.

"You are not wrong." He nodded and seemed to be considering his words. "It didn't take much for me to understand I've been kept in the dark about a great many things. For clarification and because I know how close the two of you are, I followed up the conversation with a call to Simone. Not something I wanted to do on her vacation."

"No, sir." Kyla cringed. "You needn't have done that. Simone doesn't know anything."

"The correct answer is she *didn't* know anything, which I admit was a relief. The last thing I need is my second-in-command running rogue investigations. Rest assured we are both now up to speed. She also knows that I'm removing you from the Primrose case."

The train she'd heard barreling toward her the past few days came into focus. "No, please, sir, you can't do that." Her boss fixed his stony blue-eyed stare on her.

"As District Attorney, I assure you, I can." The kindness she'd seen hovering behind his gaze vanished.

"Of course, I just meant…" She paused, took a breath and remembered what Jason had told her the other night at the police station. "I haven't let any of my work slide. I've been prepping this entire time. I've got my jury selection notes and my opening statement. I'm ready to go and as good as Simone is. No one knows this case better than I do. Please, I assure you—"

"We're past the point of assurances, Kyla. The decision's been made. I expect you to turn over all your files and pretrial notes to Simone when she asks for them. Is that understood?"

"Yes." Defeated, she sank lower in her chair. One other thing she knew about Wade Lawson: when he made up his mind, any protestations were useless.

"I've managed to talk Detective Alvarez down

from filing an official complaint," he went on. "But in exchange—"

"An official what?" Kyla tried to puzzle things out. "She doesn't have any cause—"

"Perhaps not, but she's made it clear she wants you as far away from the investigation as humanly possible." Something fierce shone in his eyes, something dangerous that sent chills down her spine. "I'm calling for an internal investigation to begin immediately."

"But that means—"

"You're suspended." Ward nodded. "Yes."

She waited for the panic. For the fear. For the hurt to descend at the idea of losing the job—possibly the career—she'd worked so hard for. Instead, she simply felt numb. "For how long?"

"Indefinitely. We'll be bringing you in to make a statement in the next few days."

"I see." She felt…odd. Everything seemed muted, surreal to her. As if she were somehow existing outside of her own body.

"I suggest you stop by your office—pick up the box Penny's packed up for you. Your personal belongings, mail, et cetera."

The knife twisted deeper. She wasn't even being allowed to clean out her own desk. "All right." She clutched her bag to her chest and stood. "Is there anything else?"

"Yes, actually." Wade motioned for her to sit again. "That conversation was obligatory for the District Attorney and one of his assistant prosecutors." He sat, leaned forward, and when he looked at her, it was as if she was seeing a different man. "Now I'm speaking as your friend. I want to hear it all, start to finish, from your perspective." His eyes glinted. "Talk to me, Kyla. What didn't Detective Alvarez tell me?"

"The fact that the police brought your car to the hospital for you must mean you're moving up in their estimation."

The cheer and optimism in Kyla's voice struck Jason as not only false, but forced. Despite reality knocking on her door, she was trying to make the best of it. Her worst case scenario had hit and hit hard. Suspension was a precursor to being fired. Jason knew it. Kyla knew it.

And yet they were both choosing to ignore the elephant in the car.

Probably because there was an even bigger elephant stomping down the road behind them. For the first time ever, he didn't plan to stop it.

"Unlikely." Jason slid the SUV into his usual spot behind The Brass Eagle and shoved the gear into Park. "You didn't notice something was missing from the car? Bess's bag for instance?" Seeing as their actions had triggered the explosion and subsequent fire at the Foxworm Storage Facility, it left their belongings—like Jason's vehicle—open to being searched. Thank goodness he'd shoved those photos of Bess's into his inside jacket pocket.

"Oh. Right." Kyla cringed. "You think maybe they'll take it to her room at the hospital?"

"If her things aren't already with Tammy in the police lab, I'll eat what's left of my jacket." On the bright side, they'd gotten the unidentified pills to the authorities so… that was a win. He reached back, let out an unintentional groan, and pulled the coat off the backseat. "Safe and sound despite our afternoon." Jason plucked the slightly damaged photos free. "You sure you still want to follow this through till the end?" He hesitated, not wanting to push.

"I'm suspended, not fired. Yet." She spoke as if her career wasn't hanging by a very thin thread. "You might have closed your case, but we haven't found who killed Julia. And for the record, no bomb or obnoxious, lying narcotics detective is going to stop me." She grabbed her stuff and shoved out of the car. "If I'm going to lose my job, I want it to be because I did everything I could to find out what happened to my friend. Not because I just sat back and waited for the shoe to drop."

Jason sat for a moment, his ears still ringing, smiling to himself. Even now, with everything that had happened, she was full steam ahead, determined to do not only what was right, but what was difficult. If he hadn't been in love with her before...

He froze, eyes wide, as the thought not only passed through his brain, but settled and took root.

"Hey!" Kyla knocked on his window. "You okay?"

"Yeah," he muttered in the empty car as he pulled his key free and opened his door. "I'm fine. Just...thinking." For once, thinking things through could get him in more trouble than his automatic impulses. "You want the box from your office?"

"I'll dig through it when we get back to Barnaby's." She glanced over her shoulder as he slowly followed. "They didn't release you from the hospital too soon, did they?"

*Probably.* Clearly his brain had been scrambled. "Just moving a little slower than usual. Not as young as I used to be."

He noticed Kyla try to hide a grin, so he caught up

with her, slipped an arm around her and drew her close as they climbed the stairs to his apartment.

"You sure you're okay?" She put her hand over his. "You seem…different."

He felt different. In fact, he felt almost invincible. "Well, I nearly got blown into the afterlife—"

"We. *We* nearly got blown there."

"Right. We." And wasn't that the point. "I—we—inhaled half a lab's worth of industrial toxins—"

"Our oxygen and blood tests came back elevated, but within normal levels," she chided.

"We found a missing sixteen-year-old girl who may have been hurt by the same person who murdered your friend—"

"I was thinking the same thing," Kyla interrupted. "Bess's face. It was her face, wasn't it?"

"It sure was. I've never been so grateful to see somebody's mug, especially one that was living, breathing" Jason pulled out his key as they reached his front door. "For the record, I've had a few hours to think about our previous conversations. I've come to the conclusion that you're right."

"Oh?" She tucked her hands behind her and smiled up at him. "Right about what?"

"Right about us." He slipped his arm around her waist, pulled her in and covered her lips with his. It was, he thought as she sighed into his mouth, the only thing he wanted. To kiss her. To touch her. To be with her. "Kyla," he murmured. He could feel every inch of her pressing against him, from her thighs to her hips, to her breasts. The sensation made him feel more alive than he ever had. He could have been facing the possibility of a life without her. Now? Now this was all he could think about. "I need to be with you."

She pulled her head back, just enough so that he could see her arch a brow and curve her lips into that teasing, knowing smile he adored. "Took you long enough." She kissed him then. Long enough to linger and tempt. "I swear if you talk yourself out of it this time—"

He kissed her back, as deeply, as completely, as perfectly as he'd dreamed of doing. "I don't want to talk at all." He felt her tremble as he nibbled and licked his way along her jaw. "I didn't see Vince's car anywhere."

"I looked, too," she said on a laugh. "Do you think we have time before they get—"

Jason's apartment door swung open to reveal Vince Sutton standing there, looking every inch the big brother he was. "No," he said in his full don't-mess-with-me marine voice. "You don't." He stepped back and waved them inside. "You were right, Simone. It's them," he called over his shoulder. "Her hearing is uncanny these days."

"Talk about bad timing," Jason muttered as they walked past him.

"Sorry we interrupted." He pointed to the couch, silently telling him to sit.

Kyla snort-laughed, covered her mouth, and was thrown into a fierce embrace by Simone. "I'm okay," Kyla whispered. "Wow, you and Eden have this suffocating thing down. Simone, really. We're all right."

"No, you aren't. You smell like smoke and cleaning fluid." She gagged, shoved Kyla away, and had to hold out a hand to stop her husband from coming to her side. "Be a sec." Simone raced into the bedroom and slammed the bathroom door shut.

"Is *she* all right?" Jason gaped at the retching coming from behind the door.

"Food poisoning's kicking her butt. She's going to the doctor tomorrow. Thankfully." Vince retrieved a few water bottles from the fridge and handed them out. Left one by the bathroom door for his wife. "Salmon is definitely off our menu for a while. So. Bess Carmody. What's the latest? You call her parents?"

"As soon as I got my phone back," Jason said. "It's incredible she's still alive. They've put her in a medically-induced coma. The beating she took caused swelling on her brain. She's got defensive wounds as well. Whoever went at her will definitely have some marks."

"They found a significant amount of PoWWer in her system," Kyla said. "Cole told us, by comparison to other overdoses, this stuff was even more potent. She shouldn't be alive."

"Neither should you two." Vince sat on the edge of the sofa beside his brother. "Jack said you were able to give him a description of the explosive device."

Jason nodded, then took a long drink. Big brother interference aside, talking about the weapon that had nearly obliterated him and Kyla was enough to douse his desire. For now. "Cell phone, clock, C-4."

"If we'd been a minute later, Bess's body may never have been found," Kyla said. "She'd have been incinerated."

Vince glanced at Jason.

"What?" Kyla asked.

"The countdown started after the call," Jason told

her. "And the call came when we went into the unit. That bomb wasn't meant for Bess, Kyla."

"It was meant for the two of you," Vince said.

# Chapter 14

"You want to hear something funny?" Kyla asked Jason as they turned the corner to Barnaby Faustus's house.

"More than I want my next breath."

"I was thinking back to when Eden went through that whole Ice Man thing, then Simone with her missing witness. And then Allie and Max had to deal with his niece being kidnapped and…"

"Greta nearly getting thrown off the roof of an art museum."

"That, too. I remember thinking how…extraordinary it all sounded. I was actually envious, you know? That all these wild things were happening to them and I was just sitting at a desk as research backup. I felt left out."

"I hear that," Jason agreed.

"Turns out getting caught up in wild things really

isn't all it's cracked up to be." Every inch of her body tingled, as if dormant cells had been awakened and re-charged. "I'm not sure I'm cut out for danger and ex-citement."

"Could have fooled me." He hit the garage door opener and when he parked and turned off the engine, faced her. "You got through it great, though. Maybe witnessing everything your friends went through pre-pared you more than you realized."

"Our."

"What?" Jason frowned.

Kyla reached over, slid her fingers through his and grabbed hold of his hand. "They're our friends, not just mine. It wasn't just me Eden came to see in the hospi-tal. She went to you first. You're part of us, Jason. It's time you accept that."

"I do accept it." He turned their hands over, lifted the back of her hand to his lips and brushed his mouth across her knuckles. "It's just not what's on my mind at the moment."

Every feeling and emotion she'd been holding back whirred to life. "Yeah?" She tried to sound casual, tried to ignore the fact her heart was beating fast. "I was afraid maybe after that stop at your apartment you'd have talked yourself out—"

The rest of her statement was caught by his mouth. That wonderful, sensual, demanding mouth of his that she couldn't wait to challenge.

"No more talking, okay?" He left a series of kisses along her jaw and down the side of her neck, something she was developing a great affinity for.

"Maybe no talking, but definitely walking." She re-leased his hand and reached up to catch his face between her palms. "I want you in that big bed upstairs, where I can enjoy every…" She kissed him. "Single." Kissed him again. "Inch. Of. You."

She felt him smile against her mouth. "Finally, we're on the same track."

Her heart nearly melted. "Get inside before I change my mind and see just how far back these seats go." Kyla watched him jump out of the car and head for the door as she let out an odd, uncharacteristic giggle. She followed.

"Kyla! Oh, hey, Kyla! Wait a second!" Lynn Wainwright burst out of her front door, waving like a maniac. Her bright pink top had Kyla blinking against the glare.

"You have got to be kidding me," Kyla said, disbelieving, and shot a sad look at Jason.

"Be a nice neighbor," he teased. "I'll be waiting upstairs."

Kyla pinched her lips together and forced herself to wait for Lynn. "Hi there."

"Hey, I'm so glad to catch you," Lynn caught her breath as if crossing the street was an effort. "You two are just go go go, aren't you? Oh, what happened?" Her green eyes shifted to concern. "Are you okay?"

"What do you mean?"

"Your face. You have scrapes and your arms are bruised."

"Oh, we went rock climbing." Kyla tossed out the first thing she thought of. "I took a bit of a tumble. Nothing serious. Was there something you wanted?"

"Forrest and I wanted to invite you and Josh over for dinner tomorrow night. Nothing fancy, just a cookout. A get to know you kind of night."

"Oh." Kyla's eyes went wide. "Well, yeah, sure. I'll

check with Josh, but I don't think we have any plans. Thank you for thinking of us."

"It's our pleasure. Alicia's going to help me choose the menu."

"Can I bring anything? I make a mean summer corn salad."

"That sounds perfect." Lynn reached out and caught Kyla's hands, squeezed. "It's so nice to have friendly neighbors. We'll see you about seven? Does that work okay?"

"Should be great."

"Great it is. I'll let you go." Lynn smiled and gave her a wink. "Sorry if I interrupted anything."

"No worries. I'm good at picking things back up."

Lynn laughed, waved and returned to her house.

Kyla spun around and hurried to close the garage and run upstairs. She paused, pressed a hand against her chest and caught her breath. "Okay. Cool. Be cool." It wasn't as if she'd been waiting for years to sleep with Jason. Oh, wait. Yes, she had.

She bit her lip against the wicked grin. She reached down, slipped off her sandals, knocked on the bedroom door and pushed it open.

"Are you thinking what I'm thinking?"

"Considering I'm spent, I'm really hoping I'm wrong." Jason let out a small moan when Kyla ran her fingers along his still buzzing skin. She sat up, just enough to look down at him, as she slid a long, bare leg between his.

When she smiled, he gave into temptation and sank the hand that had been stroking her shoulder into the thick curls of her hair. "I'm thinking we should have done this ages ago." She pressed her mouth to his and set his system to humming. It didn't matter where or how she touched him, the result was always the same. "I'm also thinking—" she kissed along his jaw, to his ear, bit gently "—that maybe we should…" Her hand moved down his chest, hovered over his navel.

"Either finish that thought or finish that thought," he teased as he drew her to him for another kiss. She laughed.

"I'm really sorry."

"I don't think you are." But he smiled anyway. If there had ever been a more perfect moment in his life, he certainly couldn't think of it.

"I was going to say I think we should get something to eat." She kissed him quick, then rolled over and grabbed for an oversize bright pink nightshirt that was tossed over the arm of the closest chair. "We need to keep up our strength, yeah?"

It could be a little damaging to the ego to admit she was right. He watched her stand and stretch, the hem of the shirt rising to indecent levels. The play of that fabric, that color against her dark skin, the way her curls draped down her back and the look she gave him over her shoulder made him push aside any regrets he might have felt.

Kyla Bertrand was as glorious as he'd dreamed she'd be.

"I'm thinking pasta," she declared. "That work?"

"Right now, you could suggest a roasted pail of garbage and I'd agree." But he didn't move. He simply lay there against the pillows that smelled like her, summer and promise, and continued to watch her move. Elegant, effortless. Entrancing. "I'll meet you downstairs. I want to check on the decryption."

"Okay."

Jason shoved out of bed, anxious for when he could crawl back into it along with Kyla. Naked, he grabbed his cell and walked down the hall to the surveillance bedroom. He tugged on a clean pair of jeans and leaned over his laptop to check its progress.

When the readable files popped up on the screen, Jason nearly let out a whoop. A few more clicks had him scanning through the list that was stored on the jump drive he'd found in Colin O'Callaghan's safe. Accounting records, properties, subsidiary and partnered companies...

"Jackpot." Jason clicked open the first file and began reading. He figured he could get through at least a portion of them before heading downstairs.

Sometime later, he lifted his chin and grimaced. Reflected in the larger monitor, he saw Kyla lounging against the doorframe, arms crossed over her chest. "How long have I been sitting here?"

"About an hour." She strode in, came up behind him and slid her arms around him from behind. "Dinner's ready. You find anything?"

"Maybe." His brain was seeing things he couldn't quite process yet. "I'm not exactly sure what we can do with all this information, but it's a gold mine as far as how the O'Callaghan business empire works."

"Empire?" She leaned down and he felt her breath against his ear.

"Alvarez and her team are right to be concerned. They've got PoWWer distribution plans already set in at least seven major cities. Los Angeles, Seattle, Miami, New Orleans…"

"Those are all port cities."

"Yep." Jason did a bit more tapping on the keyboard. "And that's just phase one. Phase two takes them overseas to Europe and from there—"

"From there there'll be no stopping them." She peered closer. "You need to get this information to the right people."

"I don't think Detective Alvarez is in a receptive mood where we're concerned." Not that Jason didn't agree with Kyla's point. "Fruit of the poisonous tree. She won't be able to use it."

"I'm not talking about Alvarez." The cool tone in Kyla's voice had Jason glancing at her over his shoulder. "We aren't just looking at statewide distribution with this. It's crossing state lines."

"You're thinking I should get this to the Feds?"

Kyla shrugged. "Might be worth running it past Slade, just to see what he thinks."

"You're thinking since he's retired from the FBI he can be more objective than say, Eamon?"

"I'm thinking Slade isn't obligated to report it up the chain of command like Eamon would be. How about we talk about it over dinner?" She shifted to sit on the edge of his desk. "Unless you want to keep working?"

Only an imbecile would choose work over Kyla and those fantasy-inducing legs of hers. "Nope." He closed his laptop, turned off his monitors and stood. "I could definitely use some…dinner."

They'd barely reached the kitchen before the view of the backyard had Jason considering other options.

"How do you feel about cold pasta?" He walked past

her and the kitchen table that she'd set, and pulled open the double sliding doors.

"Hopefully okay since it already is." She reached for the bowl filled with salad greens and veggies. "Why?"

He held out his hand.

"What?" Smiling, she came to him, then squealed when he ducked down and lifted her onto his shoulder. "Jason! What are you doing?" She could barely speak from laughing. "You're still hurt. You shouldn't be doing—"

"Tonight I feel invincible." Tomorrow might be another story. But he didn't care just then. He walked to the edge of the pool. The crystal clear cascading water transporting them instantly to their own private paradise. "Take a deep breath."

"What? No! No, Jason—"

He jumped, plunging them both into the pool.

When he came up, he found her already sputtering, shoving her thick curls out of her face. "You did it now." She kicked away from him, her smile still in place. He followed, feeling as if he'd skipped a chapter in a book. "Do you have any idea what happens to a Black girl's hair in the pool without any preparation?"

He stopped, treaded water and watched as she gathered her hair into one hand and twisted. "What hap—"

"Potential disaster," she half grumbled. "It's why I brought my swim caps."

"I guess I don't get points for romance then."

"That depends." She sighed, tilted her head back and released her hair, then swam toward him. "How fast do you think you can ditch those jeans?"

"Faster than you can get rid of that shirt." It took some doing, but he managed to extricate himself from his jeans and toss the soggy denim onto the patio. It landed with a wet plop seconds before her top did. "Now what?" he asked. Her arms encircled his neck and her legs wrapped around his waist. He groaned as he felt her warmth press against his hardness. "Kyla, wait." He kissed her once, then twice more. "Condom," he said softly against her mouth. "Jeans. Condom."

She disentangled herself and maneuvered them to the side of the pool where she retrieved his pants. She stopped, foil packet in hand. "When did you—"

"I keep one on me at all times." He nearly lost it when she ripped the packet open with her teeth. "Or at least I have since I met you."

Her eyes softened, her lashes spiked with water. "Okay, that wins you a bunch of points. You want me to—"

"No, no." He took the condom and, with the determination of a man in need, covered himself. Smiling, she followed him as he drifted toward the shallow end. "Come here." He drew her close and watched as she wrapped herself around him. As she lowered her mouth to his, she sank onto him.

After conquering the pool, she'd ducked upstairs for a shower—to wash the chlorine out of her hair. She'd never gone through her styling process so quickly. By the time they ate, the pasta was stone-cold.

It was also the best dinner she'd ever eaten.

The fact that she was sitting at a kitchen table and sharing post-lovemaking food with Jason Sutton erased a bit of what had been an exhausting and nearly traumatic day. "I feel like I could sleep for a month." She stretched her arms over her head, then pushed her empty plate away. "How about you?" As good as the sex had been, she was looking forward to simply sleeping in his arms.

"Huh?" Jason glanced up from his phone. "Sorry. Just got a text from Bess Carmody's parents. They've told me to send the final invoice and they'll pay me in full once they're back next week."

Kyla arched a brow. "Next week? But—"

"Yeah." Jason shook his head and set his phone down. "But—" that cool, intense look came into his eyes and made her shiver "—even with a weak prognosis, they're finishing their vacation."

"That poor girl. No wonder she's lost."

"She's one of thousands," Jason said as he gathered their plates and carried them to the sink. "Most of the men I was inside with had similar stories. Not as many in her tax bracket, but the lack of emotional connection to anyone real and good just drives some people to the edge."

"Not in your case, though." Kyla got up and sat on one of the bar stools on the other side of the counter. "You had Vince."

"I had me," Jason countered. "Vince was long distance. My friends were trash. I did what I had to in order to survive. I used prison as a way to do what I should have done originally. Graduated high school. Learned every computer and mental skill I could that would make me useful one day. If Simone hadn't taken another swing at my case and gotten me out early…"

"What?" Kyla asked when he trailed off. "What would you have done if you were still inside?"

Hands deep in soapy water, Jason didn't look at her. "I thought about college. But it's hard to think about the future when you aren't sure you have one. Kids like Bess, like Tristan…they already see the dead ends. It's all they see. How do we expect them to be better?" He shook his head. "Sorry. People like the Carmodys, they just…everything is possible for them and yet…" His helpless shrug broke Kyla's heart.

Kyla couldn't argue with anything he'd said. Working where she did, she'd seen cases like Bess's and Tristan's up close and personal. But there was always another one to focus on. Another crime to prosecute.

"You have options now, though. You're working for Vince. You're putting those talents—"

"You really want to call them that?"

"Jack wouldn't have found his kidnapped sister if you hadn't helped. You saved Slade, too."

"It was a team effort."

"Why do you do that? Downplay the good you've done."

"Because people only remember the worst you've done."

"You underestimate us. Eden, Simone, Allie, Jack—"

"I do." Jason nodded and set the last of the clean dishes in the rack to dry. "Because when I do, I'm not disappointed."

"Is that why you won't apply for clemency?" She took a calming breath at his shocked expression.

"How did you—"

"Simone told me. After Ashley, you could have applied to the governor for it. She even had the paperwork drawn up for you. Recommendations not only from her, but from Eamon and Slade. They've got FBI pull and were willing to go to bat for you yet you told her not to bother. Why?"

"Because it wouldn't have been right." He sounded... She couldn't be certain...defeated? "I was just doing the right thing. There shouldn't be a reward for that."

Kyla blinked. "You seriously believe that, living in the world we do? Jason, you of all people know that sometimes doing the right thing is the most difficult thing of all. Why not take advantage of opportunities that come around because of it?"

"Because I don't want to." He dried his hands, leaned against the sink and folded his arms over his chest. "Because the foundation of it would be like quicksand. Do you know why I suddenly started doing the right thing when I got out?"

The challenge in his eyes had her shaking her head.

"Because I didn't have any more excuses for getting into trouble. My father was dead. Dead and buried. And then I got luckier. I was welcomed home, not only by Vince and Simone, but by their friends. Their family. By you." He shook his head in disbelief that she didn't understand. "That's more than I could have ever asked for. I don't need anything else. It's selfish of me to think otherwise. My life is better now than I ever dreamed it could be, Kyla."

"And yet you still hide behind your conviction."

Confusion rose in his eyes. Her heart, which not so long ago had beat in rhythmic time to his, beneath his, broke open.

"You're so concerned about people seeing you as an ex-con and yet you won't even take the chance you can to change it."

"I don't need a PI license to make my life complete."

"No, you don't." Kyla folded her hands on the counter. "You need me."

Jason closed his eyes, but not before she saw the raw pain. "Kyla, don't."

"Don't what? Tell you I love you? Tell you that I fell pretty darn hard the first time I saw you tending bar at The Brass Eagle? Because I did. I love you, Jason Sutton. You're just going to have to get used to that."

"Kyla, I'm no good—"

"You're using your past as a reason for us not to have a future. I'd bet a year's salary you were already figuring this fling we had tonight would be over as soon as we packed up and moved out. I'd win, wouldn't I?" she challenged when he cringed. She got up and walked around the counter, stood in front of him, toe-to-toe, and stared into his eyes. "You're terrified, Jason. You're terrified to take the chance because we might work. Do you know that when I talked to my boss, he only asked how you were? He didn't ask about our relationship or hint that I should walk away or that you were poison. You know why?" She poked a finger into his arm. "Because you're the only one who sees yourself that way. I love who you are. Now. Today. The man your past made you. But despite what you think, despite what you've said, you haven't let your past go at all." She inched her chin up. "You're still wearing it like a broken shield."

Before she said something she'd regret, even as she felt her heart break, she spun on her heel and stalked upstairs.

# *Chapter 15*

Jason opened his eyes, was instantly awake. One glance at the still-buzzing monitor told him the twenty minute power nap he'd planned to take knocked him out for more than two hours. Now it was nearly one o'clock. Jason groaned, scrubbed the grit from his eyes and moved his neck from side to side. Sleeping at a desk was not conducive to comfort. He stretched, got to his feet, then leaned over to check the decryption program's progress.

Eighty-five percent complete.

Jason gnashed his back teeth. The NSA didn't have this much security on their files. At this rate, he expected to find the combination to Fort Knox when he could finally access Colin O'Callaghan's drive.

The sound of approaching vehicles had him peering through the blinds. The gut-wrenching, familiar sight of spinning police lights had him reaching for his cell. Slamming doors and raised voices echoed in the darkness.

A gentle knock on the door preceded Kyla's entry. "Any idea—"

"Checking now." Irritated he'd let himself fall asleep after going through the surveillance footage from when they were out, he scanned his messages. "Jack says they've got an arrest warrant for Tristan as well as a search warrant for his place of residence. Guess they aren't wasting any time." He pinched the bridge of his nose. "He sent this over an hour ago. I should have read it sooner."

"Don't blame yourself for needing sleep. You had a long day," Kyla said in that practical, no-nonsense tone of hers. She came over and wedged herself between the desk and the microphone he had set up.

"Yeah, but I could have told them Tristan isn't there." He texted Jack back now. "He took off in his car about an hour before we got back."

"Then they can put out a BOLO for his car. Tristan isn't your responsibility."

"We agreed to keep them up-to-date on the Wainwrights' movements," Jack reminded her.

"And now you are. You don't need to take the world on your shoulders, Jason."

"I'm not."

She flicked the blinds open. "Let's continue this discussion later. They're escorting Lynn and Alicia outside."

It was on the tip of Jason's tongue to suggest they hang back, but instead he found himself pocketing his cell and following Kyla downstairs.

When he grabbed the sweatshirt hanging by the door, she was already halfway down the walk.

It was like stepping into a scene from his past. Uniformed officers moved in and out of the house like choreographed dancers while others stayed by their patrol cars, guiding new arrivals through the array of cars. No surprise, the SUV that pulled up seconds later carried Jack, Cole and Detective Alvarez.

One sharp look in Jack's direction earned Jason a quick nod of approval.

"Kyla." Jason reached her as she joined Lynn and Alicia. He draped the sweatshirt around her—she was only in sleep shorts and a tank—and cast a concerned look at her bare feet.

"I don't understand." Lynn clung to Alicia, who had her arms locked securely around herself. "What's going on?"

"Mrs. Wainwright, do you know where your stepson is?" Detective Alvarez asked.

"Tristan?" Lynn croaked. "Um, no. He and my husband had a disagreement this afternoon and he left. Forrest—" She turned alarmed eyes on Kyla, then Jason. "He went to look for him hours ago."

"I have many more questions," Detective Alvarez said.

"Lynn?" Alicia lifted a wobbling chin to her stepmother. "What's going on?"

"I can take Alicia to our place," Kyla offered. "Would that be all right?"

"No." Lynn clung harder to the girl. "Thank you, but I'd rather she stayed with me."

"Then how about you talk to them inside?" Kyla suggested. "No conversation can be productive in this kind of environment."

"I'm sorry. Who are you?" Detective Alvarez asked.

"A friend," Kyla said with more ice in her voice than Jason had ever heard. "Kyla Cooper. This is my husband, Josh."

Detective Alvarez shot Kyla a look that, as far as Jason could tell, didn't have any effect. Pride and affection swept through him, even as he wondered if Alvarez was going to blow their cover. "All right," Alvarez said. "As soon as my team has finished in the kitchen, I'll let them go back inside."

"How generous," Kyla muttered as the detective walked into the house. "Lynn, do you have any idea why they might be looking for Tristan?"

Lynn shook her head. "I... I can't be sure. Tristan and I don't exactly get along."

"What about you, Alicia?" Jason asked. "Did Tristan say anything to you?"

The girl caught her lower lip between her teeth.

"Alicia, it's okay if you want to tell us something," Kyla urged and bent down beside her. "I know you might think you're protecting him—"

"I just want to go back to the way things were." Alicia's eyes filled with tears. "I want my family. I want my mom."

"Oh, honey—" Lynn squeezed her tighter.

"Not you!" Alicia pushed herself free and moved closer to Kyla. "I want my real mom. Everything was fine before she died. There wasn't all of... this."

"All of what?" Kyla asked when Alicia turned fearful eyes on her stepmother.

"She's just overtired and scared." If Lynn took offense to Alicia's outburst, she didn't let on. "We'll be fine once Forrest gets home."

"Mrs. Wainwright?" Bowie, the familiar deputy, sent Jason a side-eyed glance as he approached. "If you and your daughter would come with me?"

Lynn nodded. "Thank you," she whispered to Kyla and Jason as she and Alicia headed inside. "For checking on us."

"Of course," Kyla replied. "We can reschedule dinner."

"Oh, no, please." Lynn stopped. "We're so looking forward to it and it'll be nice to have friends over after all this. Right, Alicia?"

Alicia agreed.

"All right then. We'll see you later tonight."

Lynn and Alicia disappeared into the house, the officers continuing to carry out their tasks. "I didn't know we were having dinner with them tonight," Jason said.

"I would have told you, but I was anxious to get into bed with you." Kyla flashed him a smile that didn't come close to reaching her eyes. "Jack? What's going on?"

"Forgive me for, uh, not knowing you." Jack pulled a notebook out of his pocket and pretended to write things down. "We retrieved partial fingerprints on some of the remnants of the storage facility. They were Tristan's."

"Where would Tristan have gotten C-4?" Jason demanded.

"Can't imagine," Jack murmured. "Which means he's either deeper in this than we thought or someone's setting him up. Either way, he's witness number one against the O'Callaghans at this point. Any idea what time he left the area?"

"Yeah, three forty-five." Jason glanced at Kyla. "Forrest went out around seven, hasn't been back."

"Let's hope Dad isn't trying to get the kid out of the country," Jack speculated. "We're alerting the airports, train stations, bus stations. The usual. One thing. We got a call from Eamon. At the FBI, there's a lot of dark web buzz about the O'Callaghans making a big move and soon. Considering both Colin and Liam have all but vanished, that sounds right. If they're heading out of town—"

"They'll be looking to clean up loose ends." Kyla turned alarmed eyes on Jason. "Bess."

"Way ahead of you," Jack confirmed. "Vince is still at the hospital and we've assigned a couple of deputies to be safe. Night Crawler's still locked down, but we have eyes on it just in case. Chances are Tristan won't be coming back this way." He eyed the two of them. "Not sure there's anything left for you two to do. We've got the access we need now."

"We still don't know who killed Julia," Kyla said.

"Know? No. Suspect." Jason clarified. "I think it's pretty safe to say Liam or Colin killed her and Kevin Dowell."

"When we find Tristan, that's on the top of our list to ask about, Kyla. I promise."

Kyla's smile was strained. "I'm suspended pending an investigation and Darcy's enjoying her time with Loki." She shrugged. "Besides, it'll take a while to pack up all his tech stuff."

Was that code for something? Jason couldn't be sure. But it didn't seem wise to question her. "What she said." Jason said.

"Right." Jack smirked. "Cole bet me you'd say that. You see any sign of Tristan, you let us know, yeah?"

* * *

"I know Jack said otherwise, but I can't help but feel Julia's just a footnote in all this." Kyla shivered once they were back inside the house. Her bare feet were tingling numb. Hugging her arms around her torso, she couldn't wait to crawl back into bed.

"It's safe to say she isn't their priority." Jason's agreement deflated her already sagging balloon of hope. "Doesn't mean she can't be ours. If you still want to work with me?"

"We've gone this far together." She headed upstairs, stopped halfway when he didn't follow her. "You need to sleep."

"I will."

She let her arms drop and tilted her head. He was so…perfect. Not perfect in the traditional definition. He had flaws, glaring ones. He had moments which caused her infinite frustration. He was impulsive and reckless, but cautious when someone else was at risk. He might never see himself the way others, the way she, saw him, but maybe that was okay. Maybe she could see enough good in him that he didn't need to. No. He wasn't perfect.

But he was perfect for her.

She held out her hand.

Jason hesitated. "Kyla, I don't think—"

"Please," she said quietly. "Don't. This one time, don't think. Just feel. We both need sleep and we'll both manage that if there's one less thing to obsess over. Besides—" she took a step toward him as he stood up and took her hand "—I honestly don't have the energy to do anything but hold you."

His smile tipped those wrinkles in the corners of his eyes into the realm of irresistible. "Your wish."

"My command." She led him upstairs.

"Were you able to tweak that photo Bess had in her treasure box?"

Kyla walked into Jason's surveillance bedroom the next afternoon. He was dressed, with a good portion of his things packed, but he still had his computers and the microphone hooked up. Seeing him sitting there, at his desk, gave her an odd thrill she didn't expect. Why? She asked herself for the millionth time. Why couldn't he see what they had?

They'd slept, wrapped around each other in a way that made her heart ache. She knew once they stepped foot out of this house, the illusion of bliss they'd created for themselves would disappear. As she'd traced her fingers over his features, teased his hair, felt his heart beat against hers, she willed him to understand, to feel what she felt. To be willing to take the chance.

Until Jason, she hadn't known what it was to love another person. But because of him, now she'd never forget.

She'd awakened alone with only the sun to greet her, and waited until she was in the shower before she let the tears flow.

It had already begun.

"Not yet." Jason searched through a few piles. "Here."

"Did you scan it already?"

"It was next on my list. Hang on." He stood, froze when she didn't move, then shifted around her. When he returned, he had a small device in his hands. "It's wireless." He put the picture in, accessed an app on his phone and hit scan. "I'll have it sent to both our computers. Feel free to play around with it if you want."

"Great," she lied. Like she knew what to do with a photo editing program. She'd just needed an excuse to get a conversation going.

His smile was quick and perfunctory before he turned back to the collection of documents open on his screen.

"Jason—"

"There's an extra smoothie for you in the fridge."

"Thanks. Jason—"

"I've got a lead on some of these shell companies. I was thinking if I could get some concrete details, maybe Eamon and the FBI—"

"Jason, stop." All she wanted to do was touch him. To hold him. To tell him that it was okay to be scared. "We have to talk."

"You were right." His hands hovered over the keyboard. "About my past. I do use it as a shield. Not to protect myself. To protect you."

"To protect me from what?" She leaned on the edge of the desk and waited. She'd wait forever if she had to. "I haven't seen anything I need protection from."

"Not yet, no. But you will." He was talking to her, but he wasn't looking at her. "I am who my father made me, Kyla. I've done things…" He shook his head. "I've done things no one knows about. Things I needed to in order to survive. I don't want that darkness anywhere near you. If we tried to do this, if we made a go of things, I'd be terrified every day that I'd mess up. I know you don't believe that will happen."

"No," she said quietly. "I don't."

"But I do." Now he did look at her, and the resolve

she found in his gaze shattered the hope she'd built up the past few days. "I do love you, Kyla. I've loved you from the moment I first met you. I've taken a lot of chances over the years. I've done a lot of things I shouldn't have, a lot I'd do again. I will not take a chance with you."

"In other words, you'd rather I not be hurt than happy." It stung to say it; it was even more painful to accept it. But she loved him too much to push him into something that would make him miserable. That was the last thing she wanted for him.

"There's only one problem with that argument, Jason." She bent down and pressed her lips to his, one last time. "No one is ever completely safe. From anything."

He managed to make it until late afternoon before the walls closed in.

He'd been examining documents and spreadsheets until his eyelids drooped, all the while knowing that the only thing he really wanted in life was down the hall just waiting for him to acknowledge he was wrong.

Except he wasn't wrong. He wanted to be.

But he wasn't.

Feeling as if he couldn't breathe, he closed his laptop he'd transferred everything over to and grabbed his jacket. He expected to find Kyla across the hall, but her room was empty. It crossed his mind to leave without saying anything, but that was the coward's way out and honestly? He was already doing that in one sense. No need to pile on. They were on borrowed time as far as how much longer they'd be staying here. As soon as Tristan decided to come back home—or was apprehended, whichever came first—Jason was happy to continue the charade. For as long as he could.

He found her in the kitchen, wearing one of his favorite dresses—a brilliant pink with turquoise flowers. The fabric swirled around her bare toes and the scarf tied around her curls trailed down to the base of her spine. She was standing at the counter, making a large salad, humming along with the popular music emanating from the digital device on the counter.

He stood in the doorway, stunned into silence, as he drew in the sight he'd carry with him the rest of his life.

"If you're just going to stand there, you can at least be useful." She turned and scooped up a spoonful of veggies. "Let me know if this tastes all right?"

He set his jacket and computer on the counter, then walked over. "You didn't put any arsenic in it, did you?"

"Not yet." Kyla smirked. "Depends on what you say next."

He accepted the sample, ate and grinned at the exploding flavors. "It's delicious."

"Good answer." She glanced around him at his belongings. "Going somewhere?"

"The Brass Eagle. Vince is still acting bodyguard at the hospital and with Halloween this weekend—"

"Halloween. Right." She sighed. "I guess I'll tell Lynn you had other plans then."

"Dinner. I forgot." And he actually had. "This is probably for the best. I don't think either of us is up for pretending anymore."

"No," Kyla said. "I don't think we are."

"Kyla—"

"Have a good evening, Jason." Just before he was out of earshot he heard her say, "I love you."

He opened his mouth—the words right there—but he knew speaking them, however true they might be, would only make things harder. Before he succumbed to temptation, before he surrendered to what he wanted more than anything in the world, he turned around.

And walked away.

## Chapter 16

"Had a feeling when you weren't answering your phone I'd find you here." Jack McTavish slid into the booth across from Jason, who was nursing the same beer he'd ordered two hours ago. Laptop open, he was so focused on connecting the dots he almost didn't hear the detective. "Hey, earth to Jason." Jack leaned in and smiled. "What gives?"

"Huh?" Jason finally glanced up. The bar had filled up since his arrival and two of the employees had unexpectedly asked for extra hours. All the better for the questions Jason had spinning in his head. The noise level was about normal, meaning loud and animated, but he was used to it.

"I've been calling you for the past hour," Jack said. "What'd you turn your phone off for?"

"Oh, that. Yeah." He motioned to where it lay silent

on the table beside him. He needed the time to focus and didn't want to be tempted to call Kyla. "Distracting."

"Hey, Jack." Trudy, The Brass Eagle's lead server, popped over with her tray. "You want your usual? Double shot of Jack Daniels?"

"Uh, no, actually. I'll just have a beer. Whatever's on tap."

"Sure thing."

Jack waved at him when they were alone. "Jason, you listening to me?"

"Not really." Excitement was pumping through his blood at top speed. He didn't just have the goods on Liam and Colin O'Callaghan. He'd unlocked the brothers' entire operation. The drugs, the money laundering, the bank accounts. Emails, newspaper articles, even family history going back to Liam and Colin's father, who, it turned out, had been the instigator of the family's criminal enterprise.

"Maybe this will get your attention."

"I'm listening." He really wasn't. He clicked through the archive of articles stored in one particular folder.

"Liam O'Callaghan's dead."

It took a moment for the words to compute. "What?" Jason's head shot up. "Dead? How? Where? Wh—"

"Night Crawler. One bullet, straight to the head, then the body was set on fire. Nearly took the entire block with him. You didn't hear the sirens? Fire went to three alarms. They found him in the office. Of course, they're waiting on DNA, but…"

"That's not good."

"That Liam's dead or about the fire?"

Jason didn't have an answer to that.

"He must have ticked someone off big time," Jack said, tossing a handful of the pretzel mix from the bowl on the table into his mouth. "Who kills an O'Callaghan? And in his own place?"

"Not Tristan Wainwright," Jason said. The more he dug, the more he thought Kyla was right. The kid was being set up. "I take it you haven't found him yet?"

Jack shook his head. "What's got you so preoccupied?"

Jason scowled. "I don't think you want me to answer that question."

"About what you're working on? Or about Kyla?"

"One, you don't want the answer to…yet, and the other—"

"And the other you don't want to talk about. All right." Jack was quiet for a few seconds. "For what it's worth, Greta thinks you two are perfect together."

Jason snorted, tapped through more files. What was he going to do with all this information? Give it to Jack and hope they could somehow use it against… well, Colin O'Callaghan? Or maybe the Feds' standing was a bit more…flexible when it came to illegally obtained evidence. "Greta's wrong. Sorry," he said quickly and looked at the detective in time to see Jack's gaze sharpen.

"*You're* wrong. My wife's right. And not just because she's my wife. Because I've seen you and Kyla together. You fit. Come on, man, she's crazy about you. Don't know what you're thinking, walking away from that."

"I'm thinking she has enough career issues going on right now. She doesn't need an ex-con dragging her down."

Jack pulled out his cell. "Buddy, you keep costing me money. I have to text Cole and tell him I owe him fifty bucks."

"What does that even mean?"

"It means I had faith that you weren't deluded enough to think you aren't the one for her. Cole figured your past was getting in the way."

"I thought Eden was the gossip," Jason said. Desperate to change the subject, he clicked on the folder marked family documents and nearly shivered at the file named "parents' death." He clicked it open, then clicked on Seamus O'Callaghan's certificate. As he scanned the information, he could feel the blood draining from his face. "Jack?"

"What? I'm going to need another beer." He lifted a hand only to have Jason reach over and shove it down.

Dread pooled in his gut. "I'm going to tell you something, but I need you to promise not to ask where I got it."

"Conversations that start that way never end well. Go ahead."

"Liam and Colin's parents." He closed Seamus's certificate, opened the brothers' mother's—Maeve's. "The papers and online articles reported they died in a fire ten years ago in Boston. I'm looking at their autopsy reports." Jason stared at his friend. "Gunshot wounds. Point blank to the head. Then set on fire."

All humor evaporated on Jack's face. "That's no coincidence." Jack hesitated. "Colin?"

"Must be. Except..."

"Except what? I feel like you're existing in a completely different timeline than me. What are you reading?"

"The encrypted jump drive I borrowed from Colin O'Callaghan's office safe the other night."

"I'm sorry, the what?"

He didn't even try to excuse or explain it. Right now, he didn't care one whit about consequences. "You can decide what to do with me later, but at the moment, I'm looking at the entire O'Callaghan enterprise on my screen. You name it, it's in here." He clicked on another family file, speed-reading every single article and document. "Sister, Caitlin, reportedly died in the same fire. It was…oh, no." He pulled up a photo of Caitlin O'Callaghan, taken around the same time as the photo Jason had seen in Colin's office the other night. "It's the eyes. How did I not notice her eyes?"

Fingers flying, he opened an online window. "Don't even ask me what I'm doing right now, Jack, because I can't—"

"Not asking." Jack was out of his seat and came around to look at the computer. "Do what you need to."

It took him ten minutes, but in those minutes he hacked into Dr. Forrest Wainwright's website, rode it into his server, which in turn took him into the payments portal. Once he had Wainwright's bank account information, he found the business's revenue and billing system. From there it was a quick hop into the patient files.

"I can't believe you can do this," Jack muttered in what sounded like awe. "I thought what you did to help Ashley last year was amazing, but this… Lynn Wainwright?"

"Barnaby Faustus told us that Forrest met his second wife when she was a patient. I just need to confirm…" He wanted to be wrong. More than anything, he wanted to be wrong. But as he tapped open the before and after photo files, he had proof he wasn't. Those sharp green eyes. Despite the extensive work she'd had done, there was no hiding those eyes. "That's it—"

"I don't understand," Jack said. "What does Wainwright's wife have to do with this?"

"That's not just Forrest Wainwright's wife." Jason pulled up the photo Bess Carmody had taken of Tristan, Liam and Colin O'Callaghan, and the car. A few clicks in his photo editing program, a bit of lighting here, brightening there, and…fear locked around his throat as he stared at the woman in the backseat. "That's Caitlin O'Callaghan."

Kyla hefted the blue porcelain bowl of corn salad in one arm and pulled her front door closed with her free hand. It all felt so normal, dinner at the neighbor's. After the events of the last week, normal sounded like a perfect respite.

The sun had faded, and the cool night maintained just enough warmth that she could forego a sweater. The early evening stars were beginning to twinkle as the sky darkened and welcomed the moon. The only thing that would have made it perfect was if Jason were here.

Having dinner out—especially after the hours she'd spent distracting herself with everything from laundry to cleaning, to packing up to go home—was exactly what she needed.

She'd left her phone on vibrate for most of the day,

and only turned it on when she slid it into her purse, which she had hanging across her torso. "Gotta put Jason out of your mind," she told herself for the hundredth time. "You don't want him doing something that'll just cause him pain." Didn't mean she wasn't trying to figure out a way to get him to look beyond the unknown. She couldn't imagine the past he lived with. How could she expect him to just get over it?

She crossed the street and smiled as she spotted Alicia racing around the Halloween tombstones in her front yard. "Hi, Alicia!" Kyla stepped into the dimly lit decorations, shuddering a bit at the creepy sensation racing down her spine.

"Hi!" Alicia dived, yelped and came back up again with her arm full of dog. The grumpy looking bulldog turned its head and gave her a good, if not reluctant, lick. "Look what Lynn got me today."

"Wow. Look at him." Something niggled at the back of her mind. "Is it a him?"

"Her, actually." Alicia grinned and set the dog back down. "Her name's Doxie. I've been wanting a dog for so long. Lynn said after everything that's happened, we should have something happy. So she went out this afternoon and picked her out for me."

"Doxie." Kyla held out her hand, let the dog sniff. "Funny. I've heard that name recently." Out of the corner of her eye, the shadow of a man passed across the living room window. Tall. Thin. Red hair. Her chest tightened. The hair on her arms leapt to attention. "Any word about your brother?"

"No." Alicia dropped down to play with Doxie. "Dad's still out looking for him. Lynn said he called but not to

worry. He'd be home before we left for New York tomorrow."

"So your dad's not inside."

"No. That's Lynn's brother, Uncle Colin. He came
over for dinner, too. Where's Josh?"

*Lynn's brother, Colin. A dog named Doxie. Leaving
for New York...*

Kyla's ears roared. So much made sense and yet...

Panic attempted to grab hold, but she shoved it down,
deep down, where it couldn't hurt her. The answers to
questions buzzed in her head. Answers that only spelled
out one thing: danger.

"Kyla?" Alicia said again. "Is Josh coming?"

"Um, he had to take care of something. But you
know what?" Kyla forced a laugh. "I forgot my cell
in the house. Why don't you come check out our pool
while I find it?"

"Really?" Alicia's eyes brightened. "Okay, cool. Let
me just take Doxie inside—"

"No time." Kyla grabbed Alicia's arm and brought
her with her.

Doxie let out chest-deep barks even as Alicia cried
out.

They were halfway across the street when Kyla heard
the door to Lynn's house open. "Alicia? Kyla?"

Kyla could only think of one thing to do.

She tightened her hold on Alicia's arm and ran.

Ticking off Detective Jack McTavish really wasn't
on Jason's list of things to do, but where Kyla was concerned, rational thinking and Jason parted ways. She
was walking into the house of an O'Callaghan.

Leaving Jack behind to call in whatever reinforcements he felt necessary, Jason bolted out the back door of The Brass Eagle's kitchen and jogged to his SUV. With his laptop tucked under one arm, he dug his keys out of his pocket when he heard the click.

Jason froze.

Even after all these years, he knew the sound of a gun being cocked when he heard it.

"Whoever you are, there are cops inside." Jason raised the hand holding his keys. He turned, slowly, expecting each inch he moved to be his last. His gaze landed on the gun first, then the shaking hand aiming it directly at his chest. Jason pushed through the fear and looked at the face behind the arm. Stark blond hair, pale skin, frantic eyes in a young face. He was strung out, exhausted and clearly terrified. Definitely not a good combination for either himself or the kid. "Tristan."

The teen flinched, as if hearing his name hurt. "Shut up. Just…shut up. Do you have it?"

"Have what?"

"That!" Tristan waved the gun at the computer. "I need what you took."

"What I took when?"

"At the club. The night of the raid. You were in Colin's office."

Jason shrugged.

"There are cameras!" Tristan yelled. "I've seen the tape. Just give it to me. Please!"

It was the please that sliced through Jason's heart. "I can do that." Jason held out the laptop. "But it won't do any good. I've already sent everything to the police and FBI."

Tristan cried out in frustration, doubled his hold on the gun and pressed his finger against the trigger. Both he and Jason jumped when the bar's back door banged open.

"Tristan, don't," Jason ordered. "Don't look behind you. You look at me, okay?" Jason set the laptop and his keys on the top of his car, held up both hands and slowly closed the distance between them. "I know you don't want to hurt me. If you did, I'd already be dead. You want a way out. I can help you with that."

For the first time in his life, as he shifted his gaze from the gun, to the boy, to Jack, Jason made the intentional decision to put all his faith in a man wearing a badge.

The barely lit streetlights cast the full parking lot in shadows, but Jack had clearly assessed the situation accurately. He reached for his weapon, but Jason shook his head once, narrowed his eyes. Jack kept his hand on the gun's butt.

"Tristan, I need you to talk to me." Jason shifted his full attention back on Tristan. "Tell me what's been going on. Do you know about Bess?"

"Bess?" Tristan's eyes filled. "Bess is dead." He moved closer and the gun wavered.

"No, Tristan." Jason stepped close enough to feel the heat radiating from the young man's body. "Bess is alive. She's in the hospital and she's in bad shape, but she's there. I can prove it if you let me." He pulled out his phone. "My brother's watching over her. We didn't want anyone else to hurt her."

"She's alive?" Tristan's voice cracked, and for a moment, so did his determination. "It doesn't matter! I

have to get what they told me to get and I have to..."
he took a shuddering breath. "I have to kill you. If I
don't, they'll—"

Jack moved in behind. The sound of sirens blared in
the distance. His hand still poised on the butt of his gun.

"They'll what?" Jason asked softly. He did not want
this boy's blood on his hands. Not if there was anything
he could do to avoid it. "Tristan, tell me what they'll do
if you don't kill me? It's Colin, isn't it? It's Colin who's
threatening you?"

"No! Not Colin. They aren't threatening me." Tears
spilled down the boy's face and for the blink of a moment, Jason thought he was looking in a mirror. "My
sister. Alicia. Lynn told me she'd kill her if I didn't do
what she said."

Kyla had been right. Alicia was what grounded
Tristan. "When did she tell you that? Tonight?"

"Every night. For years. Ever since she forced my
dad to marry her. She told him she'd kill the two of us if
he didn't do everything she said. The drugs. The money.
The surgeries. I stopped believing her. I told her I was
done, finished, when I got out of rehab. I just wanted
to be free of her. I told her we had proof, that we'd go
to the cops, but..." Desperation mingled with shock in
his haunted gaze.

"But she found out about Julia Summerton and killed
her."

Tristan sobbed. "I tried to help. I tried to stop her,
but..." His vision cleared to the point Jason feared he
was having a moment of clarity. "You can't stop them."

"Tristan, look at me. Look at me!" Jason took another
step. "Tristan." He gentled his voice. "Let me help you.

Let us help you. We can stop her. Me, my friends. Let me stop her for you. Let me give you back your family."

Tristan opened his mouth, as if trying to find the words. "You can't. I've done too much. She's going to kill Alicia and I can't—"

It happened so fast. Tristan shifted his hold on the gun and turned it, brought it up under his chin just as Jack leapt at him from behind. Jason dived forward, grabbed Tristan's arm with both hands and wrenched it down just as the gun went off. Jason felt the bullet's heat as it ricocheted off the asphalt. He knocked the gun loose of the boy's grip and heard it clatter to the ground as he pulled Tristan hard toward him and into his arms.

"That's not the answer," Jason whispered as the boy sobbed against his chest. "I promise you, that is not the answer." He held onto him as Jack retrieved the gun and moved away to meet the officers who'd arrived on scene.

"I'm sorry," Tristan's cries were muffled by Jason's shirt. "I'm so sorry. For everything."

"I know you are." Jason choked back his own emotion. "I'm going to do everything I can to help you make it right. I'm going to get you help, okay?" He tightened his hold. "But you need to do one thing for me."

"What?"

"You need to trust me." He set the boy back, gripped his shoulders and looked him straight in the eye. "Please go with Detective McTavish."

Panic surged in Tristan's face.

"He'll take care of you. Won't you, Jack?" Jason's question left no room for debate, even as he saw hesitation pass across the detective's face as he joined them.

"I'm going to have these officers drive you to the station where you'll be safe," Jack assured them. "And in a bit, Tristan, Jason's going to come and we'll get this all straightened out. Bowie? Clarke?" He signaled the deputies over. "You got him? No cuffs. He's under our protection," he added under his breath and received a nod from Bowie in return.

"Wait!" Jason yelled at the last second. "Tristan, how much does Lynn know? About me and Kyla? Does she know we moved in to watch you?"

"Yeah. She knows everything," Tristan said in a defeated tone. "She always has."

"Grab your laptop," Jack ordered as he headed to his car. "I'll drive."

"I don't understand." Alicia cried as Kyla tugged her toward the house. "What's going on? Where are you taking me?"

"Someplace you'll be safe."

"Safe from what? Kyla, you're scaring me."

"I know." Kyla had seconds to check before she slammed and locked the front door. Lynn and Colin were racing their way. Doxie was yelping and jumping around in circles on the Wainwrights' front lawn. "I know you're scared and I'm sorry, but you need to trust me." She crouched down and looked into the girl's frantic eyes. "I promise, I only want to keep you safe. I think deep down you know from who, right?"

"Lynn?"

"Yes." Half right. "Come with me." Kyla ran around the staircase and into the office. The second she clicked the secret panel button, a bit of the fear eased. She keyed in the code she'd seen Barnaby use and the door popped open. "You need to stay in here." She pivoted Alicia by the arms into the room. "There's a phone inside. I want you to call 911. Tell them you need to talk to Detective Cole Delaney or Jack McTavish. Can you remember those names?"

"Yes." Alicia's eyes were wide. "Doxie...?"

"She'll be fine. If they were going to hurt her, they never would have given her to you. Cole Delaney or Jack McTavish. No one else, do you hear me? Only Cole or Jack."

"Okay." Clearly, the girl was confused, but she nodded.

"No one can get in here without the code. So I need you to stay in here and wait until we get you."

"Stay with me." Alicia pulled on her hand.

Kyla heard pounding on the front door. Her mind spun. She could just step inside, use the phone to call Jason or Jack or Cole herself, but that would give Colin O'Callaghan and whoever Lynn really was time to get away. She couldn't let that happen. They needed to be stopped. Her safety didn't matter. Not when she could delay them. Not when she believed Jason would be back soon. She'd taken an oath to protect and defend this city. Taking down the O'Callaghans would stop the flow of PoWWer. And she wanted them to pay for everything they'd done, including killing her friend. "I can't stay with you. I need to make sure they are kept away from you and that my friends can arrest them. You'll be fine." Kyla tried to reassure her.

Wood splintered as someone threw their weight against the front door.

"What if Lynn comes in?" Alicia asked as her eyes filled with tears.

"She can't. Not without the code." She needed to stall for time and get them away from this room. "The only other person who has it is Josh. We're not going to let anything happen to you, I promise. Now go make that call." Because she needed it as much as Alicia seemed to, Kyla gave her a quick hug and kiss on the forehead. "Good girl. Stand back."

Kyla pulled the door closed and waited until she heard the click of the steel bolts before she slid the panel back in place.

She ran into the hall just as she saw the front door splinter open. She ran at full speed through the kitchen and out the back patio doors before drawing them shut behind her. The light from the solar lamps lining the path seemed sunshine-bright. Kyla yanked loose as many as she could and threw them as far as she could. A few landed in the pool, but the yard dipped into darkness. The dense shrubbery that had provided the oasis setting now promised refuge. Even as she heard footsteps coming through the house, shouts and angry yells echoing dully from inside, she wedged herself into the bushes surrounding the waterfall. Hugging herself against the rock, she sank back into the protection of the trees, took out her cell and called Jason.

"We'll get there in time." Jack's assurances to Jason were like music to his ears as they sped down Highway 16 toward Rancho Murieta.

To Jason, time seemed to slow and speed up at the same time. He needed to be there. With her. Now. He never should have left Kyla alone. And why had he left her alone? Because he'd been too scared of his own feelings to do the smart thing.

His entire body pulsed like a raw, exposed nerve.

All these years, all his life, Jason thought he understood what terror felt like. The awful years spent with his father, his time in prison… It all paled in comparison to the heart-lurching realization he could lose Kyla. Lose her before he ever really gave them a chance.

"Jason?" Jack snapped as he increased speed, the siren roaring into the night. The visor lights blinked incessantly. "You with me?"

"Yes." He stared down at his phone, willing it to ring. It was nearing seven-thirty. Well past the time Kyla was due to have dinner at the Wainwrights. What he wouldn't give for Kyla to be terminally late, but if anything, she was always, always early. "I'm with you."

"I've been where you are. When Fremont took Greta onto that roof. I know the fear can be paralyzing. You need to fight that, all right?" Jack's dashboard lit up with an incoming call. He tapped a button on his steering wheel. "Cole. What do you have?"

"Call just came in from 911. Alicia Wainwright." Jason swore.

"I've got her on the other line," Cole said. "Hang on. There's backup and SWAT on the way, should be about two minutes behind you. Okay, Jason—"

"Josh," Jason corrected instantly. "She knows me as Josh."

"All right, Josh is on the line, Alicia. Go ahead."

"Josh?" The girl's voice was coated in tears. "Is that you?"

"I'm right here, Alicia." Jason tamped down his emotions. "Are you all right?"

"Yes. Kyla put me in this weird room because she's afraid Lynn's going to hurt me. She told me to call. She said you have the code to get me out."

A breath of relief escaped. "That's right, I do. And I'm almost there. Is Kyla hurt? Can you put her on the phone?"

"She's not here."

Jason's heart stumbled over itself. "She's not in the room with you? Where is she?"

"Out there with them. She said she needed to stop them from getting away."

Jack reached out and tapped the mute button. "What is she talking about? What room?"

"There's a safe room in the house we're staying in," Jason told him. "Kyla must have put Alicia in there before..." He untapped the mute button. "Them? Them who, Alicia?" Jason asked.

"Lynn and her brother, Colin. We were supposed to have dinner. What's wrong? Did I do something wrong?"

"No, sweetheart, no, you did just fine. Nothing's wrong," Jack cut in when Jason couldn't find the right words. "We're going to put you on the phone with one of our officers and they'll talk to you the entire time you're in that room, okay? We'll be there before you know it."

"Who are you?" Alicia asked with enough spark to make Jason grin. "Kyla told me only to talk to Cole or Jack."

"I'm Jack," the detective said. "And we're just a few minutes out. I know you probably can't hear anything outside right now, but you will soon, I promise. Just stay calm and talk with my officer. Cole?"

"Transferring her now, Jack."

Jack disconnected just as Jason's phone lit up. Kyla's name blinked onto the screen for a fraction of a second before the call went dead.

"How fast can this car go?" Jason posed as Jack pressed his foot down on the gas.

"Let's find out."

Kyla had just tapped Jason's number when the patio lights clicked on and the doors slid open. Afraid Jason's voice might be heard, she disconnected the call. She hit a series of icons, then placed the phone screen up, as far away from the waterfall's white noise as she could manage. The shrubs rustled as she tried to settle back in place.

"Over there!" Lynn's voice snapped like a twig through the darkness. "Kyla?" she called in a voice that had Kyla shivering. "You can either come out on your own or we can hunt you down. We'll get you either way."

Kyla stayed where she was, debating her options. She had no doubt they'd fire at will into the bushes and once she was dead, they'd have no reason to stick around, especially when they couldn't get to Alicia.

Lynn and Colin had one thing Kyla needed, something she'd sworn to get no matter what she had to do.

As she saw Colin O'Callaghan move toward her, Kyla rose, gripped her fingers hard against the rock and pushed herself out. "I'm here." She kept her hands up, cried out in pain when Colin's hand locked around her wrist and wrenched her arm behind her. "I don't have any weapons," she told him.

"Clearly," Lynn said, slowly lowering her gun to her side. She walked around the pool, coming into focus thanks to the brighter light.

The friendliness Kyla had previously been on the receiving end of was completely gone.

"Where's the girl?" Lynn demanded.

"Safe," was all Kyla said, wincing as Colin wrenched her arm higher. "Where's your brother?"

"Liam?" Lynn waved off the question as if it were a mosquito. "He's where he can't disappoint us anymore, with our parents. Thankfully. He was just another piece of baggage who couldn't get himself together. He got scared. Wanted out. Wanted all of us to get out. Men like that are always high risk to keep around for long."

An odd sense of serenity passed over her. They'd killed their brother. That meant it was only a matter of time before they killed her. "You don't like loose ends. Is that why you killed Julia and Kevin?"

Colin snorted and tightened his hold on her, pushed her toward the edge of the pool. "Like we're going to confess everything just before the heroes come blasting in to save the day."

"That reminds me, where is Jason?" Lynn strode around the pool, turning in circles as she searched high and low. "Yes, I know who he really is. Jason Sutton. Ex-con private investigator. I thought I could make this quick by getting you both over to dinner."

"He's having dinner with our friends. Cops," Kyla added. "He's already called me twice and I haven't answered, which means he'll be home soon." Never in her life had she put so much faith into a lie. "You could leave right now, probably make a decent getaway. Why are you sticking around?"

"Enough with the questions," Colin spat. "Let's just kill her and find the girl."

Kyla smirked. "Good luck with that."

Lynn stalked over, raised her gun at Kyla and pulled back the hammer. "Tell me where she is."

Kyla swallowed hard. "No."

"Just shoot her already," Colin ordered.

Lynn glared at her, then, with a sly smile, lowered her weapon. "You think you're so smart. You and your counselor friend, Julia. She's not so smart now, is she? One shot of junk and she was gone. Didn't even put up much of a fight."

Kyla fought to keep her expression neutral, even as she shifted her eyes to Lynn's hands.

Lynn's smile expanded as she examined the bruises and scrapes on her knuckles. "Can't turn that DA mind of yours off, can you, Kyla?" Lynn stepped closer. "Yes, I know who you are. Forrest recognized you right away from some charity event at that youth center Bess went to. He said it was just a coincidence but, to be safe, I had Tristan set a little trap." She made an explosive gesture with her free hand. "Boom! I should have made the call sooner. Then we could have disappeared and put this all behind us."

"You killed Julia," Kyla accused. "And tried to kill Bess."

"Tried to kill you, too, but that ridiculous boyfriend of yours yanked you out of the way of the car."

Kyla closed her eyes in relief. "It wasn't Tristan driving."

"Tristan? Please." Colin joined his sister in a laugh. "Kid's nothing more than a barely-useful tool."

"Family love," Lynn sighed mockingly. "Some people will do anything to protect the people they care about. But you know what I learned a long time ago? Family makes you weak. Now, one last time, Kyla." Lynn raised her gun once more at Kyla. "Where. Is. The. Girl?"

With lights and sirens off, Jack led the train of patrol cars and a SWAT van in through the gates of Faustus Estates. They pulled to a stop at the end of the block, quietly exiting the vehicles. Jason followed Jack's lead.

Behind them, eight armed deputies dropped into formation. Before they reached the house, Jack stopped. "Here." He crouched, pulled a small caliber weapon from an ankle holster and held it out to Jason. "I know you don't use them—"

Jason shook his head. "I won't need it."

"You can't go in there unarmed," Jack said coolly. "I won't allow it. Truth be told, you shouldn't be going in at all."

"Try and stop me." However this went down, he wasn't going to let Jack get in trouble because he'd given his backup weapon to a civilian with a criminal record. A criminal record not one person had thrown in his face.

"Don't tell me you have a gun in that computer of yours."

"Not the computer. Wait." He grabbed Jack's arm when he started for the house and saw Colin's bulldog, Doxie, racing around the front yard, barking up a storm.

"They aren't there." His heart nearly stopped when he noticed the door to his house standing open. And in the street, shattered pottery and corn salad splattered all around. "She led them inside."

"All right." Jack drew his team in and gave them quick orders. The SWAT team then dispersed around the perimeter of the property. Behind them, Jason heard another car pull in. Seconds later, not only did Cole and Vince appear, but right behind them were former and current FBI agents Slade Palmer and Eamon Quinn, respectively.

It looked, Jason thought in a bit of a haze, like watching a lineup of action movie heroes stride into battle.

"Anyone else coming?" Jason asked as the new arrivals drew their weapons.

"No one else is left," Slade said. "O'Callaghans were on my radar back before I went undercover at Folsom prison. Appreciate the chance to be part of their end."

"Thought you might like some federal cover," Eamon, his red hair glowing beneath the streetlights, tossed in. "Any idea where in the house they might be?"

"Upstairs," Jason stated. "She'd want them as far from Alicia as she could get them."

"Great. We'll go up," Jack said. "You get to the safe room and Alicia. Slade? You're with Jason."

"Understood."

"I don't need—" Jason tried.

"Need doesn't enter into this. You have backup, or you don't go in. Ready?" Jack raised his weapon. "Go."

Jason stayed low, following Jack into the house before Jack and the others broke off and Jason aimed silently for the office. He kept the door open long enough for Slade to enter.

"Where's the button for the safe room?"

"Bookshelf. Third row, center." But Jason didn't go near the bookcase. While Slade exposed the metal door, Jason hit the desk switch for the secret armory. He had a loaded Glock stuffed into the back waistband of his jeans before Slade could comment.

"You sure you want to do that?" Slade asked. The man stood a good six inches taller than Jason, and had at least thirty pounds on him. He'd spent two years in prison undercover to get evidence against one of the most dangerous human traffickers in the country, but spent the last six months happily retired and married to Jack's sister Ashley.

Jason grabbed another pistol, checked the magazine and chamber and slid the safety off. It had been years, literal years, since he held a weapon. It should have scared him, but the fear he had coursing through his system had absolutely nothing to do with the guns. And everything to do with Kyla's safety. "Absolutely."

"You know where they are." Slade glanced at the ceiling. "You sent Jack in the wrong direction."

"I sent him in the safest direction," Jason said. "This isn't his fight. It's mine."

"Understood." Slade moved toward the door. "I've got your six." He nodded to Jason. "Let's go get your girl."

It was odd, Kyla thought, as she stared at the barrel pressing against her forehead. This upwelling of emotion surged and in its wake she had only thoughts of her

parents, of her friends, of Eden, Cole and little Chloe
Ann. Of Simone and Vince and the baby Kyla would
never see. But mostly there was Jason. Jason in all his
irritating, frustrating, solitary determination to keep her
away from his heart even as he'd slid completely and
utterly into hers. She would meet her end, if not loved,
in love and there was gratitude that she'd been blessed
with that connection.

Jason. If she concentrated hard, she could almost see
him, moving through the house, through the kitchen,
beneath the...

Wait a minute. Her eyes went wide. That *was* Jason.
And... Slade Palmer? Her heart skipped a beat. Where
Jason and Slade were, certainly Jack and the others followed. She glanced up, saw shadows moving across
the back windows. Bushes and shrubs rustled in the
breezeless night.

These toxic siblings, were trying to rob her of the
life she wanted. The life she'd worked so hard to attain.
The life she needed with Jason.

She had a chance, a chance to have everything. A
chance to fight. Surrender was not an option. Not when
she was so close. "You kill me, you will never find Alicia."

"Kill her already and let's go." Colin released her
wrist and stepped away as Lynn moved closer. "The
money doesn't matter. We'll find a way to get it later."

"I want her dead," Lynn seethed. "She's just like her
friend. Just like Bess. She'll keep coming and coming
until we have no other choice."

"You're already out of time." Kyla placed her fate in
the hands of the man she loved. "They're here, Lynn.

The police. Jason. Go ahead." She came forward, raised her hands as Colin darted into the bushes only to sound as if he'd run into a brick wall. Moments later he emerged, his arms trapped behind him by two members of the SWAT team.

Lynn's finger twitched as Jason and Slade burst out the patio doors. "Police!" Slade shouted.

Kyla brought her hands down hard on Lynn's arm, knocked her hand wide and crouched as Lynn spun and attempted to catch her balance. She aimed wildly, fired off the first shot just as Kyla pivoted and caught Lynn behind the knees. More shots rang out. Kyla had never heard anything so loud. Lynn paused, and after hovering for a beat, pitched forward.

She fell face first into the pool. Blood spread like a twisting vine through the water.

"Jason!" Jack hollered from the upstairs window. "You sent us up here on purpose!"

"I wanted all angles covered," Jason said as Slade tugged the gun out of Jason's hand, shot him a look, then turned around and walked back into the house.

Kyla pushed herself to her feet as SWAT led Colin O'Callaghan out of the backyard. Suddenly, her knees went weak, but before she hit the ground, Jason's arms were there to catch her. To draw her close. To hold her.

"I've got you," he murmured as she held him, shock rippling through her body. "You're all right. I've got you, Kyla."

"I've got you, too," she said on a laugh even as the terror and adrenaline continued to course through her blood. She adjusted her hold, linked her arms around his neck and squeezed. "And guess what?"

"What?"

She tilted her head back, stared into his eyes. "I'm not letting you go."

"Guess what back?" His smile was slow, but steady and wide, and thrilled her right down to her tingling toes. "That sounds perfect to me."

# Epilogue

"Forget my Aphrodite costume," Darcy Ford grumbled from her chair in Kyla's bedroom. "I should just go to this party dressed as a third wheel."

Alicia Wainwright, arms full of Doxie with a fascinated Ninja trailing behind her, stopped in the doorway of Kyla's room. "What's a third wheel?"

"Something you'll never have to worry about being," Darcy told her with a flip of her curls. "You all settled in Kyla's guest room?"

"Yes." Wearing a costume that would have put any space princess to shame, Alicia sat on the edge of Kyla's bed and watched as Kyla finished putting on her makeup. "My dad said to thank you again for letting me stay with you until my aunt comes to pick me up next week."

"So you're moving to Los Angeles, huh?" Darcy asked. "That sounds pretty cool."

"I guess." Alicia shrugged. "My dad said he did some pretty bad things. Tristan, too. They have a lot of stuff to deal with."

"They'll both have all the help they need, Alicia, I promise," Kyla told her. "You want to give Ninja and Doxie their dinner?"

"People or dog food?" She lifted her dog to her cheek and nuzzled him.

"I think they've earned a treat."

"People then. I can do that. Come on, Ninja. The adults want to talk about me." Ninja let out one of his cute woofs as he zipped out of the room behind her.

"That's not what we're going to do!" Darcy called after her, then got up and closed the door. "Okay, that's kind of what we're going to do. Tell me the rest. And where did you come up with that costume at the last minute?" She walked up behind Kyla. "You make the real Cleopatra look like a troll."

Kyla smiled. Everyone needed a Darcy in their life. "Where did I leave off?"

"With Caitlin facedown in the pool."

"Right. With the evidence Jason turned over against the O'Callaghan organization, and since he's the only one left to prosecute, Colin O'Callaghan confessed and turned state's evidence against their business partners. Eamon and the FBI are trying to keep up with all the dominoes that are toppling."

"What's going to happen to Alicia's father?"

"That'll be up to the courts. He'll get some sympathy from prosecutors. Colin intercepted Dr. Wainwright when he left to look for Tristan, kept him drugged and unconscious so he and Caitlin could get away with Alicia."

"Why the girl? That doesn't make much sense…does it?" Darcy muttered.

"It's not obvious, no." Not right away, anyway. "Turns out, a lot of those offshore accounts Jason discovered had been opened in Alicia's name. Because who looks for banking fraud under the name of a kid? A lot of those banks required fingerprint or retinal confirmation. They needed her alive."

"Scary brilliant," Darcy said.

"You said it. Lynn, or rather Caitlin, found the perfect patsy. I wouldn't be surprised if Caitlin had something to do with Dr. Wainwright's first wife's death. The timing would make sense. Caitlin became his patient shortly after, drastically changed her appearance, then bided her time and seduced him. Easy to do to a grieving man with a penchant for the good life. She promised him everything he wanted, including a good life for his kids and living in the style he'd been accustomed to. She kept him and Tristan in line by threatening the people they cared most about. Alicia." Kyla grimaced. "I don't know how long it'll be before that family can start to heal. Even if father and son get lenient sentences, that family's going to be broken for a long time."

"It was nice of you to let Alicia stay here. Beats a foster home."

"According to Jason, pretty much anything does."

The doorbell rang. Through the closed door, Kyla heard Alicia yell, "I'll get it!"

"Speak of the devil."

"More like speaking of Marc Antony," Kyla corrected and closed up her liquid liner. "You ready to tackle this Halloween party?"

"I'll keep an eye on Alicia."

"Don't be too worried about her. Max and Allie are bringing Max's niece, Hope, and Eden and Cole are bringing the baby."

"It's about time you stop calling Chloe Ann a baby. Ha, she's probably driving by now," Darcy teased as they went out to greet Jason.

Jason, dressed to the nines in a Roman soldier's uniform, and Alicia were admiring her laser saber when they joined them. When he spotted her, his mouth dropped open. "Wow."

"Come on, kid." Darcy ushered Alicia out of the condo. "We'll head on over. Leave these two alone to smooch."

"Ooooh," Alicia teased. "Be good, Doxie! You, too, Ninja!"

*"Woof."*

Jason smiled and held out his hands for her. "You look gorgeous. Well, you always do anyway, but tonight? You take my breath away." He shook his head as his expression shifted to concern. "You doing okay?"

"I'll get there." She squeezed his hands. "Allie called me last night, gave me a quick therapy session. She suggested I see someone for a while, make sure I keep a handle on things." Every time she closed her eyes she could see that gun. Only in her dreams, it went off. "But tonight? Tonight I want to enjoy with you and our friends at The Brass Eagle."

"Vince called while I was in the car. He and Simone might be late. Said they have an announcement."

"An announcement about what?" Kyla barely had the question out before Jason was grinning. "She's pregnant?"

"Apparently it wasn't food poisoning at all. But don't let on you know. She's dying to tell you herself."

Okay, that was going to be downright impossible. "Did you see Tristan yet?"

"Tomorrow." Jason glanced at her sofa. "I got permission to take him to see Bess at the hospital."

"She's awake?"

"Awake and on the mend. Doctors think she's turned the corner. It'll be rough, but seeing Tristan will help."

"What about her parents?"

"They're…concerned," Jason said with the barest hint of irritation. "Maybe seeing their daughter in the hospital might knock some sense into them. I don't know. We'll have to wait and see. Can we sit and talk for a minute?" He motioned to the couch in front of her bay window.

"Sure." Refusing to give in to the nerves, she let him lead her over. "What's going on?" she asked once they were settled and Doxie and Ninja were busy wrestling over a rope toy.

"I called Alona Lopez today," Jason said. "I wanted to ask her about volunteering at the youth center, helping at risk kids. Sharing my story."

"Really?" Pride swelled inside of her. "I think that's great."

"It feels right. I haven't been able to stop thinking about Tristan."

She rubbed his arm. "I know. Jack told me what happened in the parking lot. He said you did really well with him." Jack had also told her how close Jason had come to dying at the hands of the young man.

"I thought before we take things between us any further," Jason went on, "I should let you know…"

The way he was hedging made her nervous. Didn't he know at this point there wasn't anything he couldn't tell her? "Did you change your mind about getting your record expunged? Do you want Simone to start up the paperwork?"

"No. No, Kyla, I didn't change my mind. And I won't. I need you to accept that. I'm not going to try to erase a past I plan to use as an advantage."

"I don't understand. You can't get a PI license without—"

"I'm not going to get a PI license." He took a deep breath. "I've discussed this with Vince and I told him I'd like to stay on as a consultant while I go back to school."

"Oh." Kyla blinked in surprise. "All right."

"I got my GED in prison, took some college classes, but I want to do more. I want to get my degree in child psychology, maybe become a therapist. I'm not sure yet, but I want to work with kids like Tristan. Kids like me," he added. "Try and stop them from making the same mistakes we did."

If she hadn't already been head over heels in love with the man, that statement alone would have done it. Kyla scooted closer and rested her head on his strong shoulder. "That sounds like an amazing idea."

"Yeah?" The relief in his voice proved they still had a long way to go in building up his confidence.

"Definitely, yeah." She tilted her chin up. "I bet Allie can help you figure stuff out. She's got some experience with all that."

"I already plan to talk to her at the party."

"The party!" Kyla yelped and jumped to her feet. "We'd better get over there. Let me grab my phone." She darted into the kitchen to collect it and half walked, half stumbled back into the living room. "Hey. I missed a bunch of messages from Ward."

"Your boss?" Jason stood. "Something wrong?"

"No, no, everything's fine. Detective Alvarez has withdrawn her complaint, which means I can go back to work!"

"Really? Even though we kept her out of the final confrontation?"

"We might have, but apparently Cole and Jack didn't. They convinced her to take a backseat and in exchange, she got most of the credit for the task force that brought down the O'Callaghans' operation. You want more good news?"

"Why not? We're on a roll."

"Alvarez has been transferred to Los Angeles to head up their new narcotics and organized crime detail. I guess taking PoWWer out of play before it had a chance to get a foothold earns some points. And the news just gets better." Kyla grinned. She ditched her phone and jumped into his arms. "We definitely have a lot to celebrate tonight."

"Even if it's Halloween?"

She pressed her mouth to his. "It's my new favorite holiday. I'm so glad you found me at the morgue that day, Jason Sutton."

He smiled, looked deeply into her eyes. "I love you, Kyla." He let out a pent-up breath. "Have to get used to saying that. And I plan to. Every chance I get."

"In that case, I'll make you a promise, right here and now." She hugged him tight. "I will never, ever get tired of hearing it."

\* \* \* \* \*

## #2219 PROTECTING COLTON'S BABY
*The Coltons of New York* • by Tara Taylor Quinn

ADA Emily Hernandez's life is at risk—so is the child she's carrying. Her much younger former lover, PI Cormac Colton, is willing to play protector to Emily and father to his child. Will their unexpected family survive, or will Emily be silenced for good?

## #2220 CAVANAUGH JUSTICE: DETECTING A KILLER
*Cavanaugh Justice* • by Marie Ferrarella

When NYC detective Danny Doyle finds DNA remains tying Cassandra Cavanaugh to the victim, the determined investigator jumps at the chance to crack her cousin's cold case. If only the detecting duo's chemistry wasn't off the charts...and a serial killer wasn't targeting both of them...

## #2221 HOTSHOT HERO IN DISGUISE
*Hotshot Heroes* • by Lisa Childs

An explosion in a Lake Michigan firehouse has exposed Ethan Sommerly's secret identity. Which means the target he avoided five years ago is now on his back again. Local Tammy Ingles is the only one he can trust. As the danger increases, is Tammy's life now on the line, too?

## #2222 UNDERCOVER COWBOY DEFENDER
*Shelter of Secrets* • by Linda O. Johnston

Luca Almera and her young son found a safe refuge at the highly secret Chance Animal Shelter. But when a deadly stalker targets Luca, undercover K-9 cop Mark Martin will risk his life *and* his heart to keep the vulnerable single mom safe.

HRSCNM0123

# HARLEQUIN
## PLUS

Announcing a **BRAND-NEW**
multimedia subscription service
for romance fans like you!

---

## **Read, Watch and Play.**

Experience the easiest way to get
the romance content you crave.

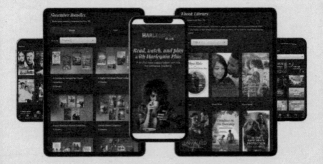

Start your **FREE 7 DAY TRIAL** at
<u>www.harlequinplus.com/freetrial</u>.